"Who are

The moon was above the water, its pale glow washing her with a brilliance that seemed to outline her whole body. His glance moved over the delicate features of her face, down the slender white neck to the ivory-colored dress.

Cassandra stopped a mere foot from him, and her next words lured his gaze back to her face like a magnet. "I'm your guardian angel, Will Alexander."

For an instant, startled, Will showed no reaction. "I'm supposed to believe that you're an angel?"

"It's the truth. You must believe it! It isn't only your soul you'll lose, but your life, as well."

"You're good—I give you that. You say you're my guardian angel. Well, if that's true, then where were you all those times in the past when I needed you?"

"I—I—"

"Forget it," he told her tersely. "We both know you aren't an angel. An angel of the night, maybe, but nothing more than that." He turned on his heel and strode off.

Dear Reader,

Once again, Silhouette Intimate Moments is breaking new ground. In our constant search to bring you the best romance fiction in the world, we have found a book that's very different from the usual, and yet it's so appealing and romantic that we just had to publish it. I'm talking about *Angel on my Shoulder,* by Ann Williams. Ann isn't a new author, of course, but the heroine of this book definitely *is* something new. In fact, she's an absolute angel—and I mean that literally! Her name is Cassandra, and she comes to Earth on a mission. Her assignment is to save the soul of one very special man, but she gets a lot more than she bargained for when she takes on an earthly shape—and starts to experience earthly emotions. I don't want to tell you any more for fear of spoiling the magic, so I hope you'll start reading right away and discover for yourself the special nature of this book.

Another book is special to me this month, too, though for a more personal reason. In *The Man Next Door,* author Alexandra Sellers not only creates some very appealing human characters, she introduces some precocious felines, as well. And if you think Lorna Doone and Beetle are too good to be true, I feel honor bound to tell you that they're actually very real. In fact, they're both living in my house, where they're more than willing to cause all sorts of trouble. But now, through the vividness of Alexandra's writing, you can get to know them, too. I hope you like them—as well as *The Man Next Door.*

Marilyn Pappano and Lucy Hamilton, two more of your favorite authors, finish off the month in fine style. And in coming months, look for Kathleen Eagle (back after a long absence), Emilie Richards, Heather Graham Pozzessere, Kathleen Korbel, Jennifer Greene and more of the top-notch writers who have made Silhouette Intimate Moments such a reader favorite.

Enjoy!

Leslie Wainger
Senior Editor and Editorial Coordinator

ANN WILLIAMS

Angel on My Shoulder

SILHOUETTE·INTIMATE·MOMENTS®

Published by Silhouette Books New York

America's Publisher of Contemporary Romance

SILHOUETTE BOOKS
300 East 42nd St., New York, N.Y. 10017

ANGEL ON MY SHOULDER

ISBN: 0-373-07408-5

First Silhouette Books printing November 1991

Printed in the U.S.A.

Books by Ann Williams

Silhouette Intimate Moments

Devil in Disguise #302
Loving Lies #335
Haunted by the Past #358
What Lindsey Knew #384
Angel on My Shoulder #408

ANN WILLIAMS

gave up her career as a nurse, then as the owner and proprietor of a bookstore, in order to pursue her writing full-time. She was born and married in Indiana, and after a number of years in Texas, she now lives in Arizona with her husband of twenty-three years and their four children.

Reading, writing, crocheting, classical music and a good romantic movie are among her diverse loves. Her dream is to one day move to a cabin in the Carolina mountains with her husband and ''write to my heart's content.''

To our own little "angel,"
our first grandchild:
Adrian Alan Buckner,
born while this book was being written

Chapter 1

"Hello?"

The deep, masculine tones filled her ear so unexpectedly that Cassandra jumped and nearly threw the phone away in surprise.

"Hello?" the voice repeated impatiently.

Cassandra cupped her hands around the mouthpiece and whispered hoarsely into the instrument, "Don't keep your appointment with Jordan Black."

"What?"

"I said—" she spoke in a louder voice, spacing her words more carefully "—don't go—"

"I heard what you said," Will interrupted impatiently, adding quickly, "Who is this? And how the hell do you know about my meeting with Jordan Black?"

"I—it doesn't matter how I know. Just don't go near Jordan Black tonight."

"Who *is* this?" Will demanded again in dangerous tones, his grip tightening on the phone.

"S-someone concerned about your welfare."

"Do I know you?"

"N-not exactly. But I know *you*."

"From where? Here? In Los Angeles? When did we meet?"

Cassandra's thoughts spun in confusion. She was becoming flustered by his rapid-fire questions and the manner in which he was taking the initiative out of her hands.

"J-just listen to what I have to say," she begged desperately. "You must *not* keep your appointment with Mr. Black."

Will listened, wondering what she was up to. He'd spoken to a lot of people in the past few months while gathering information on Black's shady past. Could it be that one of them had tumbled onto the fact that there might be money involved in his keen interest and followed him to try a little blackmail of her own?

Deciding to humor her, in order to find out if the call was a prelude to extortion, he answered, "All right, I'm listening. Tell me what you want."

"W-want?"

"Yes, what do you want from me?"

"N-nothing," she answered quickly. "That is—nothing except for you to stay away from Mr. Black. It's worth your life to—"

"My life!" Eyes narrowing on the phone in his hand, Will asked, "Are you threatening me?"

"No! Not me—Jordan Black. He plans to kill you," she blurted without thought.

Now she'd done it!

"Please," she rushed to continue, anticipating his next response, "don't ask me how I know. Just believe this—if you go to the hotel, you won't leave there alive."

"Bull!"

Cassandra winced, the explosive sound of the receiver, slammed down in anger on the other end, echoing through her head.

Ears ringing, she jerked her own receiver away from her ear and looked at it as though it were a live thing threatening to attack her. After a moment, with a despondent sigh, she replaced it, sweeping her glance apathetically around the elegant furnishings of the hotel suite.

She didn't belong in this place and was smart enough to know it. How many times before being landed here had she begged to be relieved of this assignment for just that reason? She was making a mess of things, just as she'd known she would.

Surely Barnabas could have picked someone else, someone more experienced, someone better equipped, to handle this unfamiliar territory.

It's your own fault, a small, peevish voice said inside her head. *He didn't have any more choice in the matter than you did, and you know it. He was only following orders.*

It's because you neglected your responsibilities that you're here. What was he to do?

A door banging somewhere along the corridor shattered her mood of introspection and, thankfully, drowned out any further comments from the small inner voice.

She knew that when he returned, Barnabas would expect a full and accurate account of what actions she'd taken. He wouldn't be pleased to learn she'd done nothing except aggravate the situation. A state of affairs she had better rectify if she wanted Barnabas's continued goodwill.

With an unsteady hand, she reached toward the telephone, fingers curling and uncurling in indecision a few inches short of making contact. And then, fighting an overwhelming sense of inadequacy, before her courage failed her, she picked up the instrument and dialed.

The unaccustomed clicking as the connection was made reverberated against her eardrum. Cocking her head, using her keen sense of hearing, she listened for sounds in the next suite. She concentrated hard, only to discover after a few seconds that the only sound she could make out was one she recognized as that of running water.

The water was switched off, and there followed a few moments of silence, punctuated with the *bur-r-r* of the ringing telephone. All at once she jumped in shock, reacting to the sound of a loud, concise curse, followed by a series of uneven steps, crashing against her sensitive eardrum.

"Hello?" Will shouted into the receiver.

"M-Mr. Alexander? It's me—I spoke with you a few moments ago—"

"*You* again?" he demanded in irritation, hopping on one foot, rubbing the other with exploratory fingers.

"Look, can't you get your kicks from bothering somebody else? I don't want to have to call the house detective."

He wouldn't in any case, because he didn't want to draw undue attention to himself or his stay in the hotel—but she didn't know that. "But if you don't quit bothering me—"

"Please, Mr. Alexander, I don't want to bother you.... I'm trying to save you."

"Damn it, I don't *want* to be saved."

Cassandra winced at his use of the expletive as well as the fulminating sound of his voice. "Please, I've seen your death—"

"Death?" he repeated, becoming rigidly still all at once, a sense of danger sweeping over him. "Did you say you've *seen* my death? What is this, some kind of a joke?"

"No joke—fact. I'm going to reveal something.... You may find this hard to believe, but it's true nonetheless. I—I'm a—psychic," she changed the last word in the nick of time, remembering her instructions. "I *saw* your death at the hands of Jordan Black—"

"Psychic?" he echoed skeptically, picking up on that and forgetting the rest as worthless drivel. "Listen, sister, I don't have the time, nor the inclination, to listen to this tripe. I don't know what you're trying to pull, or how you know about my appointment with Black, but take my advice. See a psychiatrist, honey. You need one. And to see *that,* I don't need to be a psychic."

Cassandra swallowed tightly and closed her eyes in quick concentration. Perhaps he needed a demonstration of what she could do. Before he could hang up, she *looked* into the next room and *saw* with her mind. He was a man built on large lines, with long and muscular limbs, and a deep chest covered with short, wavy curls the same rich brown as that on his head. His head was well-shaped, and his brown hair grew back from a widow's peak, short at the sides and back, longer on the top. A firm mouth and set chin, covered in a dark shadow of beard, suggested stubbornness. A stubbornness echoed by the glint in his golden brown eyes.

Disregarding that small, pesky voice she recognized from a few moments ago, warning her against it, she began to speak.

"What would you say if I told you I can see you, see what you're doing right now?"

"Right."

She continued as though he hadn't interrupted her. "You're sitting on the bed, wearing a white towel draped around your middle—"

"No kidding," Will murmured, unimpressed. What color were most, if not all, hotel towels? And it was a safe guess that he'd be sitting on the bed since the telephone was resting on the stand beside it.

"—water dripping down your face."

Will straightened, a frown chasing the bored expression from his damp face. "Okay, what is—"

But she wasn't through with her demonstration just yet. "Oh, yes, and you're holding the toe of your right foot. You banged it against the—"

"That's it, where are you?" Will broke across her words angrily, choosing to ignore the sudden chill in the air stirring against his bare skin as he looked toward the windows.

The curtains were drawn, as they had been since he'd entered the suite. He glanced back at the large blank screen of the television, then up toward the ceiling, as though expecting to see a camera mounted somewhere on the wall, its small prying lens focused directly on him.

"Where is it?" he barked. "Where's the—"

"Camera?" She struggled to envision the device he was thinking about. "No camera, Mr. Alexander," she whispered. "No machine of any kind. I'm in my own room, but I can still see you...with my mind. I told you, I'm...psychic."

Her words were met with silence, a long, drawn-out silence, and then he spoke, the soft words sounding as though they were being spoken directly into her ear without means of a mechanical device.

"Psychic, did you say?" he purred. "Well, tell me, are you picking up on what I'm *thinking* right now?"

Cassandra swallowed with sudden difficulty, an unaccustomed heat burning the skin of face and neck. Wishing herself anywhere in the universe except in this place, on the receiving end of this man's present thought waves, she answered in a choked murmur, "Yes, Mr. Alexander, I know what you're thinking—and I'm sorry you feel that way."

She replaced the receiver carefully before scooting back against the head of the bed, drawing her knees up beneath her chin and burying her hot face against them. She didn't like this assignment—she had known she wouldn't—and she didn't like this human male, Will Alexander, any better.

Will stared down at the phone in his hand, absently wiping the other hand down his face, removing the moisture from forehead and chin, transferring it to the coverlet on the bed. Maybe he shouldn't have used such strong language in his thoughts just now. It had sounded as though he might have hurt her feelings....

All at once he jammed the phone down onto its cradle in self-disgust and lunged to his feet. What was he thinking? Was he actually beginning to believe her crazy story? A psychic indeed!

Once he might have believed her—but not now. He'd outgrown such adolescent fantasies.

He didn't want to remember, but images from the past flashed through his brain, unwinding like pictures on a reel, and he couldn't turn them off.

Standing, tightening the towel cinched at his waist, he opened the drawer beside him and took out a crumpled package of cigarettes and a package of hotel matches. After lighting a cigarette, he blew out the match, dropped it into the wastebasket and walked over to the window fronting on the street.

It was hard for him to believe it now, but there was a time when he'd actually looked for a psychic, one he could believe in. It hadn't mattered how sleazy they appeared, or how much money they'd charged to perform their acts. He'd sought them out, one after another—looking for one who could help him contact his dead parents and ease his tormented soul.

The world was full of charlatans—as he'd soon found out—predators who fed on the gullibility of the weak.

Will took a deep drag of the cigarette, remembering, and wished he could block it all out.

Time had a way of dulling the pain, and experience had taken care of the rest. He'd learned how futile it was to seek out the dead—as futile as putting your trust in another human being.

He'd been a junior in college the last time he'd had any dealings with a psychic. She'd told him some nonsense about his being chosen for some great deed. But when he'd asked chosen by whom, and for what, her story had become garbled and filled with metaphysical hogwash.

She'd given him a rambling essay on the afterlife and its being a great unsolved mystery. And how only a privileged few were allowed a brief glimpse upon occasion, through the veil separating this world from the other.

The *Master,* she had assured him, had a plan for us all. And His plan for Will Alexander was *special.*

In other words, he had interpreted at the time, having learned by then to be cynical, she didn't know a damn thing, but didn't want him to realize it—in case he decided not to pay. He'd been hard put not to laugh in her face.

But one good thing had come from that particular experience: he'd learned the truth of the matter. The living were all alone in this great big world. There was no afterlife, no place for the dead to go, except to the grave.

And whatever we did here on Earth, good or bad, it mattered only so long as there was someone still living whom it would affect.

Will crushed out the half-smoked cigarette in the ashtray by the window and looked around at the expensive furniture filling the suite. A caustic smile marred the attractive set of his face.

Madam Whatever-her-name had predicted a special future for him. Yes, this was special, all right. A special room for a special man. Loving son—loyal friend—*blackmailer.*

Will shook his head in a moment of self-disgust and stalked off toward the bathroom. He loosened the towel

around his waist then dropped it heedlessly to the tile floor
before stepping over it and into the shower.

For all that Jordan Black had done to him alone, Will
considered that Black deserved what was coming to him.
For what Will knew he'd done to others, he deserved even
more.

It wouldn't really hurt Black to give up some of his fortune. Especially since much of it had been garnered by
stealing or cheating others out of what was theirs. What
would gall him to the bone most was the fact that Will, a
man he'd befriended, then destroyed, would be the one to
do it.

Jordan Black was about to feel the sting of retribution,
and no one, not some scatterbrained woman who claimed
to be a psychic or some money-hungry petty crook looking
to make a few thousand easy bucks, was going to stop him.

Will stood under the hot, needlelike spray and thought
about the expression he would soon be seeing on Black's
face when he learned what Will had on him. After so many
months of depression, life was beginning to take on a ray of
sunshine.

He had a meeting to attend—with Jordan Black.

"Oh, Barnabas," Cassandra whispered, lips trembling,
"I've made a mess of it. I *told* you this would happen. I'm
no good at this sort of thing. Please—" her huge blue eyes
begged "—can I go back now? Give this assignment to
someone else. Let me go back to caring for the little ones,
where I belong."

The old man shook his white head sadly, contemplating
the unhappy face before him. "You know that isn't possible. Come, child." He spread his arms wide. "Come here."

Cassandra lurched off the bed and rushed forward. As his
arms wrapped around her narrow shoulders, she felt the familiar peace she always experienced in his presence steal over
her. She had disappointed him again—like all the other
times in the past—and still he found it within himself to
comfort her. She would never attain the state of grace he
had—never—no matter how hard she tried.

"I'm sorry," she murmured against his shoulder. "Are you angry with me?" Drawing back, she looked up into his young-old eyes. "Please, don't be angry. I don't know what I'm doing. I've never had to deal with a *human* before."

Remembering exactly how rude that human had been to her a short while ago, she murmured, "You d-don't know." She hiccuped, looked startled, then continued. "You don't know what he th-thought about me."

"Thought?" Barnabas asked quickly.

Cassandra glanced down, unable to meet the sudden look of censure on the withered face.

"You aren't to use your talents, child, you know the rules." He counted them off on one hand. "No mind-reading. No moving objects about with your mind. No lying. You must not interfere with the past, nor attempt to change the present beyond the scope of your assignment. You cannot use your power to interfere with anyone's free will. You cannot suddenly disappear into thin air." Barnabas rolled his eyes. "Just think what a stir that would cause. And, above all, you must not reveal your true self to the mortals here on Earth."

"I know." Cassandra nodded, having learned those rules by heart. "But I only—" She'd broken the rules, it didn't matter what the provocation had been.

The fact that she'd wanted to scare Will into running from the city and handing what she knew he had on Jordan Black over to the authorities so she could get this job over with as quickly as possible and return home didn't count. She had fallen short of Barnabas's expectations, and that hurt.

She bit her lip in distress, chin quivering, a burning sensation stinging both eyes, and cast her glance to the floor. Twin streams of moisture began to course down her face without warning, startling her out of her mood of self-chastisement.

Cassandra laid a finger to one cheek, then looked at it. A crystal drop of water quivered on its tip. There was panic in the wide blue eyes she turned on Barnabas's face.

"What . . . ?"

The old man's expression softened immediately, and he smiled. "A tear, my child, that's all, perfectly natural under the circumstances. Crying is one of the things you'll have to learn to cope with in this world.''

He placed a bracing arm around her slumped shoulders and continued in a soothing voice. ''Don't be unduly alarmed. Tears can be a sign of many things, from great sadness to great joy. You must remember that.

''I know all this takes some getting used to—'' he swept one arm around the room ''—but you *will* get used to it. Give yourself some time.''

With a final pat of encouragement on the shoulder, he put her away from him. It would be easier to be firm, to reprimand her if necessary, from a distance. He knew he wasn't supposed to allow such a thing to happen, but somehow he'd gotten very fond of her over the years.

It was because of that fondness, he feared, and his penchant for making excuses for her, that they were both faced with this present state of affairs.

But Cassandra wasn't ready yet to concede the battle. She grasped his dry, parchmentlike hands and cried, ''Oh, Barnabas, this is all too, too complicated for me. If what I've already done to this man, Will Alexander, in Heaven is any indication, I could do something really *horrible* to him down here. Let me go back!'' she pleaded. ''I'm better off in Heaven with the children. At least the mistakes I made there didn't affect someone's life.''

''No?'' the old man said with a forced show of severity. ''Well, think about this. What might have happened to the children under your care while you were sleeping among the flowers, or wiling away the hours sculpting pictures in the clouds?

''How can you expect to teach those babes understanding and obedience to the rules when you yourself are constantly being reprimanded for breaking them?''

Cassandra hung her head and turned away, too ashamed to meet her old mentor's challenging glare. ''It's true,'' she admitted softly, recalling the many times she'd been called before him for the sin of transgression. ''And I'll foul this up, too,'' she whispered sadly.

The wizened little man stepped forward and clasped her trembling hands in both of his. ''I can't get you out of this one, child. This time, you have to see it through to the absolute end. Those are *His* orders.'' He motioned toward Heaven with a nod. "*He* feels it's time you took your rightful place in the realm of things. It's time you moved up the celestial ladder. Others who started their training with you have gone way beyond angel now.

"There are jobs to be filled. We need teachers for the little ones, as well as nursemaids. We need new planners to lay out the coming events on Earth. Someone to keep watch and gauge the needs of the Earth itself.

"We need angels who can learn to control the Past and keep it in place, those who can learn to preserve the Universal Balance that keeps the other bodies in the heavens where they belong.

"And we need Supervisors—like myself—who can keep the other angels in line. We need angels with compassion who can sift through all the prayers coming from Earth each day and decide what miracles are urgently needed among the people down here. We need new Keepers of God's Laws. And the most exultant position in Heaven—that of the angels who sit at God's feet and learn of His greatness.

"How can you expect your powers to grow, child, if you don't use them? If you don't grow with them?"

His glance focused on a point above her left shoulder, and he continued bluntly. "I don't like having to remind you of this." He paused, hardening his resolve. "But this situation is of your own making. You should have kept a closer watch on him."

He nodded toward the connecting door between her suite and the next. "There were times when he needed you, like when his father died, and then his mother so soon afterward. In his anguish, he called upon you, and you weren't there to give him the help and guidance he craved. What good is a guardian angel if you're always looking the other way when your help is required?

"He needs you now, child. And this time you are going to be there for him." He squeezed her hands in encouragement. "You *can* do it. I know you can."

"But you know I've already broken the rules. I read his mind. I lied—said I was psychic."

"Child, child..." Barnabas patted her hands calmingly. "You didn't lie about that. And I know you know the rules as I've just laid them out, but sometimes..." He paused, hoping he wasn't earning any black marks for what he was about to reveal. "Sometimes it's permitted—through extreme necessity—to use some of your talents. But you must be certain it's necessary," he emphasized strongly, "and it's only your *talents* I'm referring to, not your Heavenly gifts."

"Yes, but—"

"No, buts. You have only six days." He glanced down at his right arm, consulting the strange-looking instrument that passed for a watch. "Er, that is," he calculated swiftly, "only one hundred and twenty-six hours left now."

"What if I fail?" she asked fearfully.

"What if you don't?" he answered softly.

"He's hardheaded and stubborn—and he doesn't believe anything I say. He's over there right now," she protested, "getting ready to keep his appointment with Mr. Black. He's more determined than ever to go through with his plans—because of me."

"Then do something to stop him."

"What?" she asked helplessly.

"Use your imagination." Letting go of her hands, he walked toward the door.

"But not—" he stopped and turned back to raise a cautioning finger "—your Heavenly gifts. You know the ones to which I'm referring.

"Go with God, child," he blessed her. "And remember, your time here is short, so make the most of it."

Will checked his watch for the third time in five minutes and saw that he had an hour to get to Black's hotel. His steps quickened as he rounded the corner and hurried toward the elevator. Stepping into it, he'd hardly had time to reach toward the button marked Lobby when a young woman came hurrying, almost running, down the hallway.

He found himself eyeing her approach with interest. There was something familiar about her, and he wondered for an instant if perhaps he'd met her somewhere before.

"Wait! Please, hold the elevator—" Breathless, skirt flying, she stepped inside and leaned back against the wall. "Thank you. I—"

Before she could continue, a horde of people, seeming to come from out of nowhere but in reality emerging from the room across from the elevator, converged on them. Whatever she had been about to say was, literally, lost in the crush.

Will found himself pressed back against the glass wall of the elevator by the time he realized he hadn't punched the button marking his destination. Glancing up at the lighted display beside the door, he saw that they were headed toward the top floor. Great, he would have to ride all the way to the top of the hotel in order to get to the lobby.

Naturally, he noted in disgust a few minutes later, the elevator stopped at every floor.

He wasn't certain when—or even why—it finally got through to him, but before long he realized two things at the same time. First, no one appeared to be getting on or off the elevator; and two, there was a strange, almost *tickling*, sensation at the back of his mind.

He glanced around at the faces of the other passengers, curious as to whether anyone else was experiencing anything similar to the panic he was beginning to feel. However, as people everywhere seemed to do in elevators, even those who were with friends, everyone appeared to be staring upward, their eyes focused on the numbers beside the door.

"Will—may I call you Will?" a voice said, seemingly from inside his head.

Will shot a look at the man next to him, but the man was paying him no attention. Unlike the others, he appeared to have no interest whatsoever in the elevator's current destination. He did, however, show a marked interest in the charms being displayed by the low-cut blouse of the redhead standing in front and slightly to the left of him.

"No, he isn't the one talking to you, I am."

Will's head snapped up, and he glared in turn at everyone standing near him.

*"It's me. I called you. We spoke on the telephone. I'm
sorry to have to talk to you this way, but I can't simply forget all about it and let you go through with your meeting.
You have to understand—*

*"What are you doing? No! Don't do that. Don't block me
out. Please, I'm only trying—"*

Will fixed his eyes on the flashing numbers and began
running through multiplication tables in his head. Over and
over, faster and faster, like a computer, his brain reeled off
the answers.

He'd read somewhere that it was possible to throw up a
shield against those who sought to read your mind. And
whether he believed in ESP or not, it appeared to work.

In a short time the elevator stopped, the doors slid
smoothly open to reveal the lobby, and the small convey-
ance began to empty. Will was the last to leave. He'd
reached twelve times twelve in his calculations by that time
and decided to take a chance, open his mind and see if the
strange, probing feeling was still there.

Nothing happened. It seemed the lady psychic was gone.
Relieved, he strode swiftly across the lobby and through the
revolving glass doors to the sidewalk outside. A taxi was
waiting at the curb across from the hotel driveway. Will
made directly for it.

Before he could reach it, a young woman entered the
corner of his vision. Taking hold of the handle, she opened
the door and bent to climb inside.

Warding off his frustration as best he could, Will stopped
beside the open door of the taxi. He gave an impatient
glance up and then down the busy street. As with everything else, when you needed a taxi, naturally, there wasn't
one to be had.

"Excuse me." Soft, feminine tones filtered up from the
car's dark interior. "I see that you must be in need of
transportation. My trip isn't urgent, perhaps we could share
the ride?'

Will hesitated, gave her pale face a brief glance, then
looked down at his watch in the glow of the streetlight. It
was after seven, and his appointment with Black was for

eight and clear across town. Come hell or high water, he intended to make that meeting.

His eyes touched her face again. She looked harmless enough.

Bending at the waist, he looked in at the taxi driver. The old man appeared well past the age of retirement, but apparently he wasn't too old to get a chauffeur's license.

Hell, yes, why not take the ride being offered?

"Thanks." Will climbed inside the taxi and closed the door. "I'm headed for the Beresford Arms on Pacific, driver. You know it?"

The old man nodded without comment, shifted the gears grindingly and aimed the car, like a bullet, into traffic.

"Are you here on business?"

Will turned his attention from the scenery whizzing past to the diminutive figure beside him. "Yes."

He looked back through the window, resolving to put a quick end to any conversation between them. He wanted to concentrate on what he was going to say to Black. It would have to be good if he wanted to convince the man he meant business and that he was smart enough to cover his own tracks against police investigation.

"I've never been in Los Angeles before. I understand the words mean "city of the angels." Do you suppose there are any here? Angels, I mean."

He figured she had created an opening so he could assure her, gallantly, that there were indeed angels in the city—at least one, in any case, since she was there. But Will wasn't taking the bait. And if that was the best she could do...

His eyes met the taxi driver's in the rearview mirror as the man made a strangled sound deep in his throat. Even that old goat wasn't taken in by her machinations.

"I haven't had dinner yet," she said, following up her failed gambit with another attempt. "Can you recommend a good place to eat?"

"No," Will replied shortly. "I'd suggest getting a guidebook if you don't know the city."

"I don't like eating alone," she continued doggedly. "Could I impose on you to—"

"Look, sister." He decided some plain speaking was necessary. "I'm not interested, okay?" His eyes, like shards of topaz glass, cut her to the quick.

"I—" She couldn't seem to think of anything else to say. "Ex-excuse me." Her lower lip quivered, and her glance didn't move beyond the top of the black tie knotted at the collar of Will's white shirt.

Will steeled himself against feeling sympathy for her and turned toward the window. Women like her were a dime a dozen in cities like this one around the world. He didn't have time for them.

And that reminded him... He drew back the sleeve of his shirt and moved his arm to the window to get a look at the large, square face of his watch in the passing street lamps. He had thirty minutes to get to Black's hotel.

A car horn blared from somewhere close by, startling him into glancing at the traffic outside. Without warning, the taxi driver rammed his foot down on the accelerator, pushing it to the floorboard.

Will felt himself propelled back against the seat and fought to scoot himself forward. He peered over the back of the seat and saw the speedometer needle edging upward toward fifty—sixty...

"What are you doing?" he asked in rising alarm as the taxi swung out into the fast lane, swerving almost at once to keep from sideswiping a delivery van.

"Are you crazy?" he yelled. "Do you want to get us all killed? Slow down, man!"

The car rounded a curve on two wheels, narrowly missing a city bus and throwing the woman against the door. Will, literally sitting on the edge of his seat, gripped the back of the one in front to keep from being thrown to the floor.

If he hadn't known for certain that the action would send them directly into the path of another vehicle or flying totally out of control, he would have grabbed the little man around the neck and throttled him on the spot.

The taxi rounded another curve and careened down a street lined on both sides with flashing yellow lights. Orange-and-black signs streaked by, warning of a detour up ahead.

"Slow down, man! Stop!" Will roared as they crashed through a barricade and, without any lessening of speed, rushed toward the unfinished end of the bridge under construction.

The taxi's wheels left solid pavement, spinning wildly in thin air as the vehicle became airborne.

The last thing Will remembered, seconds before the car slammed into the bay, was a voice inside his head screaming, *"Barnabas! Barnabas, what are you doing?"*

Chapter 2

It was cold and wet, and his head felt as though it had been used for a punching bag. Will gave a massive shiver and groaned. He must be sleeping—dreaming, or drifting somewhere in between, in the twilight world where dreams took on the essence of reality.

He didn't like this dream. It was *too* real: the water, the cold, the pain inside his head, the stiffness in his neck.

Will opened his eyes, blinked, choked and coughed. It *was* water, no dream at all, but reality. And then he collected his thoughts and remembered the woman, the taxi and the crazy man at the wheel. He must be in the bay!

The stiffness in his neck, he soon discovered, was caused by a hand beneath his chin keeping his head above water. But every now and then a wave crashed over his head, and he swallowed some of the briny water stinging both his eyes and his throat.

Unable to move his head within the firm grip someone had on his chin, he managed to turn his eyes to the side and saw that they were headed toward shore. Reaching up, he touched the hand cupped firmly beneath his chin, keeping his head above water, and felt it loosen fractionally.

"Are you all right?" the young woman from the taxi asked gently, appearing to be under no strain in keeping herself and him afloat.

"Yes. Let me go—I can swim."

It amazed him that someone as small as she was could hold a man his size and swim, even with the water making him more buoyant.

"Your head . . ." she began.

"It's all right." He pushed at her hand, twisting his head in her grasp.

Cassandra let him go without further protest, and Will found himself instantly sinking beneath the waves. But in a moment he was back up top, coughing and sputtering, swimming sluggishly alongside her.

"Are *you* all right?" he felt compelled to ask under the circumstances.

"Yes," she answered at once, unhampered by the need to pant as he was doing. "I wasn't damaged. And I love the . . . swimming," she added in a delighted tone. "At first I was afraid of so much water in one place, but it's wonderful! Almost like floating in the clouds."

Will slanted her a questioning look, but decided that what she'd said probably would have made perfect sense if only he hadn't been groggy from the wreck and feeling a bit green around the gills. He was out of shape and finding it hard to breathe, and the headache was making his stomach feel queasy.

The swim seemed endless, and there came a moment, about fifty feet from shore, when he knew he couldn't go another inch. Feeling as though a plug had been pulled and all his energy, his will to live, had escaped through the hole, Will gave up and slowly began to sink beneath the choppy waves.

He was tired, so very tired, and it was so much simpler to just give up and let his body roll with the movement of the water instead of fighting to stay afloat, fighting to make some headway in the turbulent waves. Sleep . . . that was what he needed. . . . The sleep of forgetfulness . . . no painful memories . . . no wrong choices . . . no Jordan Black . . .

His leg accidentally brushed against that of the woman swimming along beside him, and all at once a renewed sense of vigor filled him. He pulled himself up without help, lifted his head and began to swim. He would not give up!

His glance sought the shore, closer, surely, than it had been a few moments before, and he knew beyond a doubt that he would make it—or die trying.

After what seemed like hours, their feet finally touched solid sand. Will found that it was all he could do, even with help from his companion, to throw himself far enough up onto the beach that the waves couldn't dislodge him and pull him back into the water.

Will felt the coolness against his cheek as he lay facedown against the wet sand, breathing in short, sharp gasps, his whole body racked with shivers. His stomach was rolling from the salt water he'd swallowed, and at first he didn't even have enough control of his muscles to speak.

When he could, he raised stinging eyes to find the woman and asked, "What...happened...to the...driver?"

The old man wasn't with them, as far as he could tell. Lifting his head, he peered along the beach on both sides of them, then looked back across the murky depths.

The waves rose and fell, renewing his bout of dizziness, but he forced himself to swallow back the nausea and scan the immediate vicinity for signs of the missing man. With a sense of sadness he realized that there was nothing within sight that looked anything like a body struggling in the water.

"He's all right," Cassandra answered calmly, from her cross-legged position beside him. She was busy pushing the fingers of both hands through the wet sand, lifting them, then watching the sand slide off each palm to disappear into the foamy water without leaving a trace.

Will studied her with bleary eyes, noting the wondrous expression on her face as she took great delight in what she was doing, making a game of it.

He frowned. What was with her? *"He's all right?"* Wasn't she the least bit concerned that a man, a human being like herself, had just drowned? He had thought the years had made him impervious to other people's troubles, but this woman was one cool customer.

He watched as, with a graceful movement, she stood and moved a yard farther up onto the dry part of the beach. Her shoes must have gotten lost sometime during their dunking, because she was barefoot. All at once, she began to dig her toes into the fine sand.

Will couldn't believe his ears. She was giggling, hopping up and down in delight, captivated by the tickling sensation on the bottoms of both feet, a sensation created by the sand being sucked out from beneath them by the outgoing waves.

Will gave her a half-disgusted, almost angry, glance, and asked in a loud tone, "How can you laugh? Do you really think that man wasn't hurt? How can you possibly know that?"

Casting aside her amusement, Cassandra looked up, realizing what she'd said. She'd said too much, and she searched for an answer that would sound plausible.

"I—" She moved her shoulders up and down awkwardly, learning to shrug. There was no plausible answer to his question—unless she told him the truth. "I just...know, that's all."

Will shook his head in vexation and tried to stand up. After a couple of false starts, because his legs felt as weak as a newborn colt's, he finally climbed unsteadily to his feet. The woman had noted his plight and moved toward him, offering her assistance, but he impatiently shrugged her aside.

Where had he gone wrong? How in the world had he gotten himself into this mess?

The answer to that was clear enough. He'd accepted a lift from this woman.

The evening was turning out to be a total disaster. First there had been the strange incidents at the hotel with the so-called psychic, and now this woman and the crash in the taxi.

He'd always heard that disasters came in threes. He shuddered to think what fate had in store for him next.

He'd missed his meeting with Black, and now it looked as though he was going to have to talk to the police. The old man was probably dead, drowned, or killed in the wreck. That was all he needed at this point, being detained and questioned by the police.

Plus, he was stuck with this crazy female, at least until they found out for certain what had happened to the old man.

"Come on," he said with a note of annoyance. "Let's go see if we can find him. Maybe, if we're lucky, his body will have washed up on shore."

"Body!" she echoed in dismay. "B-but—he isn't dead. I told you, he's fine."

"We don't *know* that," Will insisted testily.

A part of him was busy trying to figure her out. Was she for real? Or was she on something?

It would be just his luck—when he didn't want to draw any undue attention to himself—to be involved in an accident involving a death and with a junkie to boot.

"Look." Cassandra had come to stand beside him, and now touched his wet shoulder, tentatively. "You don't need to be concerned about Barnabas."

Will snapped instantly to attention, a faint thread of memory repeating the name inside his head.

Taking her by the shoulders with none-too-gentle hands, he drew her closer, staring intently at the startled expression on her upturned face. "What did you call him?"

"B-Barnabas. W-why?" The look on his face made her afraid, and all at once she found it hard to breathe with him standing so near, touching her as he was.

"You know him?"

"N—" She started to shake her head, then remembered she couldn't lie and answered in a small voice, "Yes, I know him."

"What is this?" he asked in disgust. "Were you and he in this together? Were you planning to pull a fast one on me? Don't think I didn't recognize the come-on in the taxi."

"W-what?" She shied away from the wrath she sensed boiling just below the surface.

"The old shill game, right? You come on to me—" He looked her up and down with a dubious stare, further angered by, and ignoring, the sudden leap of his pulses at the sight of her charms displayed so noticeably in the wet, white dress, clinging to her without benefit of undergarments. He continued. "You take me to a hotel, get me liquored up, and then your friend shows up, slugs me over the head and empties my pockets of my money and credit cards." He laughed without humor and tossed her aside, unmindful of the fact that she lost her footing and landed on her knees in the sand. "Well, not this time, honey. This time the game backfired. You and your friend would have been sadly disappointed, because you picked a real loser. I'm busted," he added, almost in satisfaction. "My pockets are empty, and my credit is all used up."

Without a backward glance, he marched down the beach. He would have liked to simply walk away from this evening's mess—and her. It was what he fully intended doing, despite the voice inside that kept whispering, *What about the old man? What if he isn't all right? What if he's hurt, or dead?*

"Wait!"

Will kept right on going, determined not to fall victim to her pseudo-innocent blue eyes, or the prying voice inside his head.

"Please." She ran up quickly to stand in front of him, blocking his way. But he simply changed directions and kept on going.

"Barnabas isn't hurt—or dead," she insisted.

But it was evident that she wasn't getting through to him. And that knowledge kindled a fresh flame inside her. This strange new emotion, a twinge of which she'd felt during her conversations with him on the telephone when he'd scorned her warnings, created a turmoil of feeling within her breast.

He would listen to her—he *would!* "He isn't hurt or dead, because he can't be harmed by anything here on Earth," she yelled without thought. "He's an angel!"

She had done it again! She had disregarded instructions against divulging that information to a living soul. Barnabas wouldn't be pleased—and neither would He.

Clamping both hands over her mouth, she closed her eyes, ducked her head and trembled in fright. At any moment she expected to hear a loud crash of thunder from overhead, a sure sign of God's wrath at her disobedient behavior.

Will halted, unable to let that pass, and turned without haste to face her. He eyed her for a moment in silence, wondering what she was up to, and asked, "Am I really supposed to swallow that?"

Cassandra opened one eye, gave a tentative glance upward, then straightened and looked Will straight in the eye. "Yes."

Will gave her full marks for standing her ground and looking him in the eye, no matter how crazy her story sounded, and shook his head in admiration. "I have to hand it to you, sister, you've got—" He paused and changed what he was going to say. "—imagination. So, tell me, are you his daughter," he asked, playing along with her, "or just another angel?"

"No—and yes."

"Well, that's clear enough," he commented sarcastically.

"I'm an angel," she explained, having let the cat out of the bag and attempting to straighten out some of the confusion, "but not Barnabas's daughter."

Will finally turned away, taking up his march along the beach. This female was too dizzy for him.

"I don't understand," she called to his back. "Don't you want to know why we—I'm here?"

"No!" he called back over his shoulder.

"Wait! Will Alexander, wait!"

The words seemed to stretch out across the air, echoing across the waves and coming back to his ears over and over before finally dying away into silence.

Will had stopped at the sound of his name spoken by this stranger; now he turned as the sound faded to stare at her in confusion.

"Who are you?"

The night had been calm up until then, with only a slight breeze blowing off the ocean. Now the wind began to come in strong gusts, sweeping along the beach, wafting her white skirt out behind her.

The moon was full and round, riding high above the water, its pale glow washing her with a brilliance that seemed to outline her whole body as she moved slowly toward his stationary figure. There was indeed something other-worldly about her in that moment.

His glance moved over the delicate features of her face, down her slender white neck to the white dress, resting half off one shoulder. His eyes became ensnared, held captive by the hint of her small, jutting breasts showing pink through the wet material.

Cassandra stopped a mere foot from him, her next words luring his glance back to her face like a magnet.

"I'm *your* angel, Will Alexander. I'm here as your guardian angel. No." She shook her head to halt the words she could see forming before they were spoken. "Before you say anything, listen to me, please.

"I was sent to stop you from blackmailing Jordan Black. You must not take money to forget about what he's done in the past and is planning to do in the future. He is a truly evil man, and if you do, if you help him in his evil work, you will damn your soul to hell for all eternity."

Her words seemed to be picked up and carried by the wind, echoing ominously across the beach and along the shore. And for an instant, startled, Will showed no reaction.

Then withdrawing his gaze from her *earthly* charms, he asked, "I'm supposed to believe this? Believe that you're an angel?"

"It's the truth. You must believe it! It isn't only your soul you'll lose, though that's the most important part. But you'll lose your life, as well. Mr. Black intends to get information from you, then kill you afterward."

"And you're going to save me?" he answered skeptically.

"No." She shook her head. "You must save yourself. You must take the information you have about Mr. Black's evil plans and turn it over to the authorities before he can hurt anyone else."

"You're good, sister, I'll give you that. But I'm afraid I'm not buying what you're selling. You say you're my guardian angel, right?" He waited for her slow nod. "Well, if that's true, then where the hell were you when I needed you fifteen years ago—when my father died?" he asked.

"And where were you when Jordan Black was putting a knife between my shoulders?" His voice rose with anger. "Tell me, where were you all those times in the past when I needed you?"

"I—I—"

"Forget it," he told her tersely. "I don't believe in all that religious crap anyway. And we both know you aren't an angel. Angel of the night, maybe, but nothing more exalted than that."

It had been a mistake to reveal the truth to him. Barnabas had been right to forbid it. But what should she do now? He wasn't likely to believe anything she said. Yet she had to say something—she had to stop him from making a deal with Jordan Black.

"All right—I'll tell you the truth. I'm the woman who called you at the hotel." He refused to believe her truth—perhaps he would believe the truth of what he knew to be a fact.

Will frowned a moment in puzzlement, and then a look of cynicism crept into his golden-brown eyes. "So you're the *psychic.*" He laughed without humor. "Now why doesn't that tidbit of information surprise me?" He shook his head. "Sorry, but whatever it is you have up your sleeve, psychic or not, I'm not interested."

Pivoting on his heel, he strode off, leaving her once more to stare in frustration at his rigid back.

After a short distance, Will stopped and turned back, motioning for her to follow. "Come on, Angel, or whatever you call yourself. Let's get out of here. We have a body—or your friend—to find."

There was no way he believed her story about being an angel, that was pure lunacy. But the psychic bit was something else again. It was possible for someone to know the future—despite how he'd come to deny the fact over the years, by virtue of the charlatans he'd encountered—because his mother had been able to.

However, that didn't make him believe this young woman, psychic or not. And he didn't want to become involved with her. But he still couldn't leave her there on the beach all alone after she'd saved his life.

Besides, if she truly believed what she was telling him, especially all that angel stuff, then in his opinion she needed professional attention. He'd seen the prophets of doom carrying signs and walking the streets of big cities often enough to know they were mostly people who suffered from one psychosis or another and belonged in an institution where they could receive treatment.

Maybe, just this once, he would trouble himself on someone else's behalf and see that she got it.

After he'd looked into the taxi driver's whereabouts. Angel or not, he still didn't think the old man could walk upon the water.

What a screwed-up night this had turned out to be. Will shook his head silently in vexation.

The first thing he needed to do, when he got back to the hotel, was set up another appointment with Black. But he guessed that needn't concern him overly much. Black would, he felt certain, be more than agreeable to it.

Will had something the man wanted. That in itself should keep him sweet, at least until he got it, and perhaps—as this young woman had implied—got Will Alexander, too, in the bargain.

They moved, mutely, Will in the lead, Cassandra following, toward a lighted portion of the beach. Will spotted a group of people standing around something on the ground and moved closer to investigate.

Lying on the sand, with several people in attendance, lay the taxi driver, Barnabas, quickly stirring to life under Will's eyes.

Will heaved an audible sigh of relief, realizing there was no need now to become involved with the police. It was the old man's duty to report the accident and his own responsibility for it. For a moment Will considered confronting the old man and turning the custody of the young woman over to him.

That, however, would entail his being drawn once again into the accident, and as it now stood, once he turned her over to someone at the nearest hospital, he would be free to pursue his own business.

There was no choice to be made in the matter. The old man could take care of his own problems, and Will would get rid of—see to the needs of—the woman.

The decision made, he turned to speak to her, only to find the space where she'd been standing empty. She was gone.

He scanned the ocean in the moonlight, looking for a sign of the pale glow of her dress. But the water was calm and, as before, when he'd looked for signs of the old man, empty.

He didn't have to glance down at his watch to know that time waited for no man and was quickly passing. But something kept him from turning aside and forgetting the young woman. Despite himself, he felt a sense of responsibility toward her.

And even though time for him was crucial, because he knew he couldn't trust Jordan Black to calmly sit and wait for him to name the sum of money he wanted for his silence, and even though he was living at the hotel under the threat of being tossed out on his ear because he had no money to pay his bill, Will couldn't put the woman out of his mind.

For the next hour he roamed the beach, stumbling over lovers on the sand, his head aching, looking for her. The only thing he discovered, however, was that even summer nights can bring a chill to your bones if you happen to be suffering from shock and wearing wet clothing.

Finally, exhausted, having found no trace of her, he gave up and headed back toward the lights, and signs of humanity.

Barnabas found her on the beach, sitting cross-legged in the sand, staring out across the ocean's turbulent waves.

"He's gone." She spoke first, sensing his presence.

"Why aren't you with him?"

"I think he's had enough of *my* protection for one night."

"He could still meet with Mr. Black—"

"Not tonight."

"You sound very certain of that, child."

"I told him—I told him I was an angel," she muttered softly.

"Oh, dear."

"It's all right," Cassandra hastened to reassure him. "He didn't believe me. He thinks I'm . . . crazy."

Was that a note of desolation he detected in her voice?

"Why did you dump us all in the water?"

"I was only trying to help. You were letting the situation get away from you. It was imperative for us to keep him away from Jordan Black tonight. You haven't had a chance to discover where the documents he has are being kept," Barnabas explained.

"I thought you said I had to do this on my own."

"It's permitted that I lend a hand when necessary."

"Why don't you simply read his mind and find out for yourself where the documents are? We could get them, take them to the authorities, and then we could both go home."

"Cassandra," he spoke severely, "you know it has to be his decision—strictly his decision—to turn over the evidence. That's the only thing that can save him."

"I'm sorry, Barnabas," she answered, chastened. "I told you I wasn't going to be any good at this."

Barnabas stood in indecision, wishing there was some way to comfort her, yet knowing, too, that she had to get through this test on her own. After a brief hesitation, he bent his ancient frame and sat down beside her.

"I know you're finding this assignment more than you think you can handle, but you know as well as I do that it isn't true. *He* won't give you more than you can endure."

He patted her hand comfortingly. "It will get better, child, I promise. Don't fight it. Make it easy on yourself and give in to this new form with which you've been blessed. Not every angel gets the opportunity to be human. My advice is to relax and enjoy it. It will make your task easier. Before long, you'll be thinking and acting as though you're one of them."

Cassandra glanced up at him. "Human, you mean?"

The old man nodded sagely.

"I don't think I'd like that, Barnabas." She hesitated briefly before continuing. "They're all so...isolated." She shivered. "So...alone. I reach out with my thoughts and there's no one there, nothing but a void—dead space. It's scary."

He felt her tremble. "How can they bear it?" she asked with a catch in her voice.

"It's how it must be for them—for now. They aren't ready for anything else, not yet. They have to learn to live with themselves before they can share their thoughts with others."

He could see that his words were bringing her no consolation, and he tried to explain. "This...aloofness you feel is a part of their lives from birth. It's all they'll ever know. That's how God intends it to be—for now.

"That's why he instilled them with the desire to mate. In the joining of their bodies in love, their two souls entwine. It's in that manner that they find a small measure of what awaits them in Heaven, where we love all beings—all things—equally."

On a warning note, he continued. "I know I said you should give in to your feelings and learn to function as a human, but in the process you mustn't get too caught up in their world. Remember, you're here only for a short time—and you're here on God's work."

"Don't worry, I could never get used to being like them. I feel sorry for them," she added softly.

She spoke of the human race as a whole, but in her mind it was Will's face she saw. She'd sensed *his* loneliness above all others.

Even in the little time she had spent in his presence, over and above any other emotions he inspired in her, she was aware of an aura of deep sadness. There was a wellspring of feeling buried deep inside him that he'd ceased, a long time ago, to share with anyone.

At the root of it was the feeling that he didn't belong anywhere here on Earth. Cassandra empathized with that feeling because it was so closely related to what she herself had always felt in her own world; a sense of being out of place, out of time.

She was beginning to realize that there was a lot more to being someone's guardian angel than she'd first believed. If she'd done her job and kept watch over Will as she'd been instructed to do, her job would have been much easier, because by now she would have known the man better than he knew himself.

When she'd slipped away from him on the beach, after he'd spotted Barnabas, it was to be alone, to think about all the new and surprising emotions she'd encountered since her first contact with Will.

Was this confusion of spirit, this maelstrom of sensations, a part of what being human was all about? This impossible feat of working blindly on someone else's behalf, wanting to help, but not knowing how to go about it?

She'd fought against having to come to Earth and get involved in Will's life. Her position had been that he knew good from evil, and whatever decision he made, the choice being his to make through free will, he must be judged by it.

But now, being human herself, she was beginning to understand a little of how easy it might be, living isolated from each other as they did, for a human to become tempted by the wicked things of this world. And now, after having met Will, she truly *wanted* to help him.

Will passed several taxis on his way to the bus stop, but he shook his head at their questioning glances. He'd had enough of taxis—and taxi drivers—for one day.

He caught the first bus he saw as it was gearing up to pull away from the curb. And though he received his share of dubious looks, drenched as he was in ocean water, he returned stare for stare and stuck it out until the last stop disembarking within two blocks of the hotel.

It was after ten by the time he entered his room. Going at once to the telephone, he made an attempt to reach Jordan Black. But the phone rang and rang without being answered, leaving Will no choice but to give up until later.

By the time he'd put the phone down, he was shivering in the air conditioning. In the bathroom, he forsook the shower and ran a tub of hot water. Though he was normally a shower man, he stepped into the steaming liquid and eased his tired, aching body down into the tub with a grateful sigh.

In a few minutes he could feel his bunched muscles unknot, and a kind of peace began to steal over him. Leaning his head back against the rim of the tub, he closed his eyes and relaxed for the first time since leaving his suite that evening.

Almost immediately, a picture of the woman—he didn't even know her name—flashed into his mind. She intrigued him, he admitted, despite himself.

Where had she disappeared to so quickly without leaving a trace—not even footsteps in the sand? It was strange, almost as though she had ... disappeared.

He pulled his thoughts up short. What was he thinking? Was he actually giving her fantastic story credence?

No. He reached for the soap. The whole evening had been like a ridiculous story you might read in some silly woman's magazine. All that malarkey about her being an angel was just that, malarkey.

The truth of the matter was plain and simple enough for anyone to see. She had gotten caught, her and her friend, trying to put one over on him, and that story had been something she'd come up with on the spur of the moment.

Maybe she did have the gift of precognition—that would make it easy for her to spot a mark—but if she was after anything, it was probably a little blackmailing of her own.

Still, she had saved his life. And he hadn't liked walking out on her after that. So, okay, maybe he was getting soft in his old age.

Not too soft, another part of his brain cautioned warningly. Not if you expected to hold your own with Black. He warned you once that he eats little boys like you for breakfast.

After climbing out of the tub and wrapping a large soft bath towel around his middle, Will strode into the bedroom and sat down on the edge of the bed. He could handle Jordan Black. All it took was a man who could be as big a bastard as Black himself. And Will was confident he could measure up.

He picked up the phone and dialed Black's number, for the last time that night, he decided, as he listened to the phone ring at the other end. If he didn't reach the man this time, let him wait. It wouldn't do Black any harm to do a bit of sweating.

"Yes?"

"Black? Alexander."

"I've been expecting you all evening, Will. What's happened? You haven't changed your mind, have you?"

"Not a chance. I got...unavoidably detained. It's too late to set up another meeting tonight. How about tomorrow morning? You name the time and place."

"Very well. I'm leaving the hotel early in the morning to take up residence at my new home in Laurel Canyon. Why don't we meet at my house at . . . say . . . eleven?"

"Right. I'll need directions." Will reached for a pen and the stack of hotel stationery beside the phone.

A few minutes later Will glanced at the directions Black had given him before folding the piece of paper and slipping it into the drawer. What he needed now was a good night's sleep. He wanted to be clearheaded and sharp-witted for his meeting with Black. He would need all his faculties when dealing with the man, of that he was certain from past experience.

He dropped the towel from his waist and slid neatly between the sheets. His head barely touched the pillow before he was asleep.

But his dreams were far from peaceful, and in a short while his head was whipping back and forth restlessly across the pillow. Once again he stood on the beach, feeling the wet sand beneath his stocking feet, shivering in the pale moonlight.

At first there was nothing but blackness all around him, with the pale light of the moon casting shadows in the distance. Then something, a movement at the corner of his vision, caught his attention. A figure floated above the sand toward him.

He cowered, drawing back one step at a time in fear. The figure drew closer, and Will identified it for what it was, a woman.

The woman from the taxi, draped in a long, white, diaphanous gown. Her hair, longer than he remembered it being, streamed out behind her narrow figure, seeming to clutch, like long blond fingers, at the air around her.

She was speaking, but at first he couldn't understand the words; he only saw the movement of her full, rosy lips. Her figure hovered a couple of feet off the ground, drawing closer, until, finally, her words reached his ears.

She was urging him to go—to leave the hotel and get out of the city—before it was too late. Will listened intently, the meaning of the words sinking in, and realized somehow that this was a dream.

His gaze was riveted on the delicate lines of her face; then it moved over her body slowly, taking in the slender waist, rounded hips and long, lithe thighs visible through the transparent gown.

A hot aching feeling hit him low in the stomach as the air around her seemed to vibrate with electricity. He caught his breath, feeling the sudden need to touch her, to bask in the warmth of the glow her figure appeared to generate.

When she was standing a few scant inches from him, his eyes locked with hers, and he saw a rapt expression creep into the blue depths.

Will couldn't seem to breathe when he realized that she, too, was caught up in the uncanny web of desire he could feel pulsating around them, seeming to bind them closer.

Slowly, inexorably, Will reached for her, but it was as though he were two people, one actually performing the act, and the other, standing a little way off, observing him do it. But as his hands closed around her waist, he could feel the supple warmth of bone and tissue within his grasp.

An emotion he'd thought long dead stirred to life. Will drew her closer, and she, like him, appeared powerless to resist.

As his face descended, their eyes locked in a mutual trance. Then, all at once, she blinked and gave a little jerk.

With his lips now suspended a mere breath away from hers, Will felt her resist.

As though coming out from under a deep spell, like a trapped wild thing confronted by a hunter, she began frantically to twist and turn, pushing at him as though to dislodge his hold on her.

Despite his superior strength, she managed to maintain a narrow margin of air between his determined lips and her resisting ones.

He knew he should withdraw, but somehow the fact of her fighting him began to excite him all the more. He could feel the heat of battle emanating from her body, see her pulse kicking against the hollow at her throat, sense the hysteria barely held in check below the surface of her control, and it fed his excitement, his sudden all pervasive need of her.

He could almost *feel* her lips yield to his, *taste* their inviting sweetness on his tongue.

Without warning Will's head snapped back on his shoulders. Ears ringing, he threw a protective arm up in front of his face, his body rocking back from the force of the unexpected blow.

Chapter 3

Will came to with a start, eyes wide and staring, heart bumping furiously against his ribs. It took a few moments for his eyes to adjust to the near darkness. It took a little longer for him to realize where he was: in his hotel room in Los Angeles—alone.

The woman he'd held in his arms and been about to kiss, the mind-jarring slap she had dealt him, were nothing more than a dream.

It had been years since he remembered dreaming. Maybe the dip in the ocean, the strange young woman he'd met, had made more of an impression on him then he'd realized. With a wry twist to his mouth and a slight shake of his head, he prepared to relax back against the pillows.

Something, perhaps a sixth sense, caused him to hesitate, raise his head cautiously and peer across the width of the room.

Years spent in too many hotel rooms from one end of the country to the other had taught him the advantage of leaving a light burning in the bathroom at night, with the door left partially open.

In the narrow stream of light Will saw a dim figure, dressed in what appeared to be a one-piece body stocking, bending over an open drawer in the dresser.

Without conscious thought, Will reached toward the lamp on the table beside him and pressed the small brass button at its base. A strong yellow glow flooded the room at the exact instant he shouted forcefully, "Just what the hell do you think you're doing?"

The figure in black faltered, then froze immediately in place. The air in the room became charged with tension. Will's words bounced off the walls and echoed back in the ringing silence.

His narrow-eyed glance, glued to the intruder's motionless back, showed him a silhouette of unrelieved black. The uneasy tautness in the atmosphere found a foothold in his gut, and his blood slid like needles of ice through his veins.

Suddenly the figure whirled without warning and propelled itself across the room toward him. A step from the bed, it made a flying leap and slammed across Will's chest, knocking the breath from him.

In an instant hands like steel talons were wrapped around Will's neck, choking the life from him. Gasping, face turning white and then red, colors exploding in his brain, Will clawed at the gloved hands and bucked on the bed, trying to dislodge his attacker.

A finger finally found a spot to connect, one of the eyeholes in the man's black hood, and Will ripped at the man's eye. With an animal-like roar of pain, the man in black released his hold on Will's larynx and drove a fist into his face.

Will recoiled from the blow, ears ringing, and renewed his bucking attempts to dislodge the man from his chest. With the side of his fist, Will began to deliver short, sharp vicious blows to his assailant's ribs.

If he could have gotten a purchase on the man's wiry frame, he might have been able to dislodge him. But the slick nylonlike material of the man's garb made it impossible.

Will's strength was quickly deserting him, his tongue becoming thick in his mouth, his vision blurring. In a few more minutes he wouldn't have the strength even to fight

back. And the man crouching over him knew it. Will could
see the thrill of blood lust, the light of victory, in the man's
dark glowing eyes.

They struggled in silence except for the heavy sounds of
their labored breathing, interlaced with an occasional grunt
or a sharp, muttered curse of pain. Having gained the advantage, the man in black entangled Will in the bedclothes
in a swift unforeseen move.

With a sense of panic Will looked up and saw the gleaming edge of a razor-sharp knife poised above him. In an instant of terror Will realized this was no ordinary thief
looking for an unsecured wallet filled with money or credit
cards.

For a reason unknown to him, Will was faced with the
very real challenge of fighting this man for his life. Fear, like
a live thing, crawled through his insides, and the urgency of
the struggle increased. It was either him or the man in black.
Will knew one of them wouldn't leave the room alive.

The door between his suite and the next opened, admit-
ting a pale figure in white. Neither man noticed; neither man
cared. Only two things were of importance to them, the
knife—and winning.

Cassandra had been pacing for more than an hour with
her ears tuned to the next room, thinking of Will.

Since the instant she'd cried Barnabas's name in protest
at their plunge into the bay, she'd been able to think of little else. Because it was at that moment, forgetting all about
the rules, that Cassandra had reached out to Will mentally
and experienced with him that first blinding terror at the
realization of his impending death.

Something profound had happened to her during that
moment. A new link had been forged between them, one
she'd never felt in all the years of her guardianship of him.

So attuned was she to what was happening in the next
room, it had been impossible for her *not* to be aware when
someone else, the intruder, entered the room. Every sound
he made came to her clearly through five inches of wood,
plasterboard and paint. She had known instantly who he
was and what he was about.

Now she hesitated on the threshold, seeing the weapon, understanding its significance. In a moment the knife would plunge deep into Will's chest, severing him forever from this life.

She couldn't let this happen!

If it did, she knew she was forbidden to use either of her Heavenly gifts to change what had happened or to restore Will's life to him should he die.

Her heart thumped erratically in her chest, rapidly spreading this new emotion called fear throughout her system. Its taste was bitter on her tongue.

What was she to do?

In a moment the decision would be taken out of her hands...forever.

She saw the black material across the intruder's back grow taut as the muscles of his shoulder and back bunched in readiness. Cassandra held her breath as, without warning, the gleaming blade arced downward in a deadly, lightning-swift motion.

Without realizing that she'd moved, Cassandra was there, throwing her body between the two men, taking the force of the blow in her left breast. Like white-hot steel cutting through warm butter, the cold, sharp blade penetrated her chest and violated her body.

Recoiling from the force of the blow, she grabbed at the black figure with both hands to keep from falling. Her only thought was to protect Will, to keep his body from being a clear target for the would-be killer.

But the man was stronger than she, and he dragged her from the bed onto the floor. Wrenching her hands from his shoulders, he threw her from him.

At first he appeared unable to comprehend that he'd missed his chosen target and stabbed at the unidentified woman. One, moreover, who appeared uninjured, despite the proficiency with which he'd struck what he knew to be a fatal blow.

The black-clad figure drew back in disbelief, his small, dark eyes staring in amazement at the unrelieved whiteness of the woman's gown. No blood, no wound...

It was too much for his limited intelligence to handle. The job, as far as he was concerned had been finished when he'd felt the knife penetrate flesh; all he wanted now was a way out.

In less time than it took to blink an eye, the man scrambled to his feet. Pausing only long enough to glance down as though in surprise at the knife clutched in one hand, he ran quickly from the room.

Cassandra hung suspended between pain and elation. She had defied the would-be killer and kept Will alive. But the elation was short-lived. Self-healing was a tricky business, and she needed all her concentration for the process.

The task was something she couldn't hurry, even though she knew there wasn't much time before Will would be fully recovered and alert.

In a half-kneeling position beside the bed, where the man had left her, Cassandra took slow, deep, even breaths, her heart racing in her chest. She could feel the warmth of the healing power spreading throughout her body, revitalizing, renewing, bringing relief from a pain so agonizing it crowded all else from her mind.

On the bed, groggy from the blows he'd received to the head, and the prolonged lack of oxygen he'd suffered at the man's hands, Will was slowly regaining consciousness. And although he was aware of having been attacked, he remained unaware of the fact that his attacker had fled the scene.

Rolling over onto his side, he rubbed a soothing hand over his bruised, aching throat, attempting to swallow. His glance darted around the room, searching for the figure in black, coming to rest on the small figure in white, drooping on the floor beside him, blond hair obscuring her face from his eyes.

And now he vaguely recalled seeing a crippling, if not fatal, blow delivered by the man in black to the same young woman who had rescued him that evening from the bay. A numbing coldness spread through him, filling him with dread as he stared at her inert figure, unable to detect any signs of life.

The thought that she might have lost her own life in trying to save his kept him paralyzed on the bed.

After a moment, keeping the sheet wrapped around his lower body, Will slid to his knees on the soft carpet beside her. With unsteady fingers he took her gently by the shoulders, somewhat reassured by the warmth of her skin.

"Don't be dead," he demanded urgently. "Please, don't be dead."

Cassandra lifted her head and turned glazed eyes onto his face. "I'm not dead," she answered with difficulty.

He examined her with fearful eyes, expecting to see blood, relieved when he didn't. "Where are you hurt?"

"I'm not hurt," she managed over the sudden lump in her throat. *There were tears in his eyes.*

"But I saw the knife!" he protested mildly.

"I'm not hurt," she reiterated in a stronger voice.

He could have sworn he'd seen the knife thrust to the hilt into her breast. Could it have been—it must have been—a trick of the light?

Given the reality of the dream he'd had before awakening to find the intruder in his room, he was willing to believe that his eyes had deceived him.

"Are you sure? Not at all?" he asked doubtfully.

"Yes, I'm sure."

Fear left the golden eyes, and in its place a new, raw emotion began to take shape. With a consideration that had been missing before now in his dealings with her, Will lifted her in his strong arms, swinging her across his powerful thighs as he sat down on the edge of the bed with her on his lap.

Cassandra offered no protest, even when he moved her head gently from side to side, raised and then lowered each arm, still searching for signs of a wound.

"Thank God," he murmured, at last fully convinced she was unharmed.

"Yes," she agreed heartily. "Thank God."

Her glance locked with his, the look in his golden eyes filling her with conflicting emotions. Her heart beat erratically with an excitement she found delicious, while on the other hand her body shook in the grip of a nameless fear.

"The last time I saw you, you were on the beach," he murmured deeply. "What happened to you? How did you get here?"

"I'm staying here. My room is through there." She pointed toward the door, standing partially open, between the suites.

But Will seemed unable to take his glance off her face to look where she pointed. Strange new sensations were firing his blood. A profusion of questions was running through his brain, but all he could make any sense of was the fact that he wanted to touch his lips to hers.

After what they had both just been through, he fought against his baser instincts and asked, "Why did you leave me like that, on the beach?"

Her glance dropped to his bare throat, and she shook her head, unable to explain. She didn't know what to say to him and found that she couldn't look away. As though she had no control over what they did, her eyes followed the strong lines of his throat down to the thick hair growing across his breastbone toward the edge of the sheet.

"I looked for you," he admitted, all at once unable to sustain his control under the innocent provocation of her glance.

"You did?" Her pulse accelerated as she looked into his glowing eyes. "Why?"

"I was . . . worried . . . about you."

Worried? About her? She was there to sustain him—and he was worrying about her. It might have been amusing, under different circumstances.

Will felt her tremble and knew he should let her go. Now that he'd ascertained she was uninjured, there was no need to keep her so close. But that curious warmth brought on moments ago by her scrutiny was stealing over him again, concentrating in his lower body.

He was disconcerted to discover that his fingers wanted to trace the gentle curve of her cheek, linger against the soft skin of her shoulder, smooth the mauve tips of her breasts.

The light falling on her upturned face caused it to take on a faint radiance, enhancing the perfection of her bowed upper lip and the full swell of the lower one. He couldn't help it, his eyes devoured her, dropping to take in the rosy hue of bare flesh visible beneath the thin nightgown.

His hands took on a caressing quality as they moved slowly up her forearms, sliding over the silky sleeves of the nightgown before coming to rest against the pristine base of her long, graceful neck.

Cassandra quivered like the strings of a fine instrument beneath the touch of a master's hand. Her blue glance rested yearningly on his face, the fingers of both hands itching to touch him, but remaining tightly clenched in her lap.

She longed, without quite understanding why, to stroke the gossamer threads of silver mixed with brown at his temples, to test the short stubble bristling along his cheeks and chin.

Their eyes meshed and became entangled, and her breath caught at the expression in his. The yearning grew inside her.

Without warning, Will's head dipped toward hers, the thumbs beneath her chin tilting her head back to meet his advance. At the first touch of her lips his body quickened, stirring to life long-dead ashes of desire.

His head swimming with the aroma of her perfume, a haunting fragrance he'd never encountered in any other woman, all thought became lost in some misty cloud of sensual awareness.

His mouth opened warmly over hers, deepening the kiss. One arm slipped around her, pulling her tenderly against his chest, pressing her soft breasts flat against him.

He couldn't fight it; the taste and feel of her were driving him out of his mind. He wanted her in a way that he hadn't wanted a woman since his libidinous youth.

This shouldn't be happening; his brain warned him against the folly of such insanity. He knew nothing about her. She'd come into his life under strange and unsettling circumstances.

But his body, his instincts, his heart, didn't care about any of those things. They craved satisfaction.

All at once he felt her push against him with both hands. Will released her, then drew back to look at her with a questioning tilt to one dark brow.

He could see the panic in her eyes, could sense the emotional turmoil she was going through. And though he was confused by his own actions, because he still wanted her, Will released her fully, realizing that with her it had to be a mutual need they both wanted to satisfy; nothing else would do.

Just for a moment Cassandra remained where she was, perched on his knee, surprised by his actions, but too mired in her own state of confusion to look too closely at them.

She was an angel, not a human. No matter what she appeared to be on the surface, she felt that what she was doing, her being here with this man like this, wasn't what Barnabas had had in mind when he'd told her to give in to new emotions and let them teach her about being human.

She didn't know what to do, because in this man's arms she felt helpless. He took away her ability to think. All she could do was *feel*.

This was too much for her to cope with alone. She needed Barnabas's council.

That thought had her propelling herself off Will's lap and rushing, headlong, toward the door separating their suites.

Closing it with a firm slam, Cassandra closed her eyes and, with an uneven sigh, leaned back against it, once more feeling safe now that she was in her own room. And that was the instant she realized she hadn't left Will in the next room at all. Because a crystal-clear image of his handsome face remained etched in her mind.

A series of disjointed thoughts and ideas crowded into her brain, most of which she couldn't make heads or tails of. Shaking her head back and forth against the door, she covered her face, trying to block his image from her mind.

She must concentrate on who she was and her purpose in being there, she told herself firmly.

Heaven was wonderful, and she longed to become an archangel—Will's image became stronger despite her attempts to block it out—but...oh...this man...Will...his touch...what it did to her...

What was she thinking! Her eyes snapped open, and she jerked upright, away from the door. This was the same man who had closed his mind to her in the elevator when she had tried to warn him of impending danger. Life had turned him from the gentle, loving youth he'd been with his parents and made him hard and uncaring. Look what he was willing to do to mankind's future for *money!*

But he hadn't been hard or uncaring just now. When he'd thought she was injured, he'd cared deeply. And she'd felt his despair, his fear, in the water.

She recalled how he had looked at her on the beach with contempt and knew that if he looked at her that way again, she would be cast into a pit of despair. What was happening to her?

She didn't want him to think badly of her; she was glad now that he hadn't believed her when she'd told him she was an angel. She realized she was beginning to want him to believe in her, to like her for herself. She wanted him to see her as a woman.

She wanted to see again that special expression he'd worn as he'd held her in his arms, touched his mouth to hers, only moments ago. The one that told her there was no one, nothing, in his mind at that moment—except *her.*

What was happening to her? What were these changes taking place inside this body that was on loan to her for the short duration of her stay?

Surely this was not how it was supposed to be. Was she *supposed* to feel more human than angel—and after only a few hours? She didn't think so, and she wished with all her heart that she could go back where she belonged right now, before she had to face this human, this Will Alexander, again.

Will stared at the closed door with troubled dark eyes. Who was this woman who taunted him first with her knowledge of his private doings and then with her...beauty?

Why had she followed him back to the hotel? And what had prompted her to come to his room so late at night?

He moved purposefully off the bed, forsaking the sheet, and headed for the closet. No one was supposed to know his reasons for being in Los Angeles. No one, that was, except Jordan Black.

Not even Tom Mason, the man responsible for giving him the evidence with which to nail Black, knew his present whereabouts. And if it hadn't been for Tom, Will knew he would still be searching for a means of revenge.

Will dressed quickly in a pair of faded jeans, then poured himself a stiff drink from the small bar in the corner and took it with him to the window. Gazing down on the traffic below, he reviewed the attack.

Obviously the intruder had been sent by Black. Yet Will found it hard to believe it had been Black's intention to have him killed. He wanted what Will had too badly, and feared the consequences should it fall into the wrong hands, to do away with him before he saw the evidence destroyed with his own two eyes.

It wasn't that Will thought Black incapable of cold-blooded murder—he knew for a fact the man was capable of that and more—but not when so much was at stake and could be lost through such a reckless move.

Will could prove, among other heinous crimes, that Black willingly, with malice aforethought, was scheming to build a planned community atop land that had been one of this country's first toxic waste dumps.

Will didn't worry, as a lot of people did, about the future of the world. He'd learned that it was all in fate's fickle hands, and fate played dirty. It stacked the deck against you at birth and changed everyone's future on a whim.

The only thing certain about the future was that you couldn't count on it unfolding the way you wanted it to. He'd come to face every day of his future with suspicion, wondering who would stab him in the back next.

As for the houses over the toxic waste dump, he didn't actually think there was that much to worry about, even if Black built the new town. The land took care of itself; it always had, despite man's attempts to destroy it. And in this world, as far as man was concerned, it was survival of the fittest just as it always had been.

And right now he was less concerned with this planet's future generations than with his own immediate needs.

But there were others, he knew, people of power, who would jump at the chance to find Black guilty. Preventing him from breaking ground for the project would give them a victory to rally around for a long time to come.

Despite Black's influence and money, Will was confident that the information he had would ruin the man. Ecology was a touchy subject with practically all governmental agencies. No one wanted to be caught backing a man who threw caution to the wind and deliberately jeopardized the world's future population.

It would be political suicide. And Will happened to know that Black had plans to run for office in the near future.

Taking a long drink from his glass, Will considered the woman who had come charging into his life tonight. It seemed strange to him that she should have arrived on the scene so unexpectedly, then be responsible for saving his life twice in one evening.

Could the accident earlier that evening have been staged by her and the taxi driver? They knew each other; she'd admitted as much. Perhaps it had merely been a prelude to the attack tonight, so he would have reason to feel indebted to her a second time.

Hadn't he heard, or thought he'd heard, her call out to the taxi driver just seconds before the crash? A signal?

And what did Jordan Black have to do with this? Was she working for him?

The idea didn't sit well with him. He knew virtually nothing about her, yet he felt drawn to her. And despite his gnawing suspicions, he acknowledged the growing attraction he felt for her. It didn't particularly please him.

Will stared down unseeingly at the amber liquid he was swirling around in the glass. He hadn't felt such an upheaval of emotion since . . . his parents' death.

Everyone he'd met in his adult life had wanted something from him. His eyes swerved toward the closed door as he lifted the glass and took a long pull from it.

What did *she* want from him?

Chapter 4

Cassandra paced with one ear tuned to the next room. Listening with her senses, she realized that Will felt as restless and uncertain as she did.

After a moment, feeling as though she was somehow eavesdropping, even though she wasn't actually reading Will's thoughts, only his aura, she turned her thoughts in another direction.

But that didn't last long. Thinking about Heaven and her job there caring for the young, as yet unborn souls only reminded her of what her new position would be. She would be elevated to the status of archangel and undertake the new job of mapping out the basic futures of those who were soon to be born, always keeping in mind that they would have a choice in the matter.

This elevated status was of course contingent on her completing this assignment satisfactorily. And that thought brought her full circle, reminding her about Will and her less than estimable part in his past.

Thinking about her momentary feeling of guilt a few moments ago, she realized that in all the years she'd made periodical checks on Will's life, she'd never considered knowing what he was thinking an invasion of his privacy—until now.

Her newly discovered emotional concepts were expanding in an utterly perplexing manner. And she wasn't certain she could handle all the changes taking place inside her. All at once the room began to feel as though it was getting smaller, closing in on her, making her want to run away and hide.

In Heaven she'd never had to face such feelings of uncertainty, never had to wonder if what she was doing was right. But then, in Heaven, she had never truly touched a human *life*.

Everything on Earth was so different and frightening. If it had been at all possible, she would have returned to Heaven with or without Barnabas's knowledge and agreement.

It wasn't that she didn't feel responsible, at least in part, for what was happening to Will. As Barnabas had pointed out earlier that evening, she should have known better than to leave Will to his own devices so much.

She'd been taught, as all guardian angels were, that some human beings required more help and guidance than others. Will was one of them.

And it wasn't that she didn't want to help him, because she did, very much, but she had no faith in her ability to do so. What if she only made things worse for him?

Will needed someone who knew what she was doing. Someone who could take charge and make things happen. And, sad though the knowledge made her, she knew that that person—or angel—simply wasn't her.

She'd arrived on Earth that day with the idea that she would repay her debt to him quickly and get back to where she belonged. And with that thought in mind, she'd jumped in with both feet and called him immediately upon her arrival in the hotel—and what had that accomplished?

Nothing except put black marks against her for breaking rules. And make her responsible for almost getting Will killed at Barnabas's hands.

In the taxi she'd tried again by attempting to charm, then seduce, him from his meeting with Black. The attempt had failed miserably, and as a result they had all ended up in the bay.

Barnabas had thought the accident would serve a dual purpose in keeping Will from his appointment and giving her a chance to save his life. That would put him in her debt, opening the door for a friendship that would help her accomplish her job.

Needless to say, only the part about missing the appointment had worked.

Cassandra sighed and shook her head. Some things didn't change, no matter where you existed. In Heaven she had been seen as less than perfect, and it looked as though that assessment was going to apply here, too.

There was, she supposed, ample reason for the way the other angels thought of her. It was no use denying the fact that she had a penchant for forgetting the time and failing to show up for important events, or becoming so thoroughly involved in one task that she neglected her other duties.

And there was the fact that she seemed to have a natural propensity for picking *exactly* the wrong time to interrupt an important event with some form of inept behavior.

But she didn't do those things deliberately, Cassandra insisted silently. She always *meant* well. Things just seemed to go wrong for her—all the time.

When Barnabas had informed her about the trip to Earth, she had begged him to intercede on her behalf and ask that someone else be chosen in her place. She'd only ever seen one angel who had been to Earth in human form, and she didn't want to be one of those who went.

Stories of such happenings had spread like wildfire up above, and most of the other angels had appeared intrigued by the idea. But not Cassandra. Heaven held enough untold mystery and fear for her; she hadn't wanted to even contemplate what new terrors Earth might offer. But all her pleading had been to no avail.

Cassandra plopped down spiritlessly onto the bed and stared around at the room's elegant appointments. Nothing—not one single thing—in this place was truly familiar to her. Oh, she had seen these things over the years in her visions of Earth, but her knowledge of how to use things like furniture, clothing and the telephone was purely theoretical.

It was the same with emotions. She'd heard people laugh, seen them cry, flinched at their anger and been enchanted by watching two people kiss, but it wasn't the same when you did those things—felt them—yourself.

She was finding that her ideas of what emotions were like were completely different from reality. Like a single fluffy white cloud floating in a sky of clear blue, Cassandra felt out of place and all alone.

She discovered she was rubbing in vexation at an annoying itch on her neck. The white terry-cloth robe she'd donned upon returning from the room next door was chafing at her skin.

This new form of clothing was another thing she found vexing. She was used to loose, flowing robes, spun from thread as delicate as that of a spider's web, garments that allowed her to perform physical tasks with the same freedom she experienced in both spirit and mind.

She disliked the restrictions imposed by Earth's clothing almost as much as she disliked the loneliness of spirit she'd found in being here. As far as she could see, there was little to like here on Earth.

Well, she conceded after a moment of thought, there was *one* thing she had found to her liking—the swimming. She liked the shower in this hotel suite, too. It rather reminded her of swimming. But nothing else.

Her glance drifted toward the closed door between the suites. *Not true,* that strange little voice, which seemed to have developed in accordance with this new body she wore, murmured slyly in her head. *You like Will.*

Of course she liked him. She had to; he was her charge.

It's more than that, the tiny voice continued, *and you might just as well admit it.*

But Cassandra refused to listen to what the voice might be implying—the idea was unthinkable.

She got to her feet and moved nervously around the room. Perhaps there were a *few* things about being human to like, she decided, touching, stroking, appreciating the *feel* of things.

After a moment she felt calmer. This was something she could enjoy without reservation. She became absorbed in the delightful occupation, putting her unsettling thoughts behind her for a time.

All at once the feel of the robe had become unbearable against her skin. She pulled the sash, loosening it, and moved toward the light, airy, walk-in closet across from the large bed.

As she moved, her feet made sliding movements in the luxurious pile of the royal-blue carpet. The resulting sensations fascinated her, reminding her of the feel of the beach earlier that night as the sand had been sucked from beneath her feet by the incoming tide. The two sensations were similar, yet, at the same time, very different.

In Heaven, the ability to touch was there, but without the accompanying corporeal response. In other words, you had no body, were in fact truly ethereal.

But you knew the sense of things, like the fact that a lamb's wool was soft, or an apple sweet, because the knowledge was implanted in your mind. You *knew* and *understood* about how things were without actually experiencing them.

As a human, the messages she was receiving were immediate, constant and ever-changing. She wondered how people could get anything else done when there were so many things to touch, so many new sensations to experience in everything around them.

If she were human, it would take up all her time, evaluating each new perception, separating them in her mind.

Bypassing the closet, she pulled open a drawer in the dresser and stared down at the clothing folded and arranged in three neat piles. Barnabas's doing, not hers. That was another of her many failings; she wasn't a very organized angel.

Her fingers touched and lingered over first one and then another of the garments. Closing her eyes, she took delight in experiencing the differences in their textures and the diverse sensations each caused her to feel. The novelty of this new game set her mind to tingling nearly as much as her fingertips. She became caught up in it, almost euphoric, high with the thrill of each contact.

After a while her eyes opened, and her glance fell on a small contrivance of delicate-looking lace and narrow straps, a delight to the eye that should have been a delight to wear. She grimaced in remembered revulsion.

She had almost worn one of those contraptions beneath the dress she'd had on that evening, when she'd followed Will into the elevator. But it was a terrible device of pure torture that pinched and bound her in places this body preferred left free, and she'd removed it again before leaving the room.

With a slight shudder she vowed to leave *that* particular item exactly where it was until the end of her stay.

She slipped out of the robe and grabbed the first thing that didn't immediately irritate her, then slipped it over her head and smoothed it into place, pleased with the soft, silky texture. Yes, this was much better than the robe she'd been wearing, more like what she was used to.

A slight sound from the next room jerked her out of her preoccupation with her new senses, reminding her of the task at hand. With a soft snap, she shut the drawer, reminded once again of what had taken place only a short while ago in Will's room.

Her nervous pacing resumed. Wringing her hands, she cast short, swift glances toward the door. For a little while she'd forgotten her immediate predicament. What was she going to do about the man next door?

"Barnabas, where are you?" she called to him with her mind. *"I don't know what to do! Am I supposed to feel so confused about everything? Am I supposed to feel the way I did in the arms of this man I've known, yet not really known, since his birth? Is it right to feel as though I belong there?*

"I'm supposed to protect him against Jordan Black's evil, to get him to realize the folly of his thinking. But, how can I do that now? I'm terrified just to be in the same room with him.

"What if—somehow—he should discover what I'm thinking and feeling? Oh, Barnabas," she wailed, *"come to me. Help me to understand what's happening to me!"*

She waited, listening with all her senses, hoping to get a message from the old man. But after a time, getting no reply, she threw herself across the bed and buried her face in the pillows.

Even now, in a state of abject despair, she couldn't turn off her awareness of the various scents and textures of the things around her. Even in her distress she was fully aware of the softness of the coverlet on which she lay, the clean, sweet odor coming from the white pillowcase beneath her cheek, the soft murmur of the air-conditioning blowing gently across her skin.

Her senses continued to absorb each message like a never-ending symphony, finally wearing her out. She had never experienced anything so wonderful, or so terrible, in all the years of her existence.

Her over-stimulated senses added to a feeling of being lost and abandoned without Barnabas's guidance, and her eyelids began to droop. That was another thing about Earth that was different from Heaven.... She yawned. So many things...to get used to...like this need for...sleep...

Cassandra slept—and dreamed. And in her dream Barnabas did indeed come to her, but only to repeat what he'd told her before their initial descent to Earth.

"I will be with you, help you, whenever I can, though I am limited in that. Some things," he had warned, "even *I* do not know and am not allowed to do.

"My job is to evaluate your work and to remind you of the passing of time. *Your* task is to bring about a change in Will Alexander's way of thinking that will benefit mankind. I will only be there to act as a mediator between you and the Divine.

"You must, if at all possible, work out any problems you encounter for yourself. And you must not use your Heavenly talents to make things too easy.

"Remember, for all intents and purposes, you will be human and must act as such. By all means enjoy these new experiences while you can. But always keep in mind your real purpose in being on Earth, and let all that you do further your work, both on Earth and in Heaven."

The resonant sound of Barnabas's voice faded, and Cassandra moved fitfully on the bed. There were still so many questions plaguing her.

Was this internal upheaval, this strange deluge of emotions she experienced when around Will, the natural order of what was to happen? Was this what Barnabas had meant she should give in to—and enjoy? Her head flopped back and forth on the pillow; it was all so complicated.

Time passed, a mere heartbeat compared to that of Heaven, while she slept. All at once a firm knock roused her abruptly from sleep. She lay on the bed, blinking rapidly in confusion.

"Barnabas?" she whispered. "Is that you?"

"Hey, are you in there?" Will's forceful whisper drifted through the closed door to her. "Open up. I want to talk to you."

The words were followed by a series of staccato knocks that escalated loudly toward the end.

Cassandra slipped off the bed and moved to the door. Her first instinct was to pretend she was still sleeping, or gone, and ignore him. But her fingers, she discovered all at once, had begun to undo the lock.

She hesitated. What could he want from her now?

She could always probe his thoughts to find out—*no, she couldn't.*

The lock clicked in her hand, and she automatically stepped back, opening the door wide.

Will moved cautiously inside, noting how dark the room appeared at first glance. The only light came from his own lamp, spilling through the open door, hardly penetrating the darkness within.

"Do you mind if I turn on a light?" he asked, his fingers reaching toward the switch by the door.

Cassandra murmured her assent. She should have remembered that though light was not a prerequisite for her, it was for him. Within an instant of the thought, a bright yellow glow flooded the room, causing her to blink several times before her eyes adjusted to the brightness and settled on his figure, standing less than two feet away.

She couldn't help the way her heart began to race as her eyes took in his tall, lean body, bare except for the pair of jeans riding low on his narrow hips. The dark, crisp hair, cut close to his scalp, showed a hint of waviness in the longer strands on top, and it looked as though he'd been running his fingers through it.

Cassandra's gaze drifted down over his face, the lower portion dark from the heavy beard visible just below the skin's surface. Once again her fingers itched to touch his cheeks and chin, and she quickly shielded her eyes with her lids at the thought.

Her glance moved over his bare chest to the jeans cupping his maleness like a gentle hand. Oh dear, there it was again, that strange, fluttery sensation in her insides, making her knees feel weak and her tongue too thick in her dry mouth.

Will took a quick peek at the pale blue see-through nightgown she was wearing and glanced quickly away, an image of her creamy skin and shadowy curves crystal clear in his mind. He couldn't decide if she was as bold as brass, answering the door dressed like this, or as innocent as a newborn babe.

"Look, I know it's late." He moved aimlessly around the room, doing his best to keep his eyes on the furnishings and off the provocative picture she made. "I couldn't sleep. I—" He paused and turned abruptly to face her. "What's your name?"

"Cassandra."

"Cassandra?"

She nodded, biting her lip. The room was beginning to grow small again, and she could hardly breathe.

Will shrugged after a moment when she offered no surname and said, "I'm Will Alexander."

"I know," she answered quickly.

He glanced up, meeting her clear blue eyes. Yes, so she did. "That's what I want to talk to you about."

He moved to lean back against the wall near the long window, edgily rubbing one hand up and down the other arm from elbow to shoulder, then back.

"I want you to tell me again who you are and how you know about me...." He hesitated. "And what you know about my... association... with Jordan Black."

Cassandra found herself following the movement of his hand as it slipped up and down the hair roughened skin. It took a great deal of effort for her to withdraw her gaze and focus on what he was saying.

Their eyes met. His stare was cool and direct.

A lightning-swift shaft of some nameless emotion pierced her heart like an arrow. Swallowing with difficulty, Cassandra tore her gaze from his, clasped her hands carefully at her waist and spoke. "I—I'm—"

No, an inner voice snapped so strongly that she almost flinched at the sound. *Don't tell him you're an angel! Do you want to reaffirm his earlier idea that you're crazy? And besides, it's against the rules, remember? Barnabas was very upset that you'd done something so stupid on the beach.*

Something deep inside took over, and her mind ran though several possible responses before she spoke. She couldn't lie, not even to protect him; that was one of the unbreakable rules she *had* to follow. To lie was a very great sin.

In this case, she could tell the truth with Barnabas's blessing. Before her journey she'd been provided with the details of Jordan Black's life. She knew him, and all the crimes he'd committed against his fellow man, better than she knew Will. And with Barnabas's help, she had prepared a reason to give Will for her having contacted him.

"I'm... something of an environmentalist," she responded after a moment of contemplation, reasoning that anyone concerned with what was happening to the Earth and its future, anyone involved in the preservation of its natural beauty and wonder for future generations, could be called an environmentalist.

"And a psychic," Will added coolly.

"And a psychic," she conceded after a brief pause. "Through my work, I've come across Mr. Black's name many times. I've learned a great deal about him and what he's been up to over the years."

There was little use in skirting the real reason for her being there. "I know all about that stretch of land in southern Nevada that he has earmarked for development. And I know that for a period of time that land was secretly used as one of this country's first toxic waste dumps.

"And I know, too, what the results to mankind would be should Mr. Black's plans become reality."

Her glance sharpened on Will's expressionless face. "Mr. Black must be stopped before that can happen," she stated firmly, her own natural abhorrence for any kind of destruction coming to the fore, giving her a confidence she normally lacked.

"Your concern is commendable," Will said after a long moment of silence. "But that doesn't explain what you're doing *here*. He gestured around the room with one hand.

He didn't like the fact that she knew so much about Black—that meant she probably knew more about his own plans than he liked to contemplate.

It appeared as though his fears that she had been sent by Black were unfounded, but he still didn't like the idea of anyone—especially this woman—knowing his secrets. It made him uncomfortable, and that made him angry.

"And it sure as hell doesn't explain your calling me this evening, or your little demonstration in the elevator, or what happened in that taxi. Who *are* you?" he asked in heated tones. "And what is it you want from me?"

Cassandra took a seat on the end of the bed to give herself time to think. "I told you, I've been gathering information about Mr. Black over a period of years." She glanced up and met his impatient glare. "Along the way I became aware of someone else—someone headed down the same destructive path in life."

Her glance lowered, became fixed on her hands linked together in her lap. "You. I've followed the direction your life has taken for some time now. I know all about the terrible financial setback you had at Mr. Black's hands, and I know you'd like nothing better than to get your revenge."

Her eyes found his face. "But sacrificing future generations of your own species is not the way to do it."

Will thrust his hands into the pockets of his jeans and turned away. A do-gooder, he thought with contempt. He was standing here in the middle of the night trading words with a dyed-in-the-wool, bleeding-heart radical. One of those people, no doubt, who saw Bambi in every slaughtered deer during hunting season. He had better things to do with his time.

"You don't know what you're talking about," he threw over his shoulder as he headed toward the door. "And in any case, this has nothing to do with you—so just butt out."

"I know that man in your room tonight was going to kill you—and Jordan Black sent him," she responded quickly, her eyes drawn to the strongly defined muscles of his shoulders and back.

Will's step didn't falter. He'd figured out for himself that Black had sent the man, though he still didn't believe Black wanted him dead. Not yet. So her ability to put two and two together and come up with Black's name didn't change a thing.

Cassandra frowned. "Aren't you upset by the knowledge? I can assure you it's the truth."

"Not particularly." Will shrugged.

"But he attacked you! He could have killed you when you caught him searching your things."

Will turned back to face her. "How do you know he was searching my things?"

Cassandra thought quickly. She had given too much away. "I saw him—through there," she said, nodding toward the door. It was true, after all; she had seen him through the door—though the door had been closed at the time.

Will shrugged again. "I'm not worried. Black has too much at stake to kill me *before* he gets what he wants."

"The documents you have in your keeping, you mean?" she asked coolly.

Will frowned. "How do you know about them?"

"I know more than you think," she answered almost defensively. "I know you're planning to extort money from

Mr. Black with what you have.'' Unable to maintain an appearance of being calm while seated, she stood and walked toward the window. "How can you jeopardize people's lives—for *money?*" She made the word sound vile.

Will took a threatening step toward her. "Obviously," he rasped, eyes running over her body suggestively, "you don't value money. One way or another, no doubt, you've never had to do without it." The golden eyes sparkled as they came to rest on her face. "Money, that is."

The significance of what he implied was lost on her. But she realized from his attitude that he was angry.

"Think of the children," she begged, concerned not with his opinion of her but with her real purpose in being there. "There will be babies born without arms, without legs—"

"You don't know that," he interrupted harshly, a thin thread of unease worming its way into his conscience.

"No? Haven't you ever read what some of the ingredients in toxic waste can do to the cells of a human body?"

He glared at her without answering.

"Well, I have!" she acknowledged tearfully.

"I'm not a bleeding heart," he told her stonily. "I don't *look* for trouble before it looks for me. And besides, I have enough worries of my own. I don't need to add worrying about future mankind—which I won't be around to see, in any case—to the list of what keeps me awake at night."

"I'm sorry you can't sleep at night," she told him sincerely. "But please, won't you reconsider what you're about to do?"

Will opened his mouth to tell her bluntly what she could do with her sympathy. He didn't know why he didn't simply storm from her room and forget all about her.

Perhaps it was the ingenuous glint in her blue eyes or the slight trembling of her lower lip, or maybe the desperate manner in which her body seemed to lean toward his that made him reconsider.

"When I first learned what Black was up to," he found himself explaining, "I tried to stop him. But no one wanted to know." He moved toward her, upset now himself. "Can you imagine people's reactions to accusations made against the great Jordan Black?" His razor-sharp glance sliced through her. "They all admitted there *might* be a problem with using the land if what I said was true. But they were all confident that I was wrong about the dumping and that Black would never knowingly endanger anyone's life. And do you know why they were so confident of his righteousness?"

She shook her head.

"Oh, come on, it has to do with something that's green and buys you anything you want." He made an impatient gesture with one hand, then pushed it through his hair. "It even buys innocence, if it's put into the right hands."

He bent toward her menacingly. "Power!" he almost shouted, watching with satisfaction as she flinched away. "Power and money! That's what it's all about. No one wanted to oppose a man as powerful as Jordan Black—but most of all, no one was willing to give up the money they'd gotten—and would keep on getting to support him. That's what makes it possible for Black to get what he wants."

In a quieter voice he added, "And no one cares."

"Oh, that isn't true," Cassandra protested, taking an involuntary step forward. "There are lots of people who care. Why didn't you go to one of the environmentalist groups? Or to the newspapers?"

Will shrugged his bare shoulders listlessly. "What's the use? It would only be the same thing all over again. Someone would owe someone else a favor, or someone would sell out.

"Besides, I found a better way to get at Black—and get back some of what I've lost in the process, thanks to him. I'm going to hit him right where it hurts—his money belt." He gave a dry laugh and reached for the door handle.

"Wait!" Her cry halted him.

He turned slowly, a long-suffering look on his tight face.

"Please—that land is deadly."

She closed the distance between them, her body swaying with unconscious appeal beneath the shimmering gown. "Won't you help me stop him? Please?"

"If my helping you means forgoing my own plans, lady, then the answer's no."

He hardened his resolve against her, against the strong, innocently sensual appeal he was once more aware of as he took in the delicate lines of her body revealed beneath the see-through gown.

"Oh, but surely," she protested, "when you think of all the people you'd be saving, the innocent children who won't have to suffer..."

She touched his bare shoulder tentatively, meeting his dark glance, and her voice dropped to a mere whisper of sound. "Those things are more important than revenge."

Will found he couldn't look away; he was drowning in twin pools of electric blue light that seemed to emanate from her eyes and burn through to the center of his brain.

The fingers resting on his shoulder began to feel warm, then hot, the heat radiating outward toward every part of his body. His senses began to swim in an alarming manner, and he could feel his heartbeat, the pounding sensation becoming the tattoo of a drum, inside his head.

"All right," he heard himself say. "I'll help you. It doesn't matter to me how Black gets his, just so long as he gets it."

Cassandra withdrew her touch, a luminous smile sweeping across her face. "Thank you. I know you won't regret your decision."

"No," Will muttered vaguely, still under her spell.

He wasn't certain exactly what he'd just agreed to, but after he had finished with Black, he didn't give a damn what Cassandra and her bunch did to him. He shook his head, feeling more like himself with every passing second.

Maybe his pretending to help her would be a good cover for his real intentions. He ignored the twinge of conscience he felt at the idea, rationalized it with the thought that she would be getting what she wanted and, after all, that was what mattered. Wasn't it? They would both be getting what they wanted.

"I'll get the documents to you sometime tomorrow evening. You can do whatever you want with them after that."

"Oh, no." She shook her head briskly, the blond waves bouncing around her small shapely head, capturing and reflecting the light.

"It's *you* who must turn the evidence over to the authorities. They'll believe in its validity because you know Mr. Black, you've worked with him. You can give them all the inside details about the evil he's done in the past and how he's managed to get this far with this plan.

"And you must do it quickly, before Mr. Black can make his plans a reality," she finished firmly.

Will backed away from her, both figuratively and literally. That wasn't at all what he intended to do. He couldn't afford to become mixed up with Black's downfall. With his pockets full of Black's money, there was no way he was going to the police or anyone else.

His intention was to be long gone, out of the country, when Black was confronted by the law. It was the only way he would be safe. Jordan Black wouldn't let a little thing like being behind bars stop him from seeing that Will's throat was slit.

"Look, you don't understand. I don't have the documents with me," he hedged, reconsidering the idea of giving them to her. "They're stored in a safe place, some place where no one else can get to them. It's late. Let's leave this discussion about what to do with them until tomorrow. Deal?"

Cassandra's eyes probed his face, wondering what was going on in his mind. But his expression told her nothing; his smile was remote. She could delve behind those eyes, behind that smile...if she wanted to.

But she wouldn't.

Will edged toward the door, but something inside Cassandra couldn't let him go, not just yet. Now that she'd done what she'd come to do, after tomorrow their brief time together would be at an end. She would continue to see him from afar, would still be a part of his spiritual life, but contact with him on a human level would be over.

"Please." She swayed toward him. "In the other room...you...touched your lips to mine..."

Her fingers lifted to touch her own lips as she spoke, then reached out toward his, hovering in the air, not quite making contact.

Will felt a strange tightening sensation in his middle and, knowing it was a mistake, dared to ask, "Did you like it?"

"Oh, yes...it was..." She hesitated. "It was like nothing I've ever known."

The tightness inside him grew, until he felt as though he might explode if he didn't touch her. He leaned forward a few inches until her extended fingers touched the skin of his lips, and then something snapped inside him. Closing his eyes, he reached for her.

It was no use fighting it; he'd been wanting to do this since he'd walked into the room and seen her standing there dressed so alluringly.

Cassandra ran her fingertips across his lips, noting their smoothness. His warm breath blowing against the back of her hand caused her to shiver. Her hand moved over his face, coming to rest on the shadowed skin of his chin, and her fingers slid down below the curve of his bottom lip to explore what had fascinated her since she'd first noticed it, the shadow of his beard.

As she touched the rough, prickly stubble, she withdrew her touch and cast him a look of surprise. But his eyes were closed, the skin stretched tautly over his high forehead, broad cheekbones and square jaw.

His eyelids quivered, the long, dark, curling eyelashes almost brushing against the skin of his cheeks, and her fingers had to explore them, too. Will opened his eyes at her touch and stared at her.

Cassandra caught her breath at the expression in his golden depths. She could see he was moved, and it created an odd curling sensation low in her stomach.

Will's hands at her back moved upward, sliding slowly over the smooth, silky gown. He felt her quiver beneath his hands, and his own foundations shook. Unlike other women he'd made love to, she held nothing back; everything she was feeling was there in her face for him to see.

When his hands had reached shoulder level—still keeping his glance locked with hers, so he could see the changes taking place in her blue eyes—he grasped her shoulders in firm but gentle hands and drew her closer. His lips parted as his head dipped toward hers.

Cassandra felt her heart stand still in anticipation. The *kiss*—he was going to do it. Again. With curious eyes she watched as he tilted his head slightly and, wanting to do everything just right, she tilted her own, licking her lips nervously.

Will hesitated, a question turning his eyes dark with passion. "How old are you?" he asked softly. It was hard to tell; there was an innocence about her, yet she seemed almost ageless.

"Old?"

"Yes, you aren't underage by any chance?" His hands shook with the effort of restraining his need in order to ask the question.

"Underage? No, I'm old—" She saw the glint of a smile spark in his eyes, remembering Barnabas's instructions and continued. "Old enough."

Will was holding her close enough to feel her breath catch as she spoke, to smell the perfume wafting from her bewitchingly beautiful body, and he agreed. "Yes," he murmured, impatient to know her more intimately, "you certainly are."

His face descended to capture her quivering mouth beneath his. He guided her into the kiss, moving his mouth over hers, opening her lips with his insistent tongue, tasting the sweet nectar inside.

He felt her recoil slightly when the tip of his tongue touched hers, and his brain fired him the message that this woman was too innocent for him. But when he made as though to put her from him, she wouldn't allow it.

Pressing her lips more firmly to his, slipping her arms around his neck, she leaned purposefully against him, plastering herself all down his front in an unintentionally provocative gesture.

Startled by her deliberate move, Will held back, wondering if she were a professional after all, her innocence a mere act. The thought bothered him more than he would have expected.

Was it justice for unborn babies she was after, or information with which she could do a bit of blackmailing herself?

His hands tightened on her shoulders. He shifted her away to get a good look at her face, confident that, if it existed, he would be able to read the mercenary light in her blue glance.

She looked up at him with heavy-lidded eyes, a bemused expression in their depths, a slight smile curving lips swollen from his kisses—begging for more.

"What...is it?" she asked softly, when he made no move to draw her close again. "Have I done something wrong?" The bemused expression left her face, replaced by one of innocent inquiry.

Will swallowed tautly. "No," he responded huskily. "You haven't done anything wrong."

He couldn't seem to keep from touching her. Hands that trembled ever so slightly slipped up her shoulders to her neck, lingering momentarily against its velvety smoothness before passing on to cup her face between large palms.

"Are you for real?" he murmured softly; then, realizing he was becoming bewitched by her again, he dropped his hands and took a step back.

"Yes," she answered softly. "I'm real. Touch me...and see." Taking one of his hands, she pressed the back of it against her cheek.

He shifted his hand from her grasp to smooth a tendril of hair from her cheek, placing it carefully behind one small, shell-pink ear.

His breathing became shallow as the thumb, instead of moving away, trailed slowly down the side of her neck. He watched her eyes close as she tilted her head away from him, leaving her neck vulnerable to his touch. She gave a delicate shiver all at once, and his heart responded with a sudden leap.

His glance traveled down over the shimmering skin of her shoulder, glinting palely in the light. His thumb followed suit, gliding across the velvety skin covering her clavicle, then coming to rest between her breasts at the top of the sheer, ice blue nightgown.

The gown left little to the imagination. And the sight of her budding breasts pushing against the silky material, the shadow of her lower body visible beneath the sheer veil of blue, aroused him to the point where release was fast becoming a necessity.

"Have you ever *known* a man?" His hot, whispered breath fanned her forehead and cheeks.

"I know *you*, Will Alexander," she answered precisely, her lids lifting so that her blue eyes stared directly into his.

The damp palms of both hands were at the lacy top of the gown.

"Would you . . . like to . . . know . . . me . . . better?"

"I would like to know you in all the ways there are," she answered with candid simplicity.

"Yes," he groaned, his head lowering to press hotly against the tops of her breasts. "I don't know who you are." His lips traveled across both breasts, leaving a moist trail of kisses. "Or even what I'm doing here with you right now."

His face moved upward, toward the sensitive cord in her neck, his tongue tasting her like a fine wine. "But you know exactly what to say to turn a man inside out."

Cassandra arched her neck, fingertips smoothing the soft, dark hair at the back of his head, a strange kind of spell weaving its way through her. She caught her breath as his teeth nipped at her skin while the fingers of his hand slipped beneath the neck of the gown and across one breast to its nipple.

"Is that . . . good?" she breathed with a tiny catch in her voice. "Is what I do to you . . . good?"

"Very good," he whispered, his lips just below her bottom lip. "Very good indeed."

Covering her mouth with his, he picked her up and carried her to the bed. He lowered her to stand beside it and bent to lift the hem of her gown, drawing it up over her head.

She stood before him proudly, without attempting to shield her nakedness from view.

Again a curious voice whispered doubt about her into his ear. "Doesn't it bother you, my seeing you like this?" He stood before her, hands on his hips.

Cassandra frowned. "Bother me? Should it?" she asked doubtfully.

"I . . ." Will hesitated. Was he really going to complain because a beautiful woman who was about to make love with him was standing unashamedly naked before him? Was he crazy?

His eyes moved slowly, caressingly, down over her, then back up to her face. "No," he finally responded, "it shouldn't. You're . . . beautiful."

Then she was in his arms, her mouth beneath his, and all the built-up longing he'd experienced both consciously and unconsciously since meeting her was released in his kiss.

But now Cassandra was uncertain. Was she doing something wrong? Was there something she should know about what was happening—and didn't?

Forcing her arms between their bodies, she stiffened, pushing him away.

"Was I too rough?" Will asked, still beneath the power of her kiss.

"I—is it wrong to show this—my body—to you in this way?"

"Wrong?" Will shrugged. "No, of course not. It's just—not all women are as liberated as you appear to be."

The frown on her face grew, and he took a moment to try to explain, when what he really wanted was to tumble her in the bed and stay there with her until morning.

"You want something, and you go after it. That's an admirable quality as far as I'm concerned. You want Jordan Black's head served up on a silver platter . . ." He paused, the light of suspicion in his eyes. "That is what you want, isn't it? To see Black's head on a silver platter?"

"I don't understand," she whispered in confusion. "Why would I want Mr. Black's head on a silver platter?"

"Don't play coy with me," he answered shortly. "You know what I mean. Was this romp supposed to stop short of actually getting in the bed?" he asked, angry now. He didn't like being played for a sucker.

She offered nothing in her defense, only gazed back at him, lower lip trembling.

"I was right about you in the first place, wasn't I? You and your friend—Barney, or whatever the hell his name was—you were only out to gull me."

Cassandra clasped her hands together, biting her lip, frightened by the extent of his anger.

"Answer me, damn you!"

She cowered away, eyelids fluttering in her white face, a tear finding its way over the edge of one lid and sliding down her cheek.

Seeing it angered Will even more. He whirled away and stomped toward the door, muttering imprecations beneath his breath.

Women! Janice, the woman who had been his fiancée until Black had ruined him, should have taught him something about women. She'd run like a rat from a sinking ship when he'd gone bankrupt. He should have known better.

With his hand on the doorknob, he paused. She hadn't made a sound, not even an uttered protest of innocence. Knowing he was a fool for doing it, but unable to stop himself, he twisted to look back over his shoulder.

"What are you doing?" he asked in a hard voice.

She didn't answer. Tears were cascading down both cheeks. She sat on the bed, the sheet wrapped tightly around her, shielding her from his sight, without making a sound.

Will turned. He didn't want to, but the pitiful sight of her got to him. A picture of his mother's silent grief at the death of his father flashed into his mind. Something twisted at his insides.

"I'm sorry."

He'd come to stand before her, part of him feeling like a fool, yet another part stricken with a need to stop her tears. When she refused to acknowledge him by so much as a look, he knelt before her and touched the sheet she had grasped tightly in one fist.

"If I'm wrong about you, forgive me—please." The words came hard for him; he was a proud man. "I—sometimes I jump to conclusions. If I have...about you...I'm sorry."

She hadn't looked at him, but her shoulders had stopped shaking. He dared to place a hand beneath her chin and raise her tear-stained face to his. Her lashes were stuck together in tiny points, the end of her nose was damp and red, and she was the most beautiful thing he'd ever seen in his life.

Without knowing he was going to, he leaned forward and pressed his lips tenderly to hers. After a moment he drew back, looked at her, then leaned forward again. He was lost. She was in his arms, her hands sliding around his neck, drawing him down onto the bed.

His hands roved over the contours of her body, storing the memory of her deep in his subconscious. For as long as he lived, he would remember what it felt like to cup his hands around her small, firm breasts, to press his lips to the concave hollow of her satin-smooth belly, to cradle her hips against his. She would be with him, remain a part of him, for the rest of his life.

His lips caressed, teased, taught her things about her body she could never have imagined. He placed her across his thighs, arms wrapped around her waist, bent her back and covered her breasts, her belly, with searing kisses of fire.

His tongue drew patterns around her navel, traveled down across her hip and thigh, creating an emotional response in her that had her sliding from his lap to lie atop him. Bunching his hair in the fingers of both hands, she held his head and smothered his face with kisses.

The room became washed with a glow that seemed to emanate from the bed, surrounding it, enfolding it in a cocoon of glittering, shimmering heat. Their bodies on the bed writhed, danced to the music of their senses, each learning and teaching a symphony of love to the other.

Cassandra found the hair on Will's chest a place of enchantment as she rubbed her face through it, the tickling sensation causing her to giggle like a child. Sifting her fingers through the curls, she leaned down and blew against them, feeling him shiver. She laughed, her face filled with delight, her eyes glowing like blue stars.

Will caught his breath and pulled her up to him, feeling her soft curves glide along his body, turning it to molten lava.

"The game is over," he moaned, his lips against the side of her neck, then sliding up the curve of her chin to her mouth and drawing a deeper, more satisfying response with each drought from her lips. "It's time to pay the piper."

Cassandra didn't understand his words, but she loved the tone. Her lips responded eagerly, her body already attuned to his wants and needs. She ran her hands over his face, down his neck to his chest to his waist, kissed his cheek, forehead and chin, longing to become a part of him.

Will breathed heavily and rolled her over onto her back. "God, how I want you! I don't know what you've done to me. You're like a fever in my blood."

He laughed self-consciously. He'd never allowed a woman to observe the effect she had upon him before, not that any woman had ever affected him as deeply as this one. He couldn't seem to get enough of her. His hands refused to be still; his lips were sore from the need to kiss her, to draw an ever-deepening response from her.

"Me too," Cassandra whispered. "Oh, me too!"

Shifting his weight, he moved between her thighs, felt their warm softness wrap firmly around him. Lifting her hips in both hands, he felt her eagerly accept him into her body.

Will bent over her, the muscles in his back and hips working, the veins standing out on his neck and forehead, his face set in tense lines.

Cassandra faltered, untutored in what was expected of her. But after a moment she opened to him, her responses becoming automatic. The endorsement of the act of love became a thirst for knowledge, and the thirst became a voracious hunger.

Her own body began to struggle in reply to Will's lovemaking. The fingers of both hands clutched at him, bit into the straining muscles of his arms, as their bodies meshed, became one.

For Will the experience was one of untold sensuality. Her body moved, anointing him in ways he'd never before experienced in the art of making love. Her soft, mewling cries of mounting ecstasy pushed him to untold heights of delight.

The blood pounded through his veins; the breath rasped in his lungs; sweat popped out on his face, back and shoulders, darkening the hair at his forehead and temples. And

he drove harder, striving for a height of fulfillment that remained just beyond his reach.

Cassandra was engulfed in a profusion of sensations that
at once thrilled and confused her. Something was missing
but she didn't know what. Whatever it was, she sensed that
it was what drove Will to the point of exhaustion.

Raising herself on her elbows, hardly knowing what she
was about, Cassandra drew his face to hers and bestowed a
tender kiss on his lips.

The kiss seemed of its own accord to intensify the link
between them, refusing to be broken. The rhythm of their
bodies increased, and all at once something, a bolt of light-
ning, passed between them, hurling them both over the edge
of their senses into the realm of angels. Cassandra was at
once at peace, at home, with this feeling of enchantment.

But Will drew back, struck dumb, his lips, his whole
body, tingling from contact with hers. His golden eyes
glowed with wonder as he gazed at her. He wanted to tell her
how amazing she was, that though he knew it sounded trite,
he'd never experienced anything as wonderful as making
love with her, but he found he couldn't speak.

There were no words to explain what he was feeling, and
a part of his brain, the small part that refused to believe in
anything, cautioned him against speech.

So instead he drew her silently against his chest, feeling
her heart thump against him. And wrapping the sheet
around both their bodies, Will lay back on the pillows,
staring at the ceiling.

Cassandra snuggled against him, too filled with wonder
herself to find words. Perhaps this world wasn't so bad after all—perhaps the *closeness,* sharing yourself with another like this, would in time make up for the loneliness of
being human.

A slight twinge somewhere in the vicinity of her heart reminded her that she was here, in human form, for only a
short time longer. But she couldn't deal with that right now,
not on the heels of such a wonderful experience.

As she snuggled against the reassuring warmth of his
shoulder, listening to the rhythm of Will's heart as it slowed

its furious pace, her eyes drifted shut, the peace of sleep slowly stealing over her.

Will felt her relax, heard the soft murmur she made in her sleep, and felt his heart lurch in response.

After tomorrow they would both be free of Black. Once he'd collected his money and handed over the evidence to her as promised, they could pursue their own lives, together—or apart.

But somehow he couldn't see her accepting him, a blackmailer, into her life.

What was he thinking? He almost jerked away from her at the thought, but managed to stay calm enough to relax back against the pillows after a moment.

Was he really planning to forego his revenge on Black and give in to her pleas?

Chapter 5

Will awakened slowly to the warmth of a soft body draped against his left side.

Cassandra.

He turned to look at the sleeping woman lying so peacefully beside him. Had he only dreamed that he'd made love with this extraordinary young woman all through the long night?

She looked so virginal, so untouched, in sleep. Yet he had firsthand knowledge of the profound passion she was capable of showing.

A contradiction in terms, he realized, innocence and passion, but this little lady harbored the charms of a seductress beneath her virginal guise.

A swath of pale gold hair lay across her face, hiding much of it from view. The soft whisper of air she expelled as she breathed blew against the hair like a gentle wind, making it flutter against her lips.

Will lifted the silky strands carefully away from her soft, moist mouth. As her features came into view he felt a sudden powerful urge to lean forward and awaken her with a kiss, but he restrained himself, knowing he had to leave and preferring to do so without complicated goodbyes or explanations.

His eyes traveled lower to the faint rise and fall of her chest. And again, as last night, his attention was captured by the hint of mauve tipping her creamy breasts.

With unsteady fingers he drew the sheet from her body, holding his breath as the rippling linen passed slowly over her delicate curves, exposing them fully to his eyes.

No, he answered his earlier silent question, he hadn't imagined this perfect creature, this magnificent, earthy woman. She was real, flesh and blood; he could touch her if he wanted—if he dared.

After spending most of the preceding night making love to her, he still wasn't certain if she had been an innocent when they'd begun. At the start she had approached the act with more enthusiasm than knowledge. But if she had indeed been an innocent, she learned quickly, and her capacity for giving, the sheer pleasure she took in it, had amazed him.

She made the act a new, intimate game that drove him to distraction, taking him to heights of nameless pleasure—and through all that, somehow, she had *touched* him. As though she had reached inside him with one of her small hands and taken his heart in her palm, she'd found that part of him he'd kept locked away from the rest of the world for so many years.

Playing the part of her lover had become the most important role he would ever enact—or so it had seemed at the time.

And for the first time, in all the innumerable times he'd made love to countless women, it had been more important that *she* be satisfied rather than himself. Yet somehow, in satisfying her, he'd made his own pleasure more intense, leaving him with a feeling that was so much more satisfying than mere contentment.

And he didn't even know her full name.

Will eased back against the pillows, wishing for a cigarette. This whole business with Black was making him crazy, and now he'd found—*her*.

Why *now,* at this crucial time in his life? Why couldn't he have met her last year—ten years ago—fifteen?

Why couldn't he have met her when he was as innocent as she appeared to be.

Jerking his eyes from her alluring form, he glanced at the clock on the bedside table. It was time for him to go. There were less than three hours left till his meeting with Black.

But he couldn't leave, not just yet, knowing he would never be with her this way again. There wasn't room for someone like her in the hell holes he would be forced to live in after he finished with Black—that is, if he wanted to keep on breathing.

His glance, drawn like a bee to a flower, flitted back to the sleeping woman. The memory of their heated bodies, passionately entwined on the bed, slippery with the sweet nectar of love, began to bathe him in a fierce heat.

He'd never been a morning lover, yet at this moment he wanted very much to awaken his sleeping beauty with a kiss—and more...

With fingers as gentle as soft fleece, Will skimmed a path up one shapely thigh. Her translucent skin shone with the essence of a fine pearl, and he couldn't resist lowering his head to press a brief kiss against the back of one knee.

But instead of moving away, Will's lips lingered then traveled up her finely muscled thigh toward the slender bone of her hip—and the woman beneath him stirred.

He froze, his lips a mere whisper from her delightful flesh, his eyes on her fluttering eyelids, the breath trapped in his chest. *What was he doing?* He withdrew at once, calling himself a fool, sitting back against the head of the bed.

If he awakened her now he would never get away in time to meet Black. He hardened his heart against her. After all his months of planning, he would have blown the deal—and for what? The charms of a stranger.

Black was not known for his patience; he wouldn't sit around waiting for Will. And after last night Will had a strong suspicion that Black was working on a few angles of his own. Angles that involved getting rid of Will once and for good.

Last night, when he'd interrupted the man looking for the hidden documents, he would have lost his life if it hadn't been for Cassandra.

Cassandra murmured something in her sleep, then threw an arm above her head and across Will's chest, breaking his train of thought.

Holding his breath, he kept his eyes glued to her face, looking for signs of returning consciousness. With a feeling of panic he realized that the arm draped so carelessly across him in sleep might as well be the bars of a prison. A prison whose walls he could see going up all around him the longer he remained in her company.

He didn't like walls—attachments—prisons. They were all the same thing. Attachments led to marriage, children, a regular job, car payments, house loans, doctor and dental bills....

And people died from trying to fulfill the commitments they'd made, or in trying to make a life for themselves and their families.

His father had been a good, honest, hard-working man whose family came first. And what had it gotten him? Nothing—except a grave in Crockett, Texas.

His mother had been the kindest, gentlest woman he'd ever known—and she was resting in a grave beside her husband, too fragile for the harshness of this world.

When they died, they had been worn-out, old before their time from too much work and not enough money, from trying to give everything they'd never had to their son—to him.

His pain-darkened eyes skimmed the sleeping woman. He didn't need that. He'd thought about getting married once. He'd even gone so far as to make his longtime lover, Janice Grice, an offer, and she'd accepted.

He'd done it because he'd known all along that marrying her would be almost the same as being single. They would go their separate ways, and there would be no children—no *love*—involved and that suited him just fine.

People got hurt when they cared too much, when they started putting the name *love* to their feelings for others. No one could live up to all the responsibility contained in that word. People hurt—they died—in the name of *love*.

His father had died for love of his mother and him. His mother died from a broken heart—because of her son—and for love of her dead husband.

And he was left with the knowledge that *he* hadn't loved *them* enough—because if he had, they would both still be alive.

Will shook his head, striving to clear it of the past. It did no good to dwell on things you couldn't change. Love was something he couldn't afford these days.

He grinned wryly. There wasn't much he *could* afford with his pockets as empty as they were at the moment.

His eyes traveled over Cassandra's body, then moved back up to her sleeping face.

Even if he were inclined to spend some time with her, if that were possible, what did he have to offer her? Not a damn thing—exactly what he'd had all his life.

The only good thing Jordan Black had ever done for him was to make him go back to college.

Will had been afloat in a morass of self-recrimination and pain over the loss of his parents and quit college. That was about the time he'd spent the remainder of his college funds seeking to make restitution for what he saw as his guilt over their deaths by trying to contact them through a medium and asking for their forgiveness. At that time there had still been a part of him, a very small part, not yet tainted by fate's bitter hand.

Then Jordan Black had come along, a man so confident he appeared almost God-like when compared to Will's low self-esteem. Black got Will to go back to college and get his degree, even helped him with the tuition. Will had offered him all the affection he'd found so hard to show the parents he didn't understand, and Black took on the standing of a well-loved uncle in Will's heart.

That was why it had taken such a long time—years—a great deal of soul-searching and an abundance of evidence for Will to finally admit to himself that Black was truly evil. The man's interest in him, he'd come to realize, had been spawned by Will's own eagerness to place him in the role of hero and worship at his feet.

And even then, knowing what he did about the man, Will had kept quiet. He'd separated himself from Black, made a life of his own, gone into business for himself and pretended he'd never known Jordan Black. Over the years he'd made a fortune by becoming a land speculator. And he'd done it without using Black's underhanded methods of doing business.

He should have known Black wouldn't let him alone. No one repudiated Jordan Black. He cast aside those who were no longer of any interest or use to him, but never the other way around.

Back then, Will hadn't fully relinquished his hold on the idea that there was some good left in the world, some little spot in the corner of someone's heart. He'd thought the affection Black had once felt for him would make him inviolate to Black's form of exterminating the business competition.

He'd been wrong.

Black had done his best to destroy him—and now it was Will's turn. Not that the amount of money Will was asking would seriously deplete the man's resources.

But for once in his life, Black would discover he couldn't have it all his own way—and the defeat involved in such a revelation would do more to avenge Will than Black's going to jail could. Black was about to learn what it was like to be at the mercy of a merciless man.

The fire in Will's loins had been effectively doused by a healthy dose of reality by the time he decided to leave the bed. Perhaps there might come a time in the future...

No, it was best not to fool himself, not anymore, not about this. Once he had obtained what he wanted from Black, he would be long gone. That was the way it had to be.

Oh, he would stick to his bargain and see that she got the goods on Black, but she would have to deliver the evidence to the authorities, herself. Being made a fool of by Black was enough humiliation for anyone.

Will slipped from the bed, moving on silent feet toward the door between their rooms. But it was impossible for him to leave without one final glance back over his shoulder.

Cassandra had turned onto her back, one arm wrapped around his pillow, holding it to her chest as a child might clutch her favorite doll or a stuffed animal; the sheet lay tangled around her small, delicate feet. She slept with the serenity of the truly innocent.

He closed the door softly between them.

If things had been different... if he had met her a long time ago... if he was still as innocent as she appeared to be... or as trusting... if he still believed in anything...

A short while later, downstairs at the front desk, Will left instructions with the concierge to see that Cassandra, and no one else, received the thin manila envelope locked away in the hotel safe. She was to be given it after nine that evening.

It was done. Now all he had to do was to string Black along, convince the man he was going to get what he wanted. And in the interim, Will would take the money and run. Piece of cake!

Cassandra awakened slowly, becoming aware of each separate part of her anatomy individually. First she curled and uncurled her toes, then tightened and stretched the muscles of calves and thighs, flexed her back, took a deep breath, yawned, then opened her eyes.

She was alone, she discovered quickly. And she felt...different...changed. Turning onto her side, she swept a hand over the sheet and across the pillow where Will had lain, sensitive to his lingering essence.

A smile began at the corners of her full lips, curving them upward. Leaning forward in a burst of new feeling, she pressed her face flat against his pillow, inhaling deeply.

The musky scent that was Will, captured in the fibers of the cloth, made her heart beat faster. But that was nothing compared to the heady sensation she experienced by merely recalling his touch in the wee hours of the night.

The act of mating was not exactly new to her; at least, she knew the technicalities of it. But she had never *dreamed* that it could be so...so... There were no words with which to describe it.

It was the wonder of feeling for the first time the sand on the beach beneath her toes, the delight of hearing the voices of the children in Heaven raised in laughter—the sight of Will Alexander's golden eyes filled with longing as they blazed down into hers.

Her steps were light as she climbed from the bed and hurried to the bathroom. The marvel of the shower awaited her. How she loved standing beneath the hot spray, feeling it wash away her cares as thoroughly as it cleansed the skin. When she left it, she felt as though she were a brand-new being.

Life was wonderful! She couldn't imagine why she had fought so hard against coming to Earth, becoming human—for a while.

Her steps faltered as the soles of her feet hit the cold tile floor and reality struck her a resounding blow. Her time on Earth was limited, and since Will had agreed to give the evidence he had to the authorities, she would be leaving soon...too soon....

Wrapping the heavy towel around her damp body, she became aware all at once of small twinges of discomfort from several sources. Shoulders drooping, she stepped through the bathroom door into the bedroom—and stopped short.

"Barnabas!" For a moment she couldn't get any further. "Have you come to get me so soon? I thought—perhaps I might be allowed to stay until the information has been turned over to the police."

"I've come to get you, all right." The old man fairly bristled. "But not to take you back."

Always closely attuned to what Cassandra was feeling, Barnabas stared at her keenly. Something was different about her—but there wasn't time to pursue the changes.

"Well, don't just stand there, child," he barked, watching her tuck the corner of the towel more firmly beneath one arm. "Get dressed! Have you any idea where your charge is at this very moment?"

Cassandra darted a glance toward the closed door between their suites.

"No!" he fairly bellowed, intercepting the glance. "He isn't there. At this instant he is in grave, mortal danger. He's gone to Jordan Black's estate—alone."

"But—I don't understand. Last night—he said—"

"We don't have time for that now. We must hurry! *You* must hurry! Before it's too late. Get a move on," he snapped, gesturing toward the steamy bathroom, then adding, "Time's awasting."

In a matter of minutes Cassandra was dressed and preceding Barnabas out the door of the suite. Not even the irritating limitations imposed on her by the restrictive clothing she now wore could get through the distress she was experiencing at Will's subterfuge.

The only coherent thought running through her mind was the urgent need to get to Will and discover why he'd lied to her.

Barnabas had a taxi waiting for them outside the hotel, and, once again wearing his guise as a taxi driver, he assisted her into the back seat before taking his place behind the wheel. He had mastered the art of driving very quickly and found it exhilarating, especially when he could go at top speed.

Cassandra hung on to her seat and watched the scenery rush past as they left the city behind. As Barnabas picked up speed, she became aware of a heavy pall hanging over the vehicle.

At first, in her misery over Will and his lies to her, she hadn't noticed it, but after a while it began to penetrate her own mood of gloom. She darted a searching glance in the old man's direction.

Was Barnabas displeased with her about something? She was used to coming before him in Heaven, charged with an infraction of one rule or another. It had always fallen to him to make her aware of her flaws. She was either too late, too early, unprepared, or at the wrong place altogether.

Quite recently, before the trip to Earth, she'd been called up on the carpet for a misdemeanor, and she recognized the same look he'd had then on Barnabas's face now. What had she done this time?

Adjusting her position in the seat, she noticed again the small discomforts she'd been aware of since awakening that morning. A new cloud dimmed her blue eyes.

Was that it? Was Barnabas angry with her because of what she and Will had done the night before? Had it been wrong for her, an angel, to be with Will in that way? Could Barnabas sense the changes in her?

Changes? Had she changed?

Yes, she had. At this moment, thinking about Will, she was filled with a new emotion, different from those she'd been struggling so hard to understand. It caused a knot to form in her stomach, made her want to clench her teeth, ball her hands into fists—made her eager to confront the man responsible for these new feelings.

Will had lied to her, had pretended to go along with what she had asked of him, and then gone on about his plans without a second thought for what he'd promised her. She wanted to...cry.

Barnabas had warned her not to fight the changes she would feel in this new form. He'd assured her that giving in to them would make it easier for her to understand the humanness of her charge, make it easier for her to relate to him.

Cassandra wanted to ask Barnabas if she'd been wrong to get so close to Will, but found herself unable to give voice to the question and for the simple reason that she couldn't get words past the strange lump in her throat. She sat stiffly, eyes focused on the passing scenery, blinking against the blurred images.

What would happen to her now that she had failed dismally—again? Her return to Heaven would be less than propitious.

Worry about her own future, however, quickly took second place to worry about Will, as she envisioned what might be happening to him at that very moment.

It was no use, she reflected sadly. What the other angels said about her was true. She was, indeed, a foul-up. It seemed she wasn't any better at doing things down here on Earth than she was in Heaven.

Her misery grew. Will was a far better person than Jordan Black. *Why couldn't he see that for himself?* He simply *had* to be saved from this bent for self-destruction he had developed!

It was with great sadness that she contemplated the fact that she might not be the one to do it. Where had she gone wrong?

Her lower lip began to tremble. What good had she done? She might just as well have stayed in Heaven. Will had been as well off then as he was now—perhaps better off.

She stared down at her clenched fists, feeling the bite of nails against her palms. A quick rush of adrenaline fired her blood, making her feel breathless, creating an intoxicating sensation, much as Will's lovemaking had created the night before.

How strange that two emotions, anger and passion— poles apart—could have the same effect on her. The thought frightened her. What did it mean?

"Barnabas?" She leaned forward over the seat until she could see his profile. "Is it true that love—the love humans feel for each other—and hate are halves of the same whole?"

The old man's eyes darted to the rearview mirror so he could glimpse her puzzled expression. "Yes, child," he admitted almost sadly. "It's quite true."

She was learning what it was to be human too quickly, too thoroughly. His old heart ached for her. It was going to be very hard for her to adjust to being an angel again.

"If Will dies, it will be *my* fault," she whispered in a hollow voice, feeling the pain of the words pierce her heart.

They were traveling down a paved road lined on both sides with orange and lemon trees. A tangy, sweet odor hung in the air. Cassandra sniffed, taking no pleasure in this new scent.

The gates to Black's estate came into sight. A paved road winding through gently rolling hills, visible through the tall iron spires, disappeared in the distance, flanked by neat hedges and a manicured lawn.

Barnabas stopped several yards past the entrance gate and turned to touch the back of the hand resting against the top of the seat.

"You've known from the beginning that this wouldn't be an easy assignment." He squeezed her fingers bracingly. "I have faith in you, child. I've *always* thought you had the potential to achieve glorious heights in Heaven."

"You have?" she asked in surprise.

"I have," he admitted gruffly. "But you take things too much to heart. *You* can't change the world—or those living in it. You must remember, Will Alexander has the freedom of choice. He must make his own decisions. All you can do is show him what's right, the rest is up to him. If he persists in choosing the path of folly . . ." He clicked his tongue and shook his gnarled head.

"Oh, but this is all *my* fault," she protested quickly. "You know that. If only I had taken my responsibilities more seriously . . . I should have been there when his father was killed, or when his mother died. I feel so responsible for all of this."

"Hush, child. You're an angel, not God. And even God can't change a person's destiny. It's only the individual himself who can do that. No matter what else happens, you must remember that."

"Yes." She nodded, swallowing back the tears. "I'll try to remember."

Barnabas felt his heart twist at her obvious distress. He wished he could put a reassuring arm around her shoulders, wipe the sadness from her eyes, tell her things would turn out all right—he would make it so—but he couldn't.

She'd always been his favorite, no matter how hard he tried not to show it. The mischief she got herself into only seemed to endear her to him that much more. Perhaps he'd been harder on her because of that fact—or maybe not hard enough—but it was too late to worry about that now.

"It's time to go, child. I wish I could go with you. But I have rules I must follow, too.

"You haven't much time left, only one hundred and ten hours," he cautioned, giving her hand one last pat before turning away.

Cassandra was reaching for the door handle when Barnabas stopped her with a word.

"Wait! Here." He started to hand her a package wrapped in brown paper and tied with a string, then suddenly withdrew it at the last moment. "No..." He shook his head. "I'd better keep this after all." He'd bent the rules enough as it was.

Cassandra looked curiously from the package to his face. "What is it?"

"Don't worry about that. Just take care of yourself and keep in mind what I've said. I'll be around when you need me. Go with God, child," the old man whispered, making the sign of the cross, a strange sadness in his moist blue eyes.

She left him with a long, backward glance and a slight wave of the hand, which he didn't return. She stood watching as the taxi drove slowly out of sight.

Once she was alone, her footsteps took her to the gate. If she had thought it would be easy getting onto the estate grounds, she was wrong. The tall, black iron gates were locked, guarded by a black, boxlike device mounted atop one stone pillar. She dredged in her memory for an identification of the thing and realized it was a camera.

It would be a simple matter to short out the circuits, she knew, seeing them in her mind. The ability to move objects by thought was within her power. Unfortunately it was also one of the things she wasn't supposed to do.

Perhaps she could find a simpler way to get inside. Skirting the wall, she walked for a short distance and turned down a deserted side road bereft of houses or traffic. Finding a suitable place at last for what she had in mind, well hidden by trees and bushes, she gave a quick glance around, making certain no one was within sight.

Satisfied that she would be unobserved, she took a running step and leaped to the top of the wall. No one had told her she must not defy gravity. In a moment she was standing on the estate grounds on the opposite side of the wall.

A moment later a large dog with short pointed ears rounded a corner of the estate and bounded toward her, a low, rumbling growl issuing from deep within its throat. She should have been warned by the ease of her entrance; nothing ever came that easily to her.

But Cassandra stood her ground without fear. Gazing into the dog's large brown eyes, she realized that she understood this animal's simplicity much better than she understood the human inhabitants of Earth.

The Doberman slowed its pace as it drew nearer, stopped, made a couple of side steps, and then, head lowered, teeth bared, began to close in, one menacing step at a time.

"Are you certain you want to do this?" she asked softly, blue eyes locked with brown ones.

The dog hesitated, teeth still bared.

"You're very unhappy—and angry. I can understand that. They keep you penned up in a very small enclosure when you aren't loose on the grounds. And they feed you sparingly. You have a right to be angry—but not with me."

The dog looked from right to left, its gaze falling to the ground. The bared teeth disappeared inside the black muzzle, and a soft whimper came from the strong muscular throat.

"It's all right, boy." She held out a hand. "I'm not angry with *you*." The dog dropped to its belly, whimpering softly as it crawled toward her.

Cassandra took time to pet it and scratch behind its ears. "I really have to go, you know, before someone who isn't as nice as you are comes and finds me. I'd appreciate it, if you didn't make too much racket. You see, I need to get inside the house. The men who are responsible for treating you so badly are holding a friend of mine inside.

"Listen, could you do me a favor? If anyone else comes around while I'm looking for a way inside, would you give me a signal?"

She held the dog's muzzle in both hands, her eyes fastened to its once more. And when she let it go, it followed close at her heels as she headed toward a back door to the large, imposing two-story house made of brick and stone.

At the back door, motioning for the dog to keep a lookout, she grasped the handle firmly in one hand. It refused to budge, and the door remained closed.

She wasn't going to be stopped. She balked at letting a locked door keep her from getting to Will when she was this close. Whispering a short prayer for forgiveness, she prepared to defy the laws of nature and unlock the door with her mind.

Concentrating intently on a vision of the inner workings of the device and what she wanted to accomplish, she felt the cool metal in her hand begin to heat. After a moment she twisted the knob—but the door remained closed, the lock intact.

Frowning, Cassandra tried again, with the same results. For some reason her ability to overcome something as puny as two pieces of metal fitted together wasn't working. She was puzzled but realized that if she was going to get into the house it would have to be in some other fashion.

It was broad daylight. Cautioning herself silently against getting caught, she stepped back to get a better look at the massive structure, letting her eyes rove its height and breadth.

A trellis near the far corner of the house, overflowing with a climbing rosebush filled with large blooms, caught her eye. It rose from the ground to the second story, where it fitted neatly between two U-shaped balconies. It should be a simple matter to climb the trellis and, she hoped, gain entrance to the house through one of the balcony doors.

The dog came swiftly at her soft command. She leaned over to give it a hug, whispering a few words into its ear. As a result, it sat at the bottom of the trellis, guarding her as she made a quick job of the climb.

In the act of throwing a leg over the balcony situated to the left of her, searching for a firm hold with one hand, she gave a soft cry and pulled her hand abruptly back. She stared curiously at the long black splinter embedded in her palm.

The small wound wasn't really bad or particularly painful, but the fact that the splinter didn't immediately pop out when she put her mind to its quick extraction surprised her.

After a moment, shrugging, thinking that perhaps there must be a way to remove a foreign object she knew nothing about, a method not used in the healing of a wound, she continued with her climb. There would be time to take care of such a small thing later, after she'd reached Will and seen to his safety.

This time, when she tried the door handle, there was no need to worry about getting past a lock. The handle of the French door turned smoothly, and the door opened inward.

Cassandra found herself inside a beautifully appointed bedroom done in shades of black and gray. The colors were a bit depressing to her; she loved the brightness of reds, yellows and greens.

The room, she noted with a sense of disappointment, was empty. She started toward the door that must lead to the hallway when a sound alerted her in the nick of time.

Dropping to her knees, she crawled beneath the bed as the door opened and a pair of shiny black shoes entered the room. Along with the man in the shoes came a strong, acrid odor of cigar smoke. When the gleaming shoes had stopped in front of the door to a closet, she scooted toward the edge of the bed and dared to peek out.

One glance was all it took to ascertain that this was Jordan Black. His tall, broad-shouldered back, covered in white silk, was an imposing sight to behold. She couldn't see his face, but the small pinky ring with the large *B* made out of diamonds on his left hand was as good as a signature.

Crawling back toward the center of the bed, she nearly cried out in surprise when one corner of the mattress sagged beneath the man's immense weight, crowding her down against the floor. She hadn't heard him leave the closet.

With a hand cupped to her mouth, she waited tensely, watching the bed move up and down as Black changed the gleaming dress shoes for a pair of walking shoes. It appeared as though he was about to go out.

So where was Will?

It took a few minutes for Black to finish changing his clothes and with the silent, catlike tread some large men possess, exit the room. But it took a few more minutes for Cassandra to get up enough courage to crawl from her hiding place and consider leaving the comparative safety of the room for the hallway.

Looking both ways quickly, she determined that the coast was clear. Now all she had to do was find Will. It was a very big house, and she had no idea where to begin looking, or who she might stumble into in the process.

She stepped back inside the room, closed her eyes and, concentrating hard, swept the building with her mind. This was not the time to concern herself with whatever rules she might be breaking. She was seeking a presence she would recognize, that of the man she'd come to rescue.

There were six people in the house besides herself. The minds of five of those caused her to withdraw after only an instant's brief joining. Unprepared as she was for such violence, even that brief integration was like touching a live electric wire.

Will, she had discovered, was on the same floor as she was, and very close by. All she had to do was get out of this room and continue down the corridor until she *felt* the room he was in.

And then all *they* had to do was get out of the house without being spotted.

In the hallway once more, she moved slowly, almost trancelike, concentrating, being careful to keep Will from sensing she was in the house. He wasn't alone, and she didn't want him to betray her presence to the man with him.

She was almost there! Her excitement mounted. In a moment she would be seeing Will again! A door behind her swung suddenly open. Cassandra froze. By allowing her concentration to slip, she had for an instant lost her capacity to keep everyone under surveillance, and now...!

Grasping the handle of the door behind her with a sweaty palm, she twisted frantically, felt it open and fell back into the room at the same instant that a figure stepped into view on her left. Heart racing, she couldn't concentrate her thoughts on the man long enough to discover if he'd seen her.

But her keen sense of hearing picked up two voices as footsteps approached the room where she lay huddled against the door.

Her scalp prickled as their footsteps drew close—slowed—then continued past. She sagged loosely, letting her breath out in a long, relieved sigh. She would have to be more careful in future if she wanted to get both herself and Will out of here safely.

It was hard being human. If she hadn't been bound by the rules Barnabas had set for her at the start of this journey, a few of which she had already broken, she could have simply disappeared in the hallway, or caused the two men to turn their footsteps in another direction.

But she was trying arduously to keep from breaking any more rules than necessary. Lord knew she had broken enough of them while in Heaven; she didn't want to tax His patience to the limit while she was here on Earth. And she didn't want to jeopardize her chance of getting Will out of this mess safely, either.

Even though she'd been given a specific number of days in which to complete this assignment, it was still possible for her to be recalled if she made too many mistakes. And despite her being upset at his careless treatment of her and what they'd shared the night before, she wanted very badly to be there for him now, when he needed her most.

There wasn't time to delve too deeply into her reasons for feeling such an intense, aching need to redeem his soul. She only knew that this time, unlike the blemished record she'd left behind in Heaven, she would prove herself to be a competent angel. One, moreover, who labored wholeheartedly at whatever task was set for her until it was successfully completed...

But most of all, she simply wanted to save Will.

The room was empty when she entered it and for a moment she stood unmoving in shock. It couldn't be! She'd *felt* him here!

Her eyes became huge with concern as she scanned the room—and then she saw him. He was sitting on a stool, head down, partially concealed by an open closet door.

"Will?" She spoke his name tentatively, moving toward him.

On her knees, one hand stretched toward him, heart bumping dreadfully against her ribs, she realized she was too late. He was dead....

Her hand touched the side of his head, lifted it until she could see his face. Sucking her breath in on a sob, she cried out, "Oh, no! No!"

How could someone have done this? How could one human being treat another so cruelly?

Her eyes searched his desecrated flesh, noting that both his eyes were blackened, one swollen shut. A two-inch cut ran from his left temple toward his hairline. It had bled profusely, leaving a trail of dark red down the side of his face. His lower lip was swollen, his whole face a mass of painful-looking bruises.

He was bare except for his jeans; even his belt, shoes and socks had been removed. She could see purple bruises extending down to his rib cage.

Both hands had been pulled down behind him and fastened through the rungs of the stool with his own belt. The fingers appeared thick and puffy, the wrists red and raw where he must have strained against the bonds during his torture.

Anger swept through her at the thought of the pain he must have endured, and her eyes began to glow fiercely as she was overcome with a desire to avenge his death.

Taking a deep breath, the hand beneath his chin becoming unsteady, veins standing out in her forehead and neck, she felt her mind expanding, filling with swirling black anger—and Will groaned.

His head moved within her grasp, reminiscent of the first time she'd come to his rescue, his eyes opened and looked directly into hers.

The brown eyes remained blank for a brief moment; then his face worked. His Adam's apple moved up and down as he swallowed painfully, and she realized he was trying to smile—to speak.

The anger in her died. She felt ashamed for what she'd contemplated doing. Cupping his ravaged face in both hands, tears of sorrow mixed with anger turning to tears of joy, she tried to answer his smile.

"I knew...somehow...you'd...come," he managed with difficulty through stiff, swollen lips.

Chapter 6

Cassandra leaned forward and touched Will's cheek with trembling lips, bathing his bruised skin with her warm tears. After a moment she withdrew, wiped her cheeks with the backs of her hands and cleared her throat.

She was too full of conflicting emotions to speak, and there was no time to waste if they wanted to get away without being discovered. She busied herself with releasing Will's bonds to give herself time to try to come to terms with her feelings.

The belt binding his hands had been twisted before being fastened around each wrist separately and then looped together and buckled. It took her a few minutes to figure out the unfamiliar working of it. Belts were something she had little knowledge about, and even something simple could be complicated if you were unversed in its use.

But the time involved in removing it gave her time to get herself under control. She was more than a little confused about how she was feeling toward Will, and it was easy for her to keep her eyes from making contact with his when she was working behind him.

When she had set out with Barnabas a little while ago to find Will, it had been with a sense of newly discovered anger and bitter disappointment at his betrayal of her. But those feelings had gradually been overshadowed by fear for his safety, and now, looking at him, by remorse at what had been done to him.

However, despite her sorrow at the suffering he'd endured, she felt a renewal of that earlier disappointment and anger. How could he have made himself vulnerable to the likes of Jordan Black? How could he willingly go through all this pain and abuse—for money?

"We've got to get out of here," she said at last, avoiding contact with his dark, pain-filled eyes. "Where are your things?" she asked, indicating his bare chest and feet.

"I don't know," he answered slowly. "One of Black's men . . . took them." He was rubbing his raw wrists, flexing his stiff fingers experimentally, feeling the pins and needles of returning circulation as he spoke.

"He did leave me this, though." Will patted the back pocket of his jeans. His wallet was tucked inside it. "I guess he figured that, under the circumstances, I wouldn't be carrying around a lot of cash." He tried a wry grin.

"Or maybe," he continued, "he simply wanted there to be no mistake about identifying the body."

"Come on." Motioning for him to follow, Cassandra turned away, chilled by his macabre sense of humor. Moving on soft feet toward the door, she said, "We can't stay here. Your guard is likely to return at any moment."

If he felt any curiosity about how she had known where to find him, or how she knew he'd been watched by one of Black's men until a few minutes ago, Will kept it to himself.

It was all he could manage just to stay upright. Every muscle and bone in his face and chest was on fire from the blows he'd received from Black and his compatriots.

At the door Cassandra paused to check that the coast was clear, then, still in the lead, motioned for him to follow as she darted swiftly from the room.

"Wait!" Will whispered.

Very conscious of their vulnerability, Cassandra gave him an impatient glance over her right shoulder.

"The stairs are that way." Will pointed in the opposite direction.

"We can't use the stairs. Mr. Black's men are guarding them." Cocking her head all at once in a listening attitude, she murmured, "Let's go! Hurry! Someone's coming!"

Hand in hand, their footsteps muffled by the thick pile of the carpet, Cassandra led Will to Black's bedroom. Once inside, conscious that an alert was certain to be sounded at any moment, she paused to conduct a brief search.

"What are you doing?" Will asked, watching her rifle the closet and dresser drawers.

"Here." She turned, handing him a shirt, shoes and a pair of dark socks. "You can't climb down the side of the house like that. The thorns on the roses are too thick."

Will hesitated, noting the quality of the items in his hands, suspecting they belonged to Black and wondering how she had known they were there. After donning them without comment and as quickly as his aches and pains would allow, he confronted her with his hands on his hips.

"Now what?" he asked, out of breath.

"This way."

Opening the lace-curtained French door, she stepped out onto the balcony. An instant later a loud shout rang out from somewhere inside the house.

Without pause, as though she hadn't heard it, she threw a leg over the balustrade and swung herself toward the wooden trellis almost completely hidden by green leaves and large-petaled roses. Will was right behind her, and if the thorns tore at his flesh, he kept the fact to himself.

They moved swiftly, and when they were a few feet from the ground, Will glanced down and froze. He automatically grabbed the shoulder of the woman below him.

"Hold still," he muttered insistently.

The golden head beneath him lifted, and Cassandra stared up at him with puzzled blue eyes. "What...?"

Her glance followed his to the ground beneath them.

"It's all right," she whispered, pulling loose from his hold. "He's a friend. His name is Beast."

The instant her feet touched ground, she went down on one knee beside the large Doberman, threw an arm around its strong neck and gave it a hug.

Will couldn't believe his eyes when a large, pink tongue darted out of the canine's mouth and left a long, wet streak down Cassandra's cheek.

"Well, I'll be damned," he muttered, ending his descent with a jarring leap that instantly doubled him over with pain.

"I hope not. Dear God, I hope not," Cassandra breathed, aghast at his lack of concern for his own injuries.

"How did you manage that?" Will asked, indicating the affection with which the dog regarded her.

"I . . . get along well with children and animals," she answered with an ear tuned to what was happening inside the house.

"They know you're gone," she informed him. "We must hurry!"

Across the back lawn, with Will close at her heels, Cassandra followed the loping gait of the huge, black-and-brown dog. The distance seemed to stretch out interminably, anxiety making it appear far greater than it actually was.

Without warning, a sudden, sharp pain knifed through Cassandra, halting her in her tracks. Will ran headlong into her back.

"What's . . . wrong?" he panted, an arm braced against his own aching ribs, the other steadying her. "Got a stitch?"

Cassandra knew the pain for what it was in that instant. And, feeling a sense of relief mixed with an odd sense of surprise, she nodded.

Beast came trotting back to stand beside her, licking her hand, making soft whimpering sounds deep in his throat.

"Y-yes—I know," she murmured to the dog, stroking its smooth black head absently. "They're coming after us."

Will looked up from where he was bent almost double, trying to breathe shallowly to take some of the stress off his sore ribs.

"He . . . really likes . . . you."

Cassandra smiled as she bent to press her face against the dog's right ear. A moment later they were under way again.

When they came to a place in the back wall where the trees grew thick, partially shielding a tall iron gate, the Doberman moved through the trees a short way, then stopped, giving a soft yip.

Cassandra left Will's side and followed the sound. Beast was standing below the gnarled trunk of an old elm, staring up at what was left of a small limb that had been removed with a saw. With a fond pat of thanks, Cassandra lifted the metal key ring off the limb and into her hand.

"That dog is amazing," Will said, watching the animal turn and trot back the way they'd come.

Cassandra was twisting the key in the lock when the dog suddenly began to bark furiously. Will whirled, almost stumbling in his anxiety, and at once fell back into the cover of the trees.

"Damn! I knew it was too good to be true. Your *friend* is leading them here."

"No." Cassandra shook her blond curls without turning around, still trying to make the key fit the rusted lock. All at once it grated in the lock and the gate swung open.

"He's heading them off."

"But—"

"Come on," she urged. "They won't be fooled for long."

The pair darted through the gate, hearing it close with a soft clang as they ran down the hard uneven surface of the dirt road. Seconds later the sound of the gate clanging open a second time, followed by an angry shout, alerted them to the fact that their escape route had been discovered.

Cassandra darted a quick glance back the way they'd come to see that either one of Black's men hadn't been fooled by the dog or else he'd stumbled upon them accidentally.

As she turned to run, Will at her side, the man looked back toward the house and shouted, "Here! He's here! And he isn't alone—he's got a broad helping him!"

Will grabbed Cassandra's hand while the man's head was turned and pulled her off the road, shoving her down behind a thick pile of brush.

"Where did they go?" a second man asked, joining the first.

"I don't know. They were here a second ago. Let's take a look. They can't have gone far."

The voices all but faded then except for a low murmur, and Will whispered, "I wish I could hear what they're saying."

"They're waiting for more dogs—they plan to track us," Cassandra answered without thinking.

"How do you know that?"

"I . . . have a very keen sense of hearing." Her unwavering blue glance met his suspicion-bright eyes for a long beat of silence.

"Some people do," she added, looking away, wishing she could learn to think before speaking. "What do we do now?" she asked in chastened tones when he remained silent.

"You mean you don't know?" Will asked in a taunting voice, suddenly angry for no good reason—unless it was because she always seemed to be in the right place at the right time. "I thought you knew everything."

Cassandra bit her lip to keep it steady, staring intently at something through a gap in the foliage, trying to work up her own anger against him.

"I'm sorry."

The words came from close beside her, causing her to shiver as the sound of Will's deep timbred voice played over her nerve endings like gentle fingers plucking at a guitar string.

"It's all right—"

"No, it isn't," he insisted softly, brushing at a smudge of dirt on her cheek. "You don't deserve my sarcasm."

The hand at her cheek curved around it, lifting her face to meet his. Their eyes locked as their breaths mingled, and Cassandra's head angled automatically to accommodate Will's as he bent to kiss her.

"They've got to be here!"

The harsh voice, sounding so close beside where they lay hidden, snapped them apart.

Will shoved Cassandra facedown against the hard ground, his body covering hers like a shield. If ever there was a time when he'd wished for a magic potion to make him invisible, it was now, he thought as he pressed his face against the back of her head.

Unbeknownst to him, Cassandra was wishing the same thing, but from a slightly different point of view.

Gravel crunched loudly beside their hiding place, causing Cassandra to give a start of surprise. The men were so close! The brush a short distance away snapped under the blow of a stick, as one of the men literally beat the bushes for them.

Cassandra hardly dared to breathe. And she wasn't quite certain if that was due to fear, the heavy weight crushing her, or the heady excitement of feeling Will's body plastered tightly to hers.

When the footsteps of the men had finally faded, Will spoke soft words against Cassandra's ear, tickling the short hairs growing there, telling himself not to be sidetracked by her sweet perfume and enticing curves.

"We have to move or they'll find us, either now, or when the dogs get here. Let's see if we can crawl deeper into the cover of the trees. Then, after we've put a little distance between them and us, we'll make a run for it. We won't get far if we're still here when the dogs arrive."

Somehow they made it without being spotted, and by the time they heard the dogs baying in the distance, they were on the open road. Will spent an uncomfortable few minutes as a station wagon approached around a curve, coming from the direction of Black's estate, wondering if they were about to be caught.

When it slowed and a matronly woman leaned out to ask if the *poor things* needed a lift, Will had to forcibly resist the impulse to jerk her from her seat, dump her on the road and take the car from her.

In what seemed an amazingly short amount of time, most of it spent fielding questions about the "accident" he and Cassandra had had with their own auto, Will saw with relief that they'd reached town. He directed the woman to a garage he knew and thanked her for the ride.

"Thanks again." He stepped back from the woman's window and waved.

"Are you certain, young man, you don't want me to take you to a hospital?" the older woman asked for at least the fifth time since she'd picked them up.

"No, really, I'm fine, just a little sore." Will touched his face carelessly. "I should have been wearing my seat belt— I will in future. Thanks so much for taking the trouble to drop us off here."

"No trouble, really. I just wish..." She looked at him one last time, glanced at Cassandra, then shook her head as though to say, *Men, aren't they silly?* Then she waved and drove off.

The garage mechanic who'd watched their arrival wiped his hands on a greasy cloth and ambled over.

"What can I do for you folks?" he asked, spitting a stream of brown toward the sidewalk.

Cassandra followed the action with interested eyes.

"Where can we rent a car—cheaply?" Will asked.

The man stared at his battered face, took in the dirt and grass-stained clothing that didn't quite fit, then turned his attention to Cassandra. She was still staring with a puzzled frown at the brown stain on the concrete.

"You okay, little lady?" the man asked, ignoring Will for the moment.

She glanced up at him in surprise. "Yes." She nodded, eyes captured and held by the large puffy area centered in his right jaw, noting that he spoke with difficulty. "I'm fine."

"Sure?"

She nodded again and moved a step closer to Will. The mechanic shrugged, nodded his own grizzled head and smiled with one side of his face, keeping the other side held stiffly over his teeth.

"There's a place down road about six blocks where you can rent a car, if you got a major credit card handy."

"Right." Will put an arm around Cassandra's shoulders and started to move off.

"Hey!"

Stiffening, Will came to a reluctant halt. "Yeah?" He glanced back.

"The two of you look like you been through hell, if you don't mind me sayin' so. See that brown truck over there?" He indicated a Ford parked in front of the rest rooms. "Go on over and get inside—I'll give you a lift."

A few minutes later, sitting between the two men, Cassandra almost fell asleep because she was so tired. The only thing keeping her awake was her left hand, resting protectively inside the right one. A persistent throbbing made sleep impossible. The thorn was still there.

Listening with half an ear, she heard Will and Ed, the garage mechanic, discuss the economy, cars and the merits of football over—soccer? Every now and then her glance strayed to the large swelling on the man's jaw.

When they arrived at the car lot, Will shook hands with Ed and thanked him for the lift.

Cassandra broke her silence to add her own thanks and couldn't refrain from asking, "Does it hurt?"

Ed gave her a puzzled glance, and she indicated his jaw.

He laughed, thinking she was making a joke, shook his head and spat another stream of tobacco toward the street. He waved as he shifted into first gear and pulled forward, quickly becoming lost in the traffic moving along the street.

When he'd gone, Will shoved his hand into his back pocket and removed his wallet. Flipping it open, he slipped a small, rectangular-shaped piece of plastic from one compartment and held it up.

"Well, I guess we should thank Jordan Black for leaving me this." He indicated the credit card. "I guess he didn't expect me to have any use for it in the near future." He settled her on a bench running along one wall of the building. "Why don't you wait here? I won't be long."

And then he was gone, leaving her to stare at the passing motorists and the pedestrians strolling down the sidewalk.

During her years of observing the planet and its inhabitants, she'd always assumed them to be one of two things, either good enough to get into Heaven, or evil and on their way to Hell.

But that wasn't true. She was learning that people were a mixture of the two, both good and bad. Just look at what she had been tempted to do when she'd found Will a little while ago. Vengeance was God's realm, not hers. It was a difficult lesson to learn, but she was beginning to understand that most things here on Earth were quite complicated. Nothing was either all black or all white.

Take the case of Will and the terrible thing he was planning to do. Even though she abhorred the idea that he would put money before human life, including his own, even if she had wanted to, she couldn't dislike him for it now that she'd gotten to know him.

She had been handed the job of being his guardian angel years ago, and she had always considered it an unwelcome task that would take time away from her other duties, those she enjoyed. And she had neglected him.

This trip to Earth to achieve his salvation was something she had thought of as a kind of penance for her own wrongdoing, and though she had continually balked at it, she was finally coming to terms with it.

And she was coming to realize something more. The preservation of Will's mortal life—as well as the redemption of his eternal soul—had become more important than her own needs.

She no longer thought of him as a duty she had to fulfill to make amends for her own shortcomings. She had come to care about him as a person—as a man. The thought made her very uncomfortable.

How had this turn of events come about? And what was she to do about it? Would these...feelings she harbored for this man disappear when she was once more in Heaven? How could she calmly go back to her place in Heaven and leave Will? Would Barnabas know the answers to her questions?

Even if he did, that would do her no good right now. Barnabas was gone and she had no idea where, and she was here with Will, still uncertain about what might happen to either one of them.

She suspected that Will still hadn't changed his mind about selling the information to Black. And she was stumped as to how to go about changing his mind.

She'd tried reasoning with him, tried pointing out the horror of what might happen in the future. And it had all been to no effect. He'd pretended to agree with what she wanted, fooled her into trusting him, then blatantly proceeded with his own plans for blackmail.

She had to find out what his new plan of action entailed—not just what he wanted her to believe—and accomplish it without getting inside his head to do so. And then she had to come up with a plan of action of her own, one that would make him change his mind.

The door beside her opened, and Will's tall figure moved into view. Swinging a pair of keys on a ring, he smiled and indicated a small red compact car being driven around the side of the building toward where they stood.

"That's ours. Let's go."

Will glided the car smoothly onto the street. He threw a glance in her direction, but she refused to meet his eyes. She'd been quiet, preoccupied, since rescuing him at Black's estate.

He didn't need a crystal ball to tell him that she was put out with him. And he supposed he couldn't blame her. After all, he'd lied to her, by omission if nothing else.

He'd also made love to her and gotten her into danger, and all in the space of little more than twenty-four hours.

"You know, this is far from being over," he said, breaking into speech abruptly. "Black isn't about to let me go—nor you, either, now that he knows about you.

"This isn't about money—at least, not on his part." He grinned wryly. "He doesn't give that—" he snapped his fingers "—for the paltry sum we've discussed. And it isn't fear of jail that drives him, either. He can find a dozen lawyers to keep him out. It's not even the fear of being identified in the newspapers for the criminal he is that makes him lust for blood.

"No." He shook his head. "It's me he wants, pure and simple. He wants me so badly he can taste *my* blood.

"All those men he helped to put into office in local and state government will suddenly get amnesia where Jordan Black is concerned if their culpability is made public. That means a reduction of his power—and it's power he thrives on.

"But even more than that, it's the knowledge that I would have gotten the better of him. Black can't live with that thought. He wants me safely dead."

"If you get the information you have to the proper authorities—"

"No!"

Cassandra made a startled movement and compressed her lips, turning to stare out the window so he wouldn't see how upset that one word, spoken in such an emphatic tone, made her feel.

"I guess we go back to the hotel, then," she muttered in a defeated voice.

"We can't. Black knows where I'm staying. And if I take you back there, you're sure to be recognized by one of the hoods he no doubt already has posted."

"Then what?"

"We get out."

"Out?" She looked at him questioningly.

"Of the city—out of the state—as quickly and as quietly as possible. Black will have this town sewn up within a matter of hours, leaving us no way out."

"But—"

"There's only one place we can go."

"And that is?"

"A sort of hideaway down near the border—a cabin I own in southern Arizona."

"Won't Mr. Black simply follow us there?"

"Very few people know about it. He doesn't, either—if we're lucky. It will at least buy us a little time. Maybe it will give me—" He darted her a quick look. "Us—a chance to come up with a new plan."

A green mileage sign flashed by, capturing her attention, and Cassandra sat up alertly, an idea leaping to mind. Perhaps she had been approaching the problem in the wrong manner.

She'd been appealing to his sense of fair play, counting on his being able to visualize a disaster to people who were as yet unborn.

What she really needed was to make him aware that such disasters were an ever-present danger, more horrible than the imagination could envision—and sometimes taking place in your own backyard.

"Do you have a map?"

Will narrowed his eyes in thought. "Yeah, in the glove compartment. At least, the man at the car rental agency said there was one in there."

Cassandra removed the map, unfolded it and studied it for a long moment in silence.

"Would you mind taking a small detour?" she asked all at once.

"Detour?" He glanced over at her in surprise.

"Yes, it isn't far out of the way. I know you said we were headed for southern Arizona, and the place I want to go is in the southern part of Nevada, but it's important."

Her blue eyes pleaded with him.

"You want me to take you to your family, is that it?"

"No—there's something I want to show you."

"Well..." He drew the word out, noting the tense expression on her pale face. "I suppose it won't hurt to make a short side trip," he muttered, adding, "but it will have to be a quick one. Staying on the move might be a good ploy in some cases," he said, explaining his reasons for the qualification. "But Black has a lot of friends. I think finding a hole and pulling it in after us is about what we need to do."

He shrugged when that didn't seem to change her mind and asked, "Where to?"

Cassandra moved toward the middle of the seat and pointed out the route that would take them to their new destination.

"That looks like a dirt road. You sure you know where you're going?"

"I'm sure."

"It looks like we should hit the turn off to that road in...say—" He glanced at the digital clock on the car's dash. "About half an hour."

By now, Will figured, his nemesis must have pretty well worked out the fact that he and his companion had slipped through the man's net and gotten clean away. Black wouldn't like the thought of that at all.

But Will wasn't fool enough to think Black would simply forget about them. He wouldn't rest until he'd found them and exacted his own brand of revenge on Will. And since Cassandra was with him, she would feel the lash of Black's displeasure every bit as strongly as he would.

For the second time in as many days, Will felt a twinge of doubt about what he was doing. He was willing to chance his own safety for the sake of seeing Black get a heavy dose of his own medicine. But now there was the safety of this woman at his side to consider. And that realization made him uneasy.

He hadn't really considered anyone else's needs for a long time. Not even those of Janice, his ex-fiancée. And maybe that was part of why she'd left him after his financial downfall.

Maybe a marriage of convenience hadn't been as much to her liking as he'd thought. But that didn't really matter now. They were finished; end of story.

They were on the interstate outside the city, bound for Nevada, when Will spoke again to ask if she was hungry. Cassandra shook her head, staring morosely out the window at her side, shoulders slumped in an attitude of defeat.

Just because she'd had this idea of proving to him what she'd been trying to tell him didn't mean it would work. Will was a stubborn man, and he didn't like being wrong.

And if she did manage to convince him to give up his plan for revenge, where did that leave her? She still had to leave in a few short days.

Will couldn't seem to concentrate on his driving. He found himself continually glancing at his companion, noting the pout to her full bottom lip, remembering how it had felt captured beneath his own mouth and wondering if she remembered it, too.

Was he the reason for the pout? His glance rested on her for a long moment. Who was she really?

She looked like any normal young woman, the kind you might see on any street downtown. But he'd noticed some things you couldn't find in many of those women, like her unusual sensitivity to her surroundings and the delightful pleasure she took in little things. She claimed to be psychic, and he supposed that could account for her unusual sensitivity, but not the rest.

And the thought of her having abilities outside the norm didn't sit well with him, maybe because of all the charlatans he'd met in his younger days. He didn't want her to be one of them.

Or maybe his dislike of the idea stemmed from the fact that his mother's gift hadn't seemed to help her and his father very much—and he felt certain that in the end it had even hastened her own death.

Cassandra had a fey quality about her that he'd noticed right off. And, odd as it seemed under the circumstances, it was what had drawn him to her in the beginning. That and the fact that she seemed to appreciate even the smallest pleasures life had to offer.

That part of her definitely reminded him of his mother. She was the only other adult he'd ever known with that same childlike capacity for enjoyment. All at once his grief at her death swept over him, filling him with thoughts of another time.

Will stared straight ahead, forgetting everything except how safe he'd always felt knowing his parents were around, not necessarily close by, just *there*—existing in the same world where he existed. And how quickly that had all changed in a few hours of heedless indifference.

Cassandra caught a glimpse of the faraway look in Will's eyes and misinterpreted it. She wanted to cry. Was he even now thinking up a new plan in his campaign against Black? Would nothing change his mind? Not even what she was going to show him in Nevada?

If this didn't work, she didn't know what else to do, how to make him see reason. She wanted desperately to save him, but she had to face the possibility that it might not be possible.

The thought ripped her apart, because the feelings growing inside her for this man, this mortal, kept growing stronger all the time. He was a good man down deep inside. Why wouldn't he let that part of himself out? Why was he afraid to be the man she knew he *could* be?

Was it fear driving him? Or was it something else?

Time was running out for *her* but, more importantly, it was also running out for Will—and he wasn't even aware of it. But what was worse, in his present state of mind, she didn't think he would care even if he knew.

Chapter 7

William came out of his reverie, glanced over at his companion's wan face and asked, "Why don't you curl up in the seat and try to get some rest? It's going to be a long monotonous ride from here."

Cassandra hesitated, then took his advice. She scooted down in the seat, rested her head back against the cushion, folded her hands in her lap and closed her eyes.

Perhaps in sleep she would magically come up with answers to the many questions plaguing her. More was bothering her than her fears about Will's intentions. She still shuddered mentally, thinking about how close she had come to committing an unforgivable sin herself.

When she had thought Will was dead, she'd wanted to kill the men responsible for doing it. What was happening to her? She was so terribly confused.

She tried praying for guidance, for a sign from above that would show her she was going about her job in the right manner. But something had happened to her when she'd taken on human form. She hadn't quite known how to define it at first, even to herself, but now she was beginning to realize what it was.

There was a distance between her and God that hadn't been there before. Sometimes she felt as though she were stumbling around in the dark, guessing at what was right instead of *knowing*.

What did it mean? Yes, she had broken some of the rules she'd been given by Barnabas. She was supposed to function strictly as a human, and she'd cheated a bit.

She'd used her ability to read minds, her ability to defy gravity and her ability to communicate with other species— but she was doing God's work, and He was merciful; surely He hadn't turned His back on her.

Even the possibility that He had was enough to cause her a great deal of mental anguish, and she had no one to talk to about it. No one to put her fears to rest, no one to help her decide what she must do.

Will saw her squirming in the seat and, thinking it was from physical discomfort, suggested she use the lever to adjust her position.

Instead of explaining the truth of the matter, Cassandra reached down with her left hand, searching for the lever below the bucket seat. Grasping what she thought was it, she gave a tug.

"Oh!" She withdrew her hand and cradled it in her lap.

"What's wrong?"

"Nothing, just a little sore spot from the climb."

The lever she wanted was on the other side of the seat. Finding it, she adjusted her position and settled down with her glance directed out her side window.

The splinter in her left hand throbbed. And that was another thing bothering her. Why hadn't it popped out by now? She'd had no difficulty healing from the knife wound, and that had been far more serious than this tiny injury.

Was this confirmation that God was angry with her?

She was not the most obedient of angels; she never had been. But to her knowledge she'd never done anything to cause such wrath in Him. How had she angered Him to the point of His forsaking her? How could she go on without His help?

Thinking about that reminded her of how short a time she had left on Earth. And how long a time she would have in

Heaven—after she'd left Will. Her heart sank clear to her toes at the thought.

How was she going to get by after she'd gone back to Heaven, remembering Will?

She glanced up at the sun riding high in the sky. Time was running out much too rapidly. Was she doing the right thing in taking him to Serenity? Closing her eyes, she prayed hard that she was.

Will watched the long lashes veil her eyes and wondered what she was thinking. If her thoughts had anything to do with him, from the expression on her face, they couldn't be very comforting ones.

His treatment of her over the past couple of days plagued him when he least expected it—like right now.

"You can use my shoulder for a pillow if you want."

"Thank you, this is fine," Cassandra replied stiffly, resting her chin on her shoulder so she could watch the passing scenery outside.

Why, he wondered, didn't she just yell at him, like any other woman would? No, she had to suffer in silence.

"Look, I know I shouldn't have left you like that this morning, after—I had an appointment with Black."

"Yes, I know."

"I didn't tell you about it, because...well, because..."

"Yes?" she prompted, turning to face him, making him uncomfortable beneath her steady, unblinking stare.

"I knew you'd think I was...running out on the deal we'd made—"

"And were you?" she asked shortly.

"No." He fired a quick glance in her direction, meeting her eyes. "Not exactly," he amended after glimpsing her challenging look.

Why did he feel like a guilty schoolboy standing in front of the principal?

"I was going to see that you got the stuff—*after* I finished with Black."

"I see."

What did she see? Will gripped the steering wheel tightly. She was making him feel like a heel. Why the hell didn't she tell him what she was feeling? Tell him what a bastard he was for using her and then running out on her that way?

He was treading on thin ice, and he knew it. It was his own cunning that had put this wedge between them. A wedge that, oddly enough, he resented. Yet he knew that even though he wished she wouldn't think badly of him, he wasn't ready to throw in the towel as far as Black was concerned and give up his own plans.

Stronger even than these surprising feelings toward Cassandra were the deep feelings of anger and betrayal he felt toward Jordan Black.

Black hadn't even had the decency to cloak his destruction of Will in any other form, preferring instead to tell Will he'd done it to teach him a lesson about high finance and how foolish were those who worked within the system.

Systems, like rules, Black had laughed, *were created by small-minded people afraid to take chances. Rules are good for only one thing—sharpening your teeth.*

My teeth— he'd smiled venomously at Will *—are razor sharp, as you've seen for yourself. Remember that, and if you want to make it in the big league, make certain that in the future your own teeth are honed to a fine point.*

Will knew there was only one way to deal with Black, and he didn't think the legal system was it. Men like Black could buy their way out of practically anything, because there was always someone willing to be bought.

Like you? a small inner voice whispered mockingly. It wasn't the same thing, he argued silently. He wasn't hurting anyone.

Who cared if he made a little money on something Jordan Black wanted kept secret?

Sure, the woman beside him had spouted things about the future of mankind, but, hell, man might not even be here in a hundred years....

"You don't *know,* not for certain, that the land on which Black is planning to build will actually do any harm to anyone," he challenged her abruptly, as though she'd been a party to his conversation with himself.

"Don't I?"

Will threw her an uncomfortable glance. "Come on, face facts. What with the crisis in the Middle East and new diseases springing up that we can't find a cure for, there might not be anyone around in a hundred years to worry about it. The truth of the matter is, with the way the world is going, it's up for grabs as to whether the next generation lives to see their children grown—"

"If men like Jordan Black and—" She stopped abruptly. "If Mr. Black has his way, then certainly we have no hope for a future," she interrupted, earnestly.

"And me," he added sourly. "That's what you were going to say, isn't it?"

"No."

"Don't lie to me."

"I'm not—I can't. I won't lie to you—not ever," she answered faintly, staring straight ahead, refusing to meet his doubtful glare.

"Damn it!" Will ran a hand through the short brown hair at his temples and slapped the steering wheel with the palm of his hand.

"Nothing is ever certain! If man doesn't destroy himself, there's always Mother Nature. There could be a natural disaster, like the major earthquake psychics," he spat the word at her, "have been predicting for years, causing worldwide destruction. Then where would your future generations be? I'd say they would be a moot point at best. Black deserves what he's getting," Will insisted, returning to the real subject of their conversation. "No one is going to get hurt, least of all him."

"No? Well, I disagree." She turned to face him, leaning toward him in earnest appeal. "Sure, you won't be hurting Jordan Black, but what about yourself? After you do what you're planning to, you'll be a criminal—just like he is.

"And you say you won't be hurting anyone. But what about the innocent lives that will be affected by the toxic material they'll be living right on top of? Don't you feel a responsibility toward them?"

Worry about a generation of people who *might* exist long after he'd gone? And he had only Cassandra's word that anything would happen even then.

It didn't occur to him that the danger to the Earth and its inhabitants was the very lever with which he hoped to manipulate Black. The government—at least certain areas of it—would be only too glad to know about what Black was up to. And the American public would revile the man.

Will himself was much more likely to wonder where the world would be without the products factories produced every year. Without the jobs they provided for thousands of people. That was what was important, wasn't it?

Wasn't it?

Is that a twinge of conscience you're feeling? Aren't you so certain after all that what your ex-benefactor is planning isn't morally reprehensible?

And what about yourself? How do you label blackmail?

"I don't want to discuss Black or anything about him anymore today," Will said firmly, shrugging aside the voice of his conscience.

He wanted to ignore her and what she'd said, but her presence, so close beside him, kept her words running like a litany through his head. In frustration he switched on the radio and turned it up loud enough to drown out everything—except his own thoughts.

In the long run, he reasoned, nothing mattered in this world, not people, not things—nothing really—that was what he believed. He was beginning to think life was one great big joke and the whole human race bore the brunt of it.

What had life offered a hick kid from the sticks after his parents were gone? The ranch he'd grown up on and where he'd worked alongside his father belonged to someone else. That had left Will without a home, a family, no education beyond what he'd gotten before his mother's death, and no place to go.

For a while he had drifted, trying to find a purpose in life, searching for a reason for his own existence. It had been a foolish endeavor. What he had learned was that there was nothing else beyond what you had on Earth. Only hard work while you were alive and a stone-cold grave when you died.

But when Jordan Black had come along and taken an interest in him, Will had dared to believe once more. And as long as his blinders had stayed intact; as long as he'd followed Black's rules to the letter; he had made money hand over fist.

At one time he'd had everything his father and mother had ever wanted for him, plenty of money, fast cars, a fancy home and beautiful women at his beck and call.

Something inside twisted at the thought of how his father had wanted so much for him. All the years while he was growing to manhood, his father had spoken about how proud he would be the day Will graduated from college. He would be the first one on either side of the family ever to do so.

But his father had died, and Will couldn't forgive him for that—nor himself either.

If he'd been a better son—if he'd been in the field with his father that day when the tractor overturned—he might have been able to save him.

And if he'd been at home with his mother, instead of away at college, maybe she wouldn't have died all alone of a broken heart.

We make our own pain and misery.... The thought kept running through his head.

Will forced his thoughts away from the painful past. What good did it do to relive it all again? What was done was done. Nothing could change it.

He turned his eyes to the countryside and found himself comparing the barrenness of the land with the barrenness of his life.

The area they were traveling through at the moment was full of stark contrasts. At times they traveled through towering mountains and verdant valleys filled with green. And then, all at once, an uneven stretch of rocky ridge filled the horizon.

At times the mountains looked like huge irregular blobs of puff paint, smeared on a flat canvas. Here and there mesquite, palo verde and creosote bush made a welcome change, spots of green and yellow in an otherwise dull vista done in shades of brown.

Will noticed that the needle of the gas gauge had dropped almost to empty and made a mental note to stop for fuel and sandwiches at the first opportunity.

Cassandra had fallen asleep in the seat beside him, and he didn't waken her. And after looking at the sandwiches the place had to offer, he decided he wasn't hungry himself.

A few hours later the sun dipped toward the horizon, and Will decided he needed to stretch his legs. A fleeting thought of getting a motel room for the night passed through his mind, but he dismissed it.

A blue-and-white road sign informed him that a rest area was very near, and in a short space of time the car was parked near the building housing the comfort station.

After Will visited the rest room, instead of returning to the small, confining car and the woman sleeping so peacefully inside it, he walked behind the buildings through a narrow stand of trees toward a small hill. There he stopped.

The panorama of sky, mountains and desert was breathtaking in its beauty. He stood for a long time, hands shoved into his pockets, shoulders slumped, staring at it and letting his thoughts drift.

"It's so beautiful it makes me feel all funny inside."

Will hadn't heard her approach, but he turned slightly when she spoke and looked at her, a pale blur in the fading light.

"I thought you were out for the count."

She frowned for a moment until she deciphered his meaning and then offered him a slight smile.

"I was very tired." Her steps took her closer, but she was careful not to get too close, not to touch him. "You must be exhausted, too."

He shrugged, staring at the purple mountains in the distance, seeing her face. Her nearness was affecting him, bringing his senses alive in small ways. The sharp biting odor of the creosote bush had been stinging his nostrils, but it was rapidly being overshadowed by her musky essence.

"How is your face?" she asked, breaking the long stretch of silence.

"Sore," he answered succinctly, wishing she'd stayed asleep in the car and left him to his solitude for a while longer. Her presence only served to unsettle him; for a moment before she'd come he'd found a kind of peace, a oneness with the stark surroundings.

"Is there anything we can get to put on it, to help it heal?"

"Time will take care of that." He shrugged. "This isn't so bad. I've had worse."

"I'm sorry you got hurt." She paused before adding, "But I did warn you not to trust Mr. Black. He's an evil man."

"He's a bastard," Will ejaculated harshly.

Cassandra took an involuntary step back from his anger. "Have you decided what you're going to do?" she asked boldly, wishing she could change the subject, but conscious of time running out for them both.

"No, I'm still thinking about it." He didn't want to discuss Jordan Black. The subject made him irritable, and all at once he felt lonely and in need of companionship, not dissent.

Cassandra shivered as a sudden burst of cool air blew in from the desert and hugged her bare shoulders. She didn't know if her chill was a result of the cool air or the bleak look on Will's face.

Will caught the involuntary movement out of the corner of his eye and stepped closer to shield her from the fresh wind. Without conscious deliberation, he slid one arm lightly around her, wrapping her narrow shoulders in his male warmth.

Cassandra felt as though she'd been enclosed in a toasty cocoon. Her eyes shifted upward as she turned slightly into his embrace.

They stared at each other, the sky like a velvet cloth overhead. The last vestiges of the sun's rays flared into brilliant fingers of orange, yellow, pink and blue, reaching clear across the darkening sky from one rim to the other.

But the beauty overhead went unnoticed. At that moment Will and Cassandra had eyes only for each other.

She breathed deeply in anticipation as she saw the expression on his face begin to change. And then, all at once, his eyes became hooded, and he looked away.

"Are you reading my mind?"

"Do you want me to?" she asked, somewhat startled by the question.

Moving uncomfortably he said, "About that—"

"I'm not," she added quickly. "I won't invade your privacy."

"Sometimes," Will admitted, his gaze still focused on the distant mountains, "I wouldn't mind if you did...."

Cassandra felt her pulses leap. "It...doesn't bother you—knowing that I *can?*"

"Not...anymore."

Was that his voice saying that? he wondered.

"At first—I didn't believe you could." He amended the thought. "I didn't want to believe you could."

His dark eyes turned to her face, glowed down at her in the failing light. Shifting his position so that his hands rested on her shoulders, he asked, "Do you remember when you called me at the hotel?"

Cassandra nodded.

"I—you startled me." His hands tightened as he sensed she was about to speak. "You also reminded me of the past, of my mother—she had what she called *the sight*. That's why I was so rude to you over the telephone. You remind me of things I want to forget, of people who I've failed—"

"Will..." She placed a hand on his chest in sympathy.

"It's all right." He shook his head. "It doesn't matter now. I've gotten a handle on those feelings. For a while I thought—" He hesitated. "It doesn't matter. What's past is past, and there's nothing we can do to change that. This is all there is. And when it's over..." He lifted his hands. "Well, I guess it doesn't matter what we've done. We all just live the best way we can, and when we die—that's that." Dropping his hands from her shoulders all at once, he walked briskly away, leaving her alone.

Cassandra wanted to cry out that what he said wasn't true. Everyone was supposed to help each other, because everyone was connected, and what one person did affected everyone else.

But she knew that in order for him to see that, he needed to search deep inside himself and find something that up until now he'd been missing. And he needed to have faith, in himself and in others.

She wanted to assure him that there *was* more—so much more—to look forward to after this life. But she couldn't. To do so would be a waste of breath in his present state of mind. And she had no way of proving her words were true— at least, no way she was supposed to employ.

There was only one way she could prove he was wrong, and that was to take him to Heaven and show him it was there, waiting for him. But she couldn't do that any more than she could force him into believing in himself. Some things a person had to come by on his or her own.

Will would have to reach deep down to that tiny space that made him the man he was—or could be—and realize that he was a man who could do great things if he chose.

For a while she stayed on the hillside, watching the night sky fill with billions of twinkling stars and allowing Will some time alone to struggle with his own thoughts. She knew, without having to read his mind, that he was in spiritual turmoil. And in this case that was good.

Let him worry, let him doubt, let him struggle to see the bright light at the end of the dark tunnel. A tunnel of his own making that he'd been darting in and out of since his parents' deaths.

She had faith in him, more faith than he had in himself right now, and she was trying very hard to believe he would make the right decision about Jordan Black.

After a while the air grew colder, and she returned to the car. A few yards away, sitting on top of a picnic table nearby, his head in his hands, she spotted Will. He quickly glanced up at the sound of her approach, then straightened.

"It's late. Do you want to get a place for the night? A place to sleep?"

Cassandra looked around her. "I like it here. Can we stay here?"

If he was surprised at the question, Will hid it. "Yes, of course we can, but the car isn't very big. It might be an uncomfortable night."

It was, she knew, going to be a very uncomfortable night for both of them no matter where they stayed.

"I'll chance it," she answered, taking a seat at the corner of the table across from him. Folding her hands in her lap, she gazed at him expectantly.

Will moved uncomfortably beneath her stare. "We haven't eaten all day," he remembered suddenly. "There are vending machines at the side of the building. Would you like a candy bar, some chips, a soft drink?"

On the point of refusing, she changed her mind and nodded instead. "I'd like that—I think," she added beneath her breath, climbing down from the table to follow and watch as he placed coins in the machines.

"Cola? Or a fruit-flavored drink?"

"Fruit," she decided without hesitation.

A few minutes later, loaded down with chips, a candy bar and a can of grape-flavored drink, Cassandra perched once more on her table where she started on the candy bar.

Will watched as she tore into the wrapper with enthusiasm. The glow from the security lamps cast a pale yellow nimbus around her head and shoulders as she moved, and he blinked several times in surprise.

When he looked again the radiance had disappeared, and he realized it had only been a trick of the light. But just for a moment the thought that she might *really* be an angel, his guardian angel, had darted through his mind. That was one of the crazy stories she'd told him when they'd first met, and it must have stuck in his mind.

Cassandra bit into the mixture of chocolate, raisins and nuts, chewing slowly. A frown began to wrinkle her forehead.

"Is it stale?"

She looked up and met his glance. "Stale?"

"Yeah, old. You know, doesn't taste good. We can get you another one—"

"Oh, no, it's delicious! I've never had one before, and I like the mixture of flavors."

"You've never had one before? Lady, where did you grow up? I thought *everyone* had eaten at least one candy bar in their childhood."

"Cassandra—please," she murmured with a tentative smile, holding the candy close to her mouth. "Call me Cassandra." Brushing at a strand of hair blowing against her mouth, she explained, "I meant—"

"Cassandra," Will interrupted her, trying out the sound of it on his tongue. "I don't believe I've ever known anyone by that name before. I'll bet your mother read those colorful romance novels you see in drugstores to come up with a name like that."

She made no comment. Thinking it was because of her absorption in the food, Will took a sip of coffee and watched her in silence for a time, before taking up the conversation once more.

"I'll bet I know why you've never had one of those." He gestured with his cup toward the candy she was eating. "I'll bet you grew up in one of those households where candy was considered bad for you, because it caused cavities."

"Cavities?"

"Yeah, cavities. People ought to be shot for denying kids the simple pleasures in life. Before you know it, childhood's gone, and all life's innocent pleasures go with it. Things are never the same once you're an adult."

He looked out toward the blackness, toward the windswept desert, a faraway look in his golden brown eyes. "My parents..."

Cassandra lowered the candy and leaned slightly forward. "Yes? What were your parents like?" she asked with interest.

So far he hadn't volunteered much about his past life, except for a brief insight about his feelings toward Jordan Black and his mother's gift of prophecy.

Will continued to gaze into the night without speaking. When he finally met her eyes, the brooding look had faded. He shook his head and shrugged, wadding up the empty paper coffee cup. He didn't want to talk about the past.

"Poor," he answered shortly, getting to his feet. "They were poor. We couldn't afford candy very often. So I guess our childhoods weren't so different after all."

"Come on, it's getting late. Finish your food so we can get some sleep. I want to get an early start in the morning. We still have a long way to go."

"Why don't you want to talk about your parents? They were good people." He glanced at her sharply. "I can tell that just by the little I've come to know about *you.*"

"My parents are dead. I don't want to talk about them. They're gone—"

"Oh, but they aren't," she insisted, getting to her feet. "As long as they remain in your memory, as long as there's a place for them in your heart, they'll never be gone."

"I don't believe in that stuff. When this body is gone—" he tapped his chest "—there's nothing left. This—" he spread his hands to indicate their surroundings "—is all there is."

"You don't believe in Heaven?"

"Heaven?" He looked at her as though she'd said something outrageous. "Heaven is a fantasy. It's make-believe, an ideal place, like Utopia, where everyone can have what they want and be what they want without question. It's someplace everyone would like to believe exists, but it only exists in the minds of those who can't face reality—and their own mortality."

Cassandra felt a small spark of anger stir inside her. "And what is reality? Your reality?"

He stared at her, knowing his words were upsetting her and feeling almost glad of it. She was beginning to like him too much. He could see it in her eyes, feel it in her manner toward him, and he rejected the idea.

He didn't want to get close to anyone. He was a loner, always had been, except for the few years when he'd allowed himself to be taken in by Black. And of course there had been Janice, his ex-fiancée—if you could count that relationship. He wouldn't be taken in again.

"Reality," he said slowly, enunciating each word carefully, "is a hard life, little pleasure, a quick death, a cheap

WE EVEN PAY THE POSTAGE!

It costs you nothing to send for your free gifts—we've paid the postage on the attached reply card. And we'll pay the postage on your free gift shipment. We charge nothing for delivery!

If offer card is missing write to: Silhouette Reader Service, 3010 Walden Ave., P.O. Box 1867, Buffalo, NY 14269-1867

DETACH AND MAIL CARD TODAY

BUSINESS REPLY MAIL
FIRST CLASS MAIL   PERMIT NO. 717   BUFFALO, NY

POSTAGE WILL BE PAID BY ADDRESSEE

NO POSTAGE
NECESSARY
IF MAILED
IN THE
UNITED STATES

SILHOUETTE READER SERVICE
3010 WALDEN AVE
PO BOX 1867
BUFFALO NY 14240-9952

casket and six feet of dirt shoveled in your face. It's an eternity of nothingness.''

"You don't believe that."

"Don't I?" His eyes were cold, resolute.

"There is a Heaven." She touched his arm urgently. "Believe me, it exists."

There was so much conviction in her voice that it irritated him all the more. Fastening his hand over hers in an iron grip, he threw it from him.

"Oh!" she cried out, clasping the hand protectively against her chest.

Will had turned to stomp away, but at her cry he turned back. "What's wrong? Did I hurt you?"

"No." She shook her head, eyes glistening in the light. "It's all right."

"Then what?" he asked, coming back to tower over her.

"Nothing."

Will grabbed her hand impatiently and opened the fingers, then stared at the palm. In its center the flesh was red, and a black object, about a quarter of an inch long, was embedded just below the skin.

"Why didn't you tell me you had a splinter in your hand?" His eyes met hers. She looked almost frightened, and he didn't understand why. "Do you have a pin anywhere on you?"

"Pin? N-no." She shook her head.

"What about a purse? Don't you have a purse? I thought every woman in the world carried a purse with all kinds of useless things in it."

"I don't have one," she told him in a small voice, feeling as though she'd committed some terrible sin by not having one with her.

A truck had pulled up on the far side of their vehicle, and a tall man in a T-shirt, jeans and cowboy boots gave them a nod as he passed close by. Will followed the man's progress with his eyes, told her abruptly to stay put and followed in the stranger's wake.

Another car had pulled up beside the red compact when Will came into view, walking beside the trucker. Cassandra watched curiously as the two men strode toward the huge truck.

The stranger climbed up inside the the cab. After a moment his head reappeared as he handed something out to Will. They talked for a moment, shook hands, and Will gave him a brief wave.

Will motioned for her to follow him inside the building as the big truck moved off down the road.

Will waited until she'd joined him to open the door and head toward the ladies' room.

"What are you going to do?" she asked apprehensively, peering around at the empty stalls.

"I brought you in here because I figured you'd be more comfortable in the ladies' room than in the men's."

He was holding a small blue-and-white box marked with a red cross, and he set it on the sink and opened it, removing a small shiny object. "I'm going to take that splinter out of your hand with these tweezers before it becomes infected."

After lifting a small brown bottle from the box, Will twisted the lid off and poured some liquid over the end of the tweezers while holding them over the sink.

"You don't have to do that," she told him, trying to pull her hand away as he captured it with his.

"I know I don't *have* to," he answered shortly, "but I'm going to. Now, hold still."

He didn't understand, Cassandra thought, but how could she tell him there was no need? Later on, how would she be able to explain the absence of a wound?

"Ouch!" Curling her fingers over his as the sharp points of the instrument bit into her skin, she gave it a jerk.

"Sorry. Hold still." Will glanced up briefly before going back to the job at hand. "I almost had it. I don't think it's a splinter," he said peering closer. "Looks more like a thorn."

After that first murmur of protest, Cassandra kept silent, but she watched his every move as he poked and prodded, now and then muttering beneath his breath in frustration. It wasn't long before her gaze was drawn to his face, bent in deliberation over her hand.

All at once she found herself noticing irrelevant things, like the way his eyebrows drew together above his nose in concentration to create one long, dark line across his forehead. The dark gash at his temple had closed over, but she felt a stab of pain at the sight of the purple bruising around it.

Her glance moved over the one puffy eye, nearly swollen shut, to the other one, which looked as though it had been painted with rings of red and blue. His eyelashes, she noted, were a shade lighter than his hair. It was impossible to see how thick they were, or how they curled upward, unless you were seeing them like this, up close. She felt a lurch of excitement within her.

A tingling sensation started in the hand he held, working its way through her body. It wasn't caused from the prick of the tweezers but from the hand holding hers so carefully. It scorched her skin, branding it with his touch.

She forgot to fear the discomfort, forgot to worry about what she would say if he discovered the secret of her unearthly ability to heal in an amazingly short period of time. All she felt was the sheer magnitude of the emotions sweeping through her at his touch. Entirely caught up in her own inner turmoil, she deliberately shut out the reality of their situation. "There," he muttered in satisfaction, holding something up for her to see. "I knew I'd get it—all it took was patience."

The half-formed smile on his face faded as his eyes touched and locked with hers. She was staring at him as though he'd performed a major miracle. And all he'd done was remove one small thorn.

But he was, after all, a man, and not immune to the look of adoration shining from her eyes. She was stirring feelings inside him that were better left alone. He could feel his determination to keep her at arm's length beginning to crumble.

What man wouldn't welcome being thought of as a hero by such a beautiful, desirable woman?

Tearing his gaze from hers and holding her hand out over the sink without warning her of the consequences, he poured some of the antiseptic over the small wound. He felt her slight jerk at the sudden sting of the medicine and couldn't keep his glance away from her face.

The liquid shine in her blue eyes as they met his squarely made him feel ashamed, but he kept his glance impersonal as he finished the job.

When he'd fixed a small bandage over the wound and put everything away, he said, ''There, you're all fixed up. I'm going to put this,'' he indicated the first-aid kit, ''in the car. And we'd better think about getting some sleep. It's going to be a long day tomorrow.''

But Cassandra couldn't let him go that easily. She caught up with him at the picnic tables. ''Will, wait—''

He hesitated before turning to face her, a closed expression on his face.

She stopped beside him and raised a hand toward his face. ''Your own wounds—I can put some of that on them.''

Will captured her wrist before she could touch him. ''I cleaned them with cold water. That's good enough.''

He almost flung her wrist from him as he turned quickly away.

With sad eyes Cassandra watched as, back and shoulders stiff, he walked determinedly away. What had she done now? The expression in his eyes had told her that he wanted nothing from her, not even the same impersonal care he'd given her.

Her heart ached with the knowledge that she was no closer to softening his hard heart than when she'd first landed in the hotel in Los Angeles. And though Barnabas wasn't there to count down the hours, she felt a sense of panic at the thought that the passage of time on Earth appeared to have speeded up considerably since her arrival.

Chapter 8

She'd been watching him for the last fifty miles, and Will was beginning to feel restless. What did she want from him? Did she think that because they'd been to bed together he owed her something?

All right, maybe she *was* in this jam because of him, and maybe he did owe her something because of that. But *he* hadn't been the one to initiate their relationship. And he certainly wasn't the one who'd come charging into danger at Black's estate.

The memory of how glad he'd been to see her flashed into his mind, and he adjusted his thinking a bit.

It wasn't that he didn't appreciate what she'd done. That was why he was taking her to his hideaway in southern Arizona, to keep her out of Black's merciless hands.

Black had made it abundantly clear that he had no interest in paying Will to keep quiet about what he knew. The beating he'd taken at the hands of Black and his men hadn't been able to make him reveal the secret of where he was hiding the information, or where he'd obtained it.

Will knew that to mention the name of his friend in Las Vegas was to sign the man's death warrant, and he couldn't live with that on his conscience. He also knew that if Black discovered the identity of the woman with him, she was as good as dead, too.

He'd persuaded himself, when he'd undertaken this little venture, that no one was going to get hurt. No one except Black. But if Will thought his own ironclad determination to make Black pay was unbending, it was nothing compared to Black's vicious anger.

His thoughts took an unexpected turn, and he berated himself for what he was doing. He should have known better than to try something as stupid as blackmail. Maybe what Black had in store for him was nothing more than he deserved, and maybe—he gave the woman beside him a sidelong glance—he was only beginning to see that when it was too late.

And it *was* too late for him. Black would never let him live. Even if he was put behind bars, the man would reach him and see that he was punished. The only hope Will had was to force Black into paying the money and then get as far away from him to whatever tiny corner of the world he could find and hide for God knew how long.

Will slapped the steering wheel with the heel of his hand in self-disgust, drawing a surprised glance from the woman at his side. It wouldn't have been so bad if he'd been alone.

Even if he paid for his stupidity with his life, it would be no great loss to the world—but he couldn't go out of this life taking anyone else with him. Not his friend Tom Mason in Las Vegas, nor this woman who had saved his life.

Will gave her a sidelong glance, saw the pensive way she studied her folded hands in her lap and wished *he* could read *her* thoughts. Was she thinking how sorry she was that she'd tried to help him?

He sincerely doubted that when she'd had her dreams or visions or whatever form her psychic abilities took, she'd considered the possibility that she would one day be running for her life. Or that the man responsible for the danger she was in would treat her with such a lack of consideration.

The responsibility his actions had saddled him with was beginning to take root in his mind, increasing the foul mood with which he'd awakened that morning to greet the new day.

Climbing from his place in the front seat, his whole body one large bruise, he'd moved stiffly to the back of the car, opened the door and bent inside to awaken his traveling companion.

It was at that precise moment that her eyes opened, and she'd smiled up at him with a look on her face that had wrenched his heart. And that had been the instant when he'd begun to realize exactly what he was giving up because of his little venture into crime.

His anger at the world had disappeared in one fell swoop as he'd looked down into Cassandra's face, and all he'd felt in its place was shame—and regret.

He'd left her abruptly in order to hide what he was feeling, after telling her to make a quick trip to the john, so they could get an early start. When he returned, the feelings he couldn't cope with firmly shut away from the world and his own conscious mind, it was to find the car empty and Cassandra nowhere around.

He'd known a moment's blind panic, thinking all kinds of improbable things, such as Black's having found her and dragged her away. He'd searched everywhere for her, including the ladies' room, without luck. He'd about reached his wit's end when he spotted a glimpse of gold through the trees and, somehow, known it was her.

He had found her sitting cross-legged on the hill where she'd found him the night before, staring in rapture at the first bright rays of the sun coming up over the mountains. He had wanted to be angry with her, but her solemn enthusiasm for the dawn's breaking light had infected him against his will.

Dropping beside her, he'd watched the gray sky begin to grow lighter. And as golden bands were thrown across the expanse above, reaching out like gentle fingers to bring a glow to the heavens, he'd turned to stare at her face.

Her eyes had been closed, her chin lifted, as though to allow those fingers of light to stroke her fair skin. And as they did, her face began to glow, as though catching and reflecting the light.

Watching her, he'd found himself considering the crazy idea that the glow, the warmth he felt sitting this close beside her, was actually coming from somewhere inside her and not from the sun.

He had wanted to touch her in that moment, both to test his theory and to somehow share in that warmth. But he'd been afraid.

It was beginning to seem as though there were a lot of things to be afraid of in this world. When had the fear started? In his childhood?

Even though he'd learned early in life to wear the brave, macho-male mask most men wore, he felt lost down deep inside—and the fear that Cassandra might see that fear in him kept his arms firmly clasped around his knees when what he really wanted was to hold her.

When the sunlight had burst across the desert floor, Will had told her abruptly that they needed to leave. She had accompanied him to the car silently, and he'd been fighting her silence ever since.

Everywhere he looked, he kept seeing the first beam of sunlight as it had fallen onto her face, enhancing her loveliness, opening up a chasm of need in him as wide as the Grand Canyon.

It was disconcerting to feel so captivated by a woman when he knew there was nothing he could do about it. It had to be that way.

He owed her his life, but what was more, he owed her her own life, intact, just the way it had been before she'd charged onto the scene to his rescue. Whatever else they had found together, the brief closeness they'd shared that one night was all there could ever be between them.

And that was what was haunting him. He knew he would never forget her. For the rest of his miserable life, he would live, over and over again, the few hours they'd spent in each other's arms. The first real shared emotions he'd experienced in years.

He laughed at himself silently, knowing that his blackmail scheme, intended to make Jordan Black pay, had turned into a life sentence for himself. Because the only thing that would get him off the hook now with Jordan Black was his own death—or Black's.

It was ironic, and if he hadn't been hurting so much inside, he might have laughed out loud. Life was never what you wanted it to be, but what others made of it for you.

He wasn't very good with one-on-one relationships...never had been...just ask his former fiancée...or his dead mother and father....

Cassandra wondered what had put such an unhappy look on Will's face, why he'd hit the steering wheel of the car with his hand so fiercely. But, though curious, she didn't ask, nor did she make an attempt to part the veil shielding his thoughts from hers. She was learning that sometimes it was better if you *didn't* know what others were thinking.

Sighing, she squirmed in the seat until she had found a more comfortable position from which to stare out at the passing scenery and thought about how uncomfortable a night it had been. This body was susceptible to discomforts she had never imagined in Heaven.

During the night, however, she had learned a few new facts. Cars weren't made to sleep in, and desert nights got chilly this time of the year, especially if all you had to combat the cold was the clothes on your back.

The back seat had seemed very large indeed, despite Will's warning to the contrary, when she'd been trying to find warmth. But it shrank considerably when she thought about how much easier the long hours of darkness would have passed if she had been sharing it with Will.

On the tail end of those thoughts had come the worry that she might be letting her feelings for him interfere with her purpose for being here. How was she to save him, to show him the error of his ways, if she put other thoughts and needs in the way of developing a plan to that effect?

Granted, her idea to take him to their present destination was a good one, but she had to be on her toes every minute. She had to make certain she presented the purpose for their going there in the correct manner.

This would probably be her last chance to make him see what he was doing. How he was becoming a man like Black, a man without a conscience, a transformation that would be complete if he continued on his present path.

She simply *had* to make him change his mind. There were only four days left and—oh, she didn't know how many hours; that was Barnabas's sphere, measuring time.

Speaking of Barnabas, where was he? He'd said he would be around to keep an eye on her work.

"What—"

The car made a sudden sharp turn to the left, leaving the interstate and entering the access road. Cassandra flopped over in the seat toward Will. She put out a hand to steady herself and found her fingers grasping his thigh.

Will swung his head in her direction, a look almost of despair in their depths. Surprised, Cassandra opened her mouth to ask what was wrong. The car bumped against the rocky shoulder of the road, drawing Will's attention back to his driving, and sensing his chagrin at revealing even a small part of his innermost feelings to her, she pulled back her hand without speaking.

The car stopped, and they sat in silence, staring outside, pretending that none of the tension filling the atmosphere between them existed.

"Why are we stopping?" Cassandra asked in a small voice, the first to break the silence.

Gazing around at the large trucks filling the small parking lot and overflowing along the road in front, she swallowed back what she really wanted to say. Making a fist of the hand with which she'd touched him, its palm throbbing with heat, she closed her mind to the memory of rough material and hard muscle bunching beneath her touch.

With an effort, she then opened her mind to other sensations, hoping to fill the void. For the past several miles she'd been trying to identify the sharp pain she'd been having in her stomach.

"Breakfast," her companion snapped shortly.

And now she knew the pain for what it was—hunger.

Will pocketed the keys before climbing from the car. Pushing down the lock, he slammed the door and moved around the hood to wait impatiently for her to join him.

She did so swiftly, wishing he would look at her instead of simply sliding his gaze across her face without really seeing her.

The building was small, and it looked as though there would hardly be enough room to accommodate the large number of people she surmised there must be inside. She and Will walked across the hard pavement, skirting two gas pumps, and up to the glass doors.

The loud hum coming from the air-conditioning unit sitting at the side of the building drowned out any sounds coming from inside. Feeling uneasy for some unnameable reason, Cassandra scanned the parking lot, noting the large trucks, a couple of smaller pickups and one car—theirs.

As Will opened the door and they started to enter, a sound, overshadowing that of the air conditioner, drew her attention. She looked back over her shoulder.

A group of two-wheeled machines—motorcycles—was pulling into the parking lot and heading directly toward the front of the building. She counted ten of the machines, some of them holding two riders. As the door closed behind her, she wondered how this place would accommodate so many more people.

Inside the small restaurant, appetizing aromas assaulted her, causing her to forget the arriving customers outside. She heard a rumbling sound coming from her midsection and placed a hand across her stomach in surprise.

Each time she experienced a brand-new sensation she felt an immediate sense of wonder—accompanied by a small twinge of regret. Six days was hardly enough time to get a start on all there was to learn and enjoy about being human. And two of those days were already gone.

A sign tacked to the wall inside the front door informed everyone that they would have to find a seat for themselves. Cassandra, following Will, stopped when he stopped, then peered curiously over his shoulder at the other occupants of the room.

It was filled almost to capacity with a rough-looking group of diners. Cassandra noticed that they were all male and felt another twinge of unease. But another bout of hunger pains hit her, and, sniffing the air like a hungry kitten searching out a saucer of milk she decided she was more interested in investigating the appetizing scents than in who her dining companions might be.

All at once her attention was captured by the unusual silence in the room, and she noticed that all eyes were turned in her direction. She turned to stare at what everyone else appeared to be looking at, and the twinge of unease grew to a full-blown feeling of fear.

Taking a step closer to Will, she bumped into him in order to keep from rubbing against the group of strange-looking individuals piling into the small entranceway where she and Will were standing.

Will jerked away from her abruptly, and Cassandra saw that he was heading toward a table with two chairs. It was situated near a window on the edge of the thick cloud of cigarette smoke that nearly filled the room.

She followed him hurriedly, refusing to glance behind her again. The seconds passed, but instead of turning back to their meals and conversations, everyone continued to stare.

Before long, once she'd taken a seat across from Will, unable to stop herself, she glanced back over her shoulder. Her eyes were immediately captured by a big man standing head and shoulders above the others. He was dressed in green military fatigues, army boots and a black leather jacket. And he was staring at her, a small grin showing through the chest length black beard nearly covering his whole face.

After a moment, his companions pushed past the man she had already labeled as Blackbeard in her thoughts. A slight commotion drew her glance from the doorway to the center of the room. She saw two of the men who'd arrived with Blackbeard jerk two men who were already seated up from their table and take their places.

The two who'd been ejected from their seats moved toward the door. Skirting the big man still standing there, they threw some money on the counter near the cash register and left.

The same scenario was taking place all over the room. Some, anticipating being relieved of their seats, perhaps fearing something worse, stood and left voluntarily. In a matter of minutes all the bikers—with two exceptions—had taken over tables and chairs.

Cassandra glanced back toward the door and the big man still standing there. He was now bent almost double listening to what his companion, a much smaller man dressed in studded black leather pants and a matching jacket, and wearing a horned Viking's hat, was whispering intently in his ear.

Something told her, without her having to read his thoughts, that trouble was brewing.

Cassandra turned back to the table. A large man with a potbelly, wearing a white apron decorated with a colorful rainbow of spills tied around his ample waist, arrived to ask, "Coffee?"

Will nodded, and the man turned to her. Cassandra quickly nodded her head in response to his impatient glare.

Dropping her eyes to stare down at the menu without really taking note of what she was reading, Cassandra swallowed tightly. She was profoundly aware of the strained tone dominating the buzz of conversation going on around her.

"Okay, folks, what will you have?"

The man with the apron had returned, bringing coffee, to take their order. He placed a steaming cup at each place, then stood beside them, hands on his broad hips, looking from one to the other questioningly.

Will glanced across the table at Cassandra, but she only stared back at him without speaking. With a slight shrug he gave his own order, glanced at her again, then, when she remained silent, added, "Make that two of everything."

When they were alone again, she asked, "Are you angry with me?"

"No, of course I'm not angry. What do I have to be angry—"

"Well, well, what have we here?" a loud, gruff voice said from directly behind Will's right shoulder.

Cassandra looked up into small dark eyes, nearly hidden beneath twin bushes of hair. Blackbeard was staring at her.

When no one answered, he moved his bulk to stand at the side of the table between them. Indicating Will's injured face with a nod, he asked, "Did you do that, honey?"

"No, I—"

"Beat it." Will's cold voice suddenly rang out, but his eyes remained fixed on the mug in his hand.

Will lifted the steamy brew to his lips, still without giving Blackbeard so much as a glance. When the cup was an inch from his mouth, a heavy weight knocked against his arm, spilling the coffee down his shirtfront and onto the table.

"Oops, sorry." Blackbeard laughed, glancing around at his cronies sitting at various tables around the room and laughed louder as they all joined in.

"Looks to me like you're kinda clumsy. Maybe sweet cheeks here didn't do that to your face, after all.

"Maybe, you're just a big—" He leaned closer. "—dumb jock who can't keep from stumbling over his own two feet."

The atmosphere in the restaurant grew thick with tension. Not a sound could be heard except for the noise of crockery being banged together in the kitchen.

The men sitting at the tables close to Will and Cassandra stood and moved back, or left. The waiter, who'd been heading toward their table with a tray of food, gauged the situation at a glance, then made a detour back toward the kitchen.

"Are you looking for a fight?" Will asked, acknowledging the man's presence at last with a challenging glare.

"Well, now, that depends." The smirk, visible beneath the black beard, grew wider—and meaner—as he glanced around at his friends.

"On what?" Will asked obligingly, knowing the man wouldn't let it rest until he'd played out his little game.

"Why, on whether or not the fight is with *you*—or with this little beauty," he indicated Cassandra with a hand, "sitting across from you."

Blackbeard bent his hefty bulk until his face was only inches from Will's. "'Cause, you see, I don't think—from the looks of your face—that I could beat *her*." He crooked a thumb in Cassandra's direction.

"But if the fight is with *you*..." He ran a disparaging glance down over Will. "Then I think the fight's already pert near won."

A chorus of guffaws caused Will to scan the room. But it was a look of resigned acceptance that he turned on Blackbeard.

Obviously the man was spoiling for a fight. And since Will looked as though he'd already been the loser in *one,* it was a pretty safe bet, as far as this guy was concerned, that he would be the loser again.

Heaving a resigned sigh beneath his breath, Will placed both hands on the tabletop in preparation for getting to his feet.

"You know, I didn't do that to him at all." Cassandra spoke all at once in a confiding tone of voice, drawing Blackbeard's glance. "The man who's responsible had my friend's hands tied behind his back before anyone dared touch him. And he didn't have the nerve to do it by himself. He had his friends along to help. In my book that makes him—and anyone like him—a bully and a coward."

No one dared breathe as her words rang out in the silence of the room. After a moment, placing a hand on the big man's beefy forearm, she asked, "Don't you agree?"

At her touch, a change began to take place in the big man's dark eyes. His gaze became fixed on Cassandra's tranquil blue stare.

"I don't know, little lady," he answered uncertainly. "Maybe you're right."

Cassandra gave him a gentle smile. "I knew you'd agree with me. I can tell you're a man with principles. And we—" her glance included Will "—appreciate your concern."

"Right...uh..."

Blackbeard backed away from the table, withdrawing his arm from beneath Cassandra's light touch. Shaking his head slightly, as though he felt a little strange, he moved across the room. He didn't stop until he found a spot at a table in the farthest corner of the room.

Cassandra peered across the room at the short biker, the one who'd spoken so urgently to Blackbeard at the door. He'd joined his friend at his table and was once again whispering to him.

But this time it seemed the big man didn't want to hear what the other one had to say. Getting to his feet without so much as a glance in their direction, he strode back across the room, skirting their table, and out the way he'd come. The other tables emptied as his compatriots followed in his wake.

The last of the group had hardly left when Cassandra suddenly scraped her chair back from the table and stood.

Will looked up in surprise, and she met his glance, explaining, "I need to—" her eyes darted around the room for an instant "—visit the ladies' room," she finished hurriedly, and then she was gone.

She could feel his eyes on her back as she rounded the corner and entered the dark, narrow hall at the back of the restaurant. A small shadow near the end of the short hallway was making for the door marked Exit.

"No you don't!"

She grasped him by the arm. Somewhere he'd lost the Viking hat with the horns. She could barely make out the coal black hair ringing the wizened little head, but she recognized him all the same.

"What did you think you were doing back there?" she asked in a puzzled tone. "Barnabas, you nearly caused Will to get another beating—and he hasn't even healed from the last one yet."

"I'm sorry, child. I realize now that it was a foolish mistake. I was only trying to speed things up a bit, get something going for you. I thought if the police were called to stop an altercation..."

"Fight!" Cassandra insisted stubbornly.

"Ah, well, yes, ah, anyway, that would get the authorities involved..." He shrugged. "I thought maybe with them already on the scene, it might make things easier—simpler, so to speak—for you—Will—to hand over the evidence to them."

The faded blue eyes evaded her stare and angled toward the floor. He'd made a mistake. He wasn't above making them, but that didn't make him feel any better.

"I'm sorry," he murmured. "I should have let you in on what I was doing. It's just that time is getting short." He placed a hand on her forearm. "And I do so want you to succeed with this task. It's very important that you do."

"Yes," she agreed after a long moment of silence. "I know how important it is. And I have a plan. I'm taking him to visit Serenity."

Barnabas's face brightened. "Oh, that's a good idea."

"After that we're going to his cabin in the mountains near Bisbee, Arizona. You know where that is?"

"Yes, of course I do. Watch for me. I'll get in touch with you there."

"Barnabas..."

"Yes, child?"

"I—"

Should she mention what was happening to her? The new feelings for her charge growing inside her? Perhaps this was not the time. But then again, she might not get another chance before she had to leave.

"Barnabas, I've been wanting to ask you something—"

"He's coming!" Barnabas shrank as far back into the shadows as possible. "He must not see me. He might recognize me from the taxi."

Sliding along the wall toward the exit, he kept his eyes on the opposite end of the hall. "I'll speak with you soon."

Cassandra darted a swift glance toward the restaurant and then back toward Barnabas. "Wait! Barnabas, I need to ask you—"

"Later."

The door opened a few inches, and Barnabas slid outside just as Will's tall figure crowded out what little light there was in the hall by filling the doorway. Cassandra turned to face him, hoping he hadn't spotted the little man.

"Are you all right?" Will asked, waiting for her to come to him.

"Yes, fine."

"Your food is getting cold." He gave the exit door a long glance. "I came because I thought maybe all the bikers hadn't left. One might have slipped back here and be giving you a hard time."

"Oh, no—no bikers here." She lifted her hands palms up and gave a fluttery glance around. "I'm fine." Placing a hand over her middle, she added, "And very hungry."

"Right."

He moved so she could precede him back to the restaurant. As she moved in front of him, Will threw another swift glance down the hall toward the door. He could have sworn he'd seen a small stream of light at the edge of it as he'd entered the hallway.

Thirty minutes later they were on the open road, headed for a showdown, Cassandra hoped, between Will's stubbornness, his conscience and reality.

Chapter 9

The flat, monotonous desert landscape slowly gave way to the mountains. Following Cassandra's directions, Will turned onto a two-lane blacktop road, leaving the interstate behind, and the traffic became almost nil. Another hour of driving, climbing from one mountaintop to another, and he began to feel a little anxious about their destination.

"Are you certain we're headed in the right direction?" he asked as the road began once more to spiral upward.

"I'm sure," she said from her corner of the front seat.

"What's the name of this place where we're going?"

"Serenity."

"Serenity? Never heard of it."

"That's because it came into existence when you were little more than a baby and disappeared before you left college."

Will gave her a quick glance. It sounded eerie sometimes, the way she spoke. He had an inkling he wasn't going to enjoy the next few hours, but he was curious about what the place meant to the woman at his side—and her reasons for wanting to take him there.

"You mean we're going to a ghost town?"

"Yes."

A few minutes more and they'd reached the top of the mountain. The road disappeared around a curve up ahead, and looking into the distance, you could see for miles.

"Stop!" Cassandra cried without warning.

Will slammed on the brakes and twisted his head to stare at her. She was sitting straight on the edge of her seat, staring out her side window at something below them.

"There." She pointed. "That's where we're headed—right down there."

Will eased the car onto the dirt shoulder, stopped and leaned over to look out her window. Below them stretched a magnificent valley. Its outer reaches were lined with craggy rock formations and sandstone arches carved by eons of passing time, helped, no doubt, by considerable wind and rain. The valley was completely hidden by the mountains surrounding it.

If nature had been kinder, Will thought, it would be lush and green, fed by cool waters flowing down along the valley floor. But nature had not been kind. All that was left to testify to a river's past existence was a dry sandy wash, gouged with deep ruts caused by seasonal flash flooding. The only vegetation it now supported was the grayish green sagebrush growing across the valley floor.

Will's glance traveled slowly from one end of the valley to the other. It looked as though the loss of the river had done more than merely destroy vegetation.

It looked as though it might be responsible for the abandonment of a town as well. Buildings in various stages of deterioration stood like stone sentinels in stark relief against the otherwise barren backdrop.

Without commenting on the scene, he turned the wheel and began the slow descent toward the valley floor.

"Is there some place in particular you want to see?" Will asked, unable to keep the curiosity out of his voice.

"No. Just drive for a little while, if you don't mind."

The town had been laid out in a grid pattern, making it a simple matter to get from one section to another. They drove for a while without talking, up and down small side streets, down a few narrow alleys, past the remnants of another time, another way of life.

"Over there," Cassandra said, indicating the left side of the street. "That was originally the grade school."

Will slowed to a crawl as they drew close to the one-story L-shaped building. It stood all alone in the middle of a large, concrete lot littered with cans, bottles and debris.

The screens that had once been fastened onto the windows, allowing a cool breeze to blow through the building, giving a little relief from the sun's blistering heat, now littered the ground outside.

"It's hard to believe that at one time there were seventy-five students enrolled there, isn't it?"

"You said 'originally'?" Will asked.

"Yes, later it became a kind of hospital for those who couldn't afford to go to the better ones in the city."

"The town didn't have a medical facility?" Will asked.

"A small one, but it couldn't accommodate all those who. . . became ill."

"Some kind of an epidemic go through here?" he probed, sensing her reluctance to answer his questions.

"Not exactly," she answered slowly, wondering just how she should go about explaining what *had* taken place here.

Would her bringing him here make a difference in the decision he made about Black? Would anything be able to do that now, even something as devastating as this ghost town?

The thought of Jordan Black being punished didn't bother her in the least, but the manner in which it was accomplished did. It must not be at Will's hands.

They were passing a corner where a grocery store had once been located. The sign, Kiosky's Grocery, was still faintly legible. But the large plate-glass window that had fronted the store lay scattered in a million tiny pieces on the concrete, reflecting the glare of the sun's rays. A single gas pump out front still had the price of gas from fifteen years ago visible on the meter.

"Where to now?" Will asked, going along with her game of silence.

Obviously she would tell him what this was all about in her own good time. He just hoped it would be soon. They wouldn't have all that long before Black discovered where they were going. And he needed time to make his plans.

"Before we leave, there's one more place I want to show you. It's what we really came to see," she admitted.

"How do you know about this place?" Will asked. "Did you live here?"

"No. But I know someone who...had a lot to do with the beginnings of the town."

"What happened to it, and to the people who lived here?"

Cassandra remained silent.

A moment later Will forgot his question as the car slowed almost to a stop. They were passing what was left of a house that reminded him a lot of the one in which he'd spent his youth.

The remnants of a rusty metal swing-set sagged in the backyard, the green and red paint almost completely obliterated by time. The swings were gone; all that remained were the broken chains dangling in the breeze.

The fence that had once enclosed the play area lay in sections on the ground. A scooter and a tricycle, looking like junk in a junkyard, lay overturned against the rotting steps of the back porch.

Will had an instant's flash of a small boy, about five years old, falling off a bicycle. The child, who'd been trying to learn how to ride without training wheels, scraped his knees on the rough ground and bellowed in childish rage.

There was another figure in the picture, too. A woman. She ran to cradle the child in her arms, blowing on the skinned knees, kissing his tear-stained cheek, promising to "fix the hurt up."

Will's foot slammed down hard on the accelerator. He didn't want to remember the boy who had been him. And the picture...a reminder of a much happier time in his life. A time of joy and innocence.

"Now what?" he asked tersely, stubbornly refusing to allow the eerie atmosphere surrounding the place to take hold of him.

Cassandra gave him a questioning look but only pointed toward a small dirt road, a little more than a track, really, at the edge of town. It wound out of sight, upward toward the mountains.

They drove for the next few minutes in hushed silence, each caught up in his or her own thoughts.

All at once Will stopped the car with a jerk, kicking up a cloud of brown dust in the still afternoon air.

"Why?" he asked curtly.

"You wanted to know where the people are." She spread out a hand, gesturing toward the abandoned cemetery. "Here—most of them lie here."

He didn't want to ask it, didn't really want to know the answer, but the question seemed to pass between his stiff lips without his consent. "What happened to them?"

"It doesn't make a very pretty story," she warned, climbing from the car, then stopping to look back to where he was still sitting stiffly behind the steering wheel.

After a moment of staring back at her without moving, contemplating the idea of leaving her there and simply driving off alone, he reluctantly joined her in front of the tall black wrought-iron gates.

She waited for him to push against them, forcing their rusty, long-unused hinges to creak loudly in the hushed silence of the place. Will stood back, waiting for her to precede him, wishing he had the courage to turn and run. He didn't like graveyards; they reminded him too clearly of his own mortality.

Cassandra stopped just inside the gate, her eyes scanning the neglected graves. "It's sad to think that another human being could be responsible for all this pain and suffering.

"It may not look like it now, but the valley below us was once teeming with life. There was a river then, you see, the water sparkling clear and cold, purified by the mountains from which it flowed. Plants grew along it in a profusion of color. It was a beautiful sight to behold. Purple larkspur, pink balloon flowers and white sego lily... There were trees, too, cottonwood, desert willow and honey mesquite. And the tall grasses, growing on the valley floor, waving in the gentle wind, sheltered animals and insects.

"It was a place of unsurpassed beauty, lying hidden, like a jewel, among these mountains. But, like all beautiful things," she sighed sadly, "once discovered, it attracted attention. The wrong kind. An unscrupulous man found it one day and immediately decided he had to own it, because he was positive it would make him rich. He bought up the land as far as you can see, valley, desert, mountains.

"Once he'd purchased the land, however, his cash reserves were depleted, and he had nothing left with which to improve it. So, in order to make a profit, he decided to divide the valley into small parcels of land and sell shares in a planned community, designed and built—naturally—by him. Then he went looking for investors who had a limited amount of cash to invest. People who wouldn't ask too many questions about the whys and wherefores of what he was doing.

"He sought people who wanted a good, clean, healthy atmosphere, away from the crime and strife of city life, in which to raise their families. Or, in some cases, to retire. Those who couldn't afford the expensive apartments, condos and houses in the big cities.

"He found more than enough to satisfy his needs and sold them on the idea of his peaceful hideaway in the desert. He named it Serenity, after the kind of life-style he was certain they all wanted.

"While making his pitch, he made commitments to improve the community a little at a time. The early investors moved into houses that were barely finished, with no schools or medical help nearby. They had to drive through the mountain pass to shop for necessities, because there were no stores here in the beginning, either.

"But Serenity's founder promised to pave roads, build schools and attract small business to the valley. And the people believed him…" she murmured softly. "Believed he had their best interests at heart."

Cassandra left Will to move slowly among the graves, staring down at the headstones, an expression of deep sorrow in her blue eyes.

"What happened?" Will couldn't help asking as he stopped to read the message on the nearest tombstone, that of a child of seven.

"The community grew by leaps and bounds. And for a while the people were happy. But as time passed it became apparent, even to the most liberal-minded, that the town's founder, the man they had all listened to and trusted, wasn't living up to his end of the bargain. The promise of schools remained unfulfilled until the parents of the school-aged children became desperate. Eventually they had to build and support the school themselves.

"They also paid for the equipment to furnish a medical facility. And as far as attracting business was concerned . . . well, a couple of people got the money together and opened a drugstore and a grocery.

"Before long it became apparent that something was happening in the mountains around them. East of town, a mining operation was being established. The working men were pleased at the thought of getting jobs closer to home. And when the mine was opened, some *did* find jobs there.

"Meanwhile, because of the added expense of medical and educational materials, the drain on the people living here was extensive. The local leaders began to feel desperate. And as the months passed the men working at the mine became concerned about the way the waste products were being disposed of.

"It seemed that a lot of it was being dumped into the river. The same river from which the people living here obtained their water for drinking, cooking and bathing.

"Letters were sent and phone calls made to the owner of the mine, but to no effect. Finally, in desperation, a delegation of the town's leaders went to approach the owner with plans they'd worked out for disposing of the waste without utilizing the river to carry it away.

"But when the men arrived on the appointed day to meet with the owner, they were told he was unavailable. The man in charge listened patiently to their complaints and read their proposal. He agreed with everything they said. And he promised to see that the new methods were put into effect."

Will had come to stand beside her. They were looking down at the graves of a family of four buried side by side. He looked into her face and saw the tears standing in her eyes.

"He lied," she whispered with a catch in her voice. "Nothing changed. Not long after that, the people began to notice a marked decrease in wildlife in the area.

"The flowers and trees growing along the river's edge were either dead or dying. The banks of the river became littered not with the tracks of animals who'd come seeking its water to quench their thirst but with the dead carcasses of those who'd dared to drink.

"Within months the older residents were becoming ill. Soon someone called attention to the fact that the birthrate in town had dropped to zero, despite several young married couples who were trying to start families.

"And shortly after that the number of smaller children infected with childhood diseases increased alarmingly. The infant mortality rate increased, and anemia was prevalent among all the children.

"For the second time a delegation tried to reach the mine's owner. All that accomplished was to get the men who lived in Serenity and worked at the mine fired.

"Finally the town leaders went to the man from whom they'd purchased their homes, the founder of the town, hoping to get him to intercede on their behalf. That's when they learned the truth.

"The owner of the mine and the founder of Serenity were one and the same. They learned that this man had sold the land to them, then used their money to start the mining operation in the mountains around them, fully knowing what the results would be for the people living in the valley.

"When they protested and told him what was happening to their children, to the older residents, he told them in no uncertain terms that if they didn't like it, they could get out."

Turning her eyes up to Will's rigid face, she swallowed tightly before continuing. "Only they couldn't, because they'd used their life savings to purchase their homes. They had no place else to go." She spread her hands and looked around at the mountains and the valley below. "No place except here, a haven that had become a hell.

"One of the town leaders decided to go to the state and try to get the mine closed. But somehow the founder knew about the plan ahead of time and blocked him. He knew that a copper mine, one of the nation's leading providers, wasn't going to be put out of business by a few hundred people who might or might not be affected by its operation.

"At his wit's end, the same man who'd gone alone to the state agency went to beg, cajole and finally threaten the founder with public exposure unless he did something to alleviate the pain and suffering he was causing.

"But it was all to no avail. On his way home from that visit, his car mysteriously veered off the road and plunged over the side of an embankment, killing him instantly.

"The message was clear to the whole town, either they put up with what was going on around them and took their chances living there, or picked up what they could carry and left."

As her story wound to a close, Will stood for a moment without moving, his hands in his pockets. And then he left her to make his way out of the cemetery. He walked to the edge of the cliff and stood staring at the valley below.

A dust devil swirled down the empty riverbed, headed toward town, scattering dirt and debris in all directions. Will watched it until he couldn't see it any longer. The man responsible for this catastrophe was like that dust devil, stirring up trouble, leaving nothing but chaos in his wake.

Will knew the man's identity as surely as he knew his own name. There was only one man he knew of with enough charisma to make a whole town believe in his words as though they were gospel, one who thought nothing of stabbing an individual—or a town—in the back to make a profit.

"Jordan Black," he murmured through clenched teeth.

"Yes."

Cassandra had followed him, and now she stood close at his side, looking where he looked, but seeing, instead of the ruined town, the many faces of those who had lived—and died—there.

"Why have you brought me here?" Will asked almost angrily, his hands knotted into fists at his sides. "What does all this have to do with *me*?"

"I wanted—hoped—you'd understand that without my having to explain it."

"You're showing me what toxic waste can do to a town—"

"No!" Cassandra seized his arm and towed him around to face her. "People!" she all but shouted, tears staining her cheeks. "The effect it can have on *people!*"

Indicating the graveyard with her other hand, drawing him a little way toward it, she cried, "Look! Look at what it can do to *people!* Can you look at that and not understand that Jordan Black is a dangerous man? He has to be put away where he won't have the opportunity to do that to anyone else."

Will shook his head and laughed bitterly. "Where have you been all your life? I thought you said you'd studied the man? You know nothing about how he works if you think locking him up in a jail cell will stop him."

Shrugging her hands off his arm, he said, "I'm sorry about what happened here, but I had nothing to do with it. And besides," he added callously, "I didn't know these people. You didn't know them, either. What difference do their deaths make to you?"

"*Know* them?" she asked incredulously. "You didn't know them? And that makes a difference?

"They were men...women...children. They lived... breathed...laughed...loved...dreamed dreams—just like you." She spoke vehemently. "How can you stand there and say you didn't *know* them? What does *that* matter? Have you no compassion for your fellow man?"

Will held her glance. "If you mean," he asked stonily, "am I my brother's keeper, then the answer is no, I'm not. One thing I've discovered over the years is that my brother doesn't *need*, nor does he *want*, a keeper."

Pivoting on his heel, shoulders held rigid, Will marched toward the car, leaving her to stand alone on the edge of the hill.

Cassandra watched him go, a new batch of tears stinging her eyes. It was no use; nothing she said to him, or showed him, made any difference. All this had been nothing— nothing—but a waste of time.

He didn't listen to what she said. Oh, his ears picked up the sound of her words, but he steadfastly refused to understand the meaning *behind* them.

She had the sinking feeling that all was lost. Because of her—and her own lack of listening and understanding—Will was lost. *And so was she.*

She would return to Heaven as decreed, but only in spirit. The heart and soul of her would remain forever here on Earth, locked within this man's indifferent care.

Brushing the backs of both hands across her eyes, she moved as if in a trance toward the cemetery and the abandoned graves. She couldn't leave them like this. Even knowing they held but the shell of what each man, woman and child had been, the graves were monuments to them and their brief existence on Earth.

Swinging the tall gates back, she entered and knelt beside the nearest grave. Grasping the crooked headstone firmly in both hands, she twisted it into place.

For the first few minutes she could barely see what she was doing through the thick curtain of tears filling her eyes and washing her face. She didn't know if she was crying for the lost town, for Will's lost soul, or for her own lost hopes—perhaps it was for all three.

She passed from one grave to another, working diligently to remove a generation of accumulated rubble from each gravesite.

After what seemed like hours of feeling the merciless hot sun beating down on her, she began to feel light-headed. A wave of dizziness assaulted her without warning, and she stopped to lean back on her heels for a brief rest.

Licking dry lips, she tasted salt and felt another, stronger, wave of dizziness sweep over her.

"Are you all right?" a deep voice asked from nearby.

Cassandra opened blurry eyes and looked up into the sun. Shading her eyes with a forearm, she answered, "Yes. It's just...so hot."

"You don't have to do this—"

"Yes," she interrupted him. "I do."

"Why? Why is it so important to you? Will it get you 'another star in your crown' in Heaven?" he asked sarcastically, recalling the term his mother had used to get him to do something he didn't particularly want to do.

"Perhaps." She answered him seriously, knowing it was what she did toward his salvation that would accomplish that for her. "But that doesn't matter. What matters is how I feel inside. I *want* to do this for these people."

"Why? They won't know about it—they're all dead."

"Won't they? How do you know whether the dead can see and hear what's happening or not?"

"I know because—" He hesitated, unable to tell her how he'd once wanted desperately to believe in the dead's ability to hear and understand him. "I just know, that's all. When you die, you're dead, just like that." He snapped his fingers. "End of story."

"Well," she bent once more to the work at hand, "I firmly believe—no," she looked up at him, "I'm *convinced* the dead don't really die. They merely change forms, exist on a different plane from the living."

"Rubbish!"

How sad his mother and father must feel to hear him talk so insensitively, she thought.

"Tell me." She held his skeptical glance. "Is there anything you believe in—anything at all, besides money?"

"Yes."

Dropping to his knees, he grasped her shoulders and jerked her against him. "I believe in *this*." He crushed her angrily in his arms, his mouth coming down harshly over hers.

Too stunned at first to resist him, she rested acquiescently against his chest. But the new emotion—anger—that she was experiencing more and more in his presence, came quickly to the fore.

Stiffening in his embrace, she was preparing to wrench her mouth from his when, without warning, he let her go.

He got to his feet without meeting her eyes and moved to the far side of the graveyard. He stopped to stand beneath the branches of an old, twisted mesquite tree, his back to her.

When she'd composed herself, put the cruel ravishment of his kiss out of her mind, knowing he hadn't meant it, she stood and went to join him beneath the tree. She raised a tentative hand to touch him, then hesitated, undecided about what to say, how to help him.

She knew that his grabbing her that way, the anger behind the act, wasn't really directed at her—but at himself.

"I'm sorry." He spoke in a restrained tone, sensing her presence. "I don't know what got into me. Your only sin has been in trying to help me. Somehow, I keep forgetting that."

"It's all right." Her hand continued to hover, not quite making contact with his shoulder. She wanted to comfort him. She wanted to hold him in her arms and whisper soothing words against his ear. "I understand."

Will twisted to face her, a hint of amazement in the brown eyes looking deeply into hers. After several long seconds without speaking, he said, "You really do—don't you? Somehow I think you really do."

This time his hands were gentle, a little uncertain, as he drew her toward him, giving her ample opportunity to pull away. When she didn't, he felt his pulse rate increase, but forced himself to ignore the desire for her running rampant in his blood as he pressed his lips to hers, caressing her mouth more than kissing it.

Cassandra caught her breath at the gentleness of the act and raised herself on her toes to press her lips more firmly to his.

But passion wasn't what he wanted from her right then. Drawing back, his eyes moving over her face as though memorizing it for future reference, he smoothed a strand of sweat-dampened hair from her cheek and smiled.

"Come on, we have a lot of work to do if we're going to get this place in order and get out of these mountains before sunset."

They worked in silence, but every once in a while Cassandra couldn't help sneaking a peek at him. And every time she did, her heart turned over at the sight of him, working with his shirt off, the strong muscles of his shoulders and back flexing in the sunlight.

The sun began to make its descent toward the west, and a few clouds moved into the area, hanging like smoke over the mountain peaks in the distance. A slight breeze began to stir the branches of the mesquite near the entrance gate.

"Here." Cassandra looked up in surprise as Will came down on his haunches beside her, offering her a plastic container of water. "Take a sip. You look as though you need it."

She accepted the water gratefully and took a small drink before handing it back.

"Good?"

"Yes," she answered, her eyes focused on the ground, though she wanted to stare at the bare muscles rippling so close to her face. "Thank you."

Seeing how flushed her cheeks had become, Will poured some water into his hands and laid them against her hot cheeks.

Her eyelids fluttered as she looked up, surprising a look of tenderness in his glance.

"It's amazing how cool even tepid water feels after working in the sun for a while, isn't it?" he murmured, capturing and holding her gaze.

"Yes," she agreed faintly, unable to look away.

Pouring more water into his hand, he told her to tilt her head back. When she did, he held his hand cupped over her face and let the water drip slowly onto her cheeks and chin.

Cassandra closed her eyes, head tipped back, throat extended, and felt the water course down over her sun-kissed skin, marveling at how refreshing it felt. The only thing that would feel better was the luxury of stepping naked into the shower back at the hotel in Los Angeles.

As the water slid beneath the neck of her blouse, pooling between her breasts, she gave a small sigh and a shiver of delight.

Will's eyes traveled to the loose neck of the white cotton blouse. They followed a crystal drop of water as it rolled slowly down over the pale skin to the tops of her breasts where they swelled above the neckline of the blouse. His breath was arrested by the sight of twin points standing hard against the underside of the thin material.

Swallowing tautly, he tore his glance away from the sight of her, all the while thinking how he would like to bend over and touch his tongue to the tantalizing path left by that drop of water, to lick it from her salty skin....

He could feel himself becoming aroused. His glance moved over the surrounding graves. This was no place for such thoughts.

What was she doing to him? What was he to make of her? She'd made him feel a whole range of emotions since he'd met her, anger, frustration and shame among them.

She wanted to instill in him a feeling of responsibility for his fellow man, and he'd spent the better part of his adult life learning to ignore such feelings. Every time he gave in to that brand of thinking, it got him into trouble.

Just look at what his overdeveloped sense of values had done to his relationship with Black. If he'd been able to overlook the man's dishonesty and greed—if he'd been able to forget the values his mother and father had taught him as a kid—he wouldn't be in this predicament today.

And he might never have met Cassandra, either.

She never seemed to give up—on anything. God only knew how long she'd been on Black's trail.

And she'd dogged *his* footsteps until she'd gotten him to listen to her, to believe in what she said. She'd put her own life in jeopardy to save his. He couldn't figure her out.

Then there was this place. He glanced around at the work they—well, she mostly—had done. She'd worked all afternoon in the hot sun to make this place look as though someone cared, because someone did. *She* cared.

And he'd let her do most of it alone, soothing his conscience by telling himself it was nothing to him if she wanted to get heatstroke by undertaking such a useless task. In a few weeks the place would look just the same. Who would clean it up then?

But it was already too late to go back to his uncaring attitude; something inside him had been stirred to life by this woman. Was it guilt? Or perhaps...shame?

Cassandra opened her eyes and felt her hot cheeks grow hotter. She'd seen that look in his eyes before—the night he'd first kissed her.

Will tore his gaze from hers, got to his feet and walked away. He needed time to reevaluate his thinking.

Cassandra let him go. She wasn't ready to deal with any more of his kisses just yet. The work was almost done. Just one more headstone, a really big one, to adjust, and that was it.

It slipped.

"Ouch!"

"Here, let me get that." Will was beside her, taking the weight of it from her hands. He couldn't help wondering about the man who rested beneath it. Husband? Father? Son?

Cassandra's words about the people buried here, had she but known it, had struck a sympathetic chord within him. What, he wondered, had this man's dreams been like?

He was still puzzled by the intensity of Cassandra's feelings about the death of the town. True, Black was involved, and she wanted to see Black pay for his crimes, but why did it matter so much to her?

"Why do you *care?*" He couldn't help blurting the thought aloud.

She looked up at him over the top of the headstone. "Why *don't* you?"

A muscle flexed in his jaw. "Touché." He stood and bowed before striding away.

Cassandra started to call him back, sorry she'd been so abrupt, but when she looked at this place, it was the children she thought about. And she found herself wishing that she might change the past, bring the young to life again.

But that was not to be, she reminded herself with a heavy sigh, turning back to finish her work. She was here to deal with the problems of the living, not the dead.

Her eyes, full of yearning, shifted to find Will. He was looking at her, and she glanced hurriedly away.

The sun was riding low in the sky when he came to tell her it was time to leave.

"Here."

Cassandra stared at the hand he had extended toward her. "Thank you," she said as she accepted it, feeling the roughness of his fingers closing around hers.

He pulled, and she stood unsteadily. "O-o-h..." Her hands flew to his shoulders, her eyes to his face. Off balance, Will let go of her hand and reached for her waist to steady them both.

She looked away, removed her hands from his shoulders. "Thank—"

"I know, I know," he interrupted her, letting her go without haste. *"Thank you,"* he mimicked as he turned away.

Hands hanging determinedly at his sides, he glanced back at what they'd accomplished. "I hope someone appreciates this."

"They do," she replied softly, a secret smile on her lips.

Will glanced at her but made no comment. She was doing it again, making him feel as though she knew something he didn't. Well, this time she wasn't going to get to him.

"Are you ready to head south now?"

"Yes," she whispered over the lump in her throat, feeling the pain he tried to hide with his brisk behavior. "I'm grateful for your help."

"It needed doing," he conceded. "And I needed the exercise."

Inside the car, instead of starting the engine right away, Will sat with his hands gripped together on his lap, staring down at them.

"Can I ask you something?" he finally said softly.

"Yes, of course."

"How did you know about this place?"

Cassandra caught her breath lightly. "I told you—before undertaking this...assignment I read quite a lot about Jordan Black."

"Assignment?" His head turned in her direction. "You make it sound as though you were hired to bring Black to justice." Suspicion darkened his eyes. "Are you a Fed?"

"Fed?"

"Yeah, are you from the government? Is it your job to get something on Black?"

"No—I told you, I'm nobody. Just someone who wants to see Mr. Black brought to justice for what he's done. I don't work for the government."

"I know what you *said.*"

He ran a tired hand over his face as he turned back toward the front of the car. "But if all the people here died, how do you know the facts about what happened to them?"

"I didn't say *everyone* died," she said, sidestepping the question.

"What about this...psychic business?" he demanded quickly.

"What about it?" she asked, a slight tremor in her voice.

Without looking at her, he asked, "Do you really believe in...an afterlife?"

"You mean, in Heaven?" she asked gently, feeling her heart miss every other beat.

"Yeah, I guess that's what I mean—Heaven. My...mother..." He hesitated, looking down at the hand now lying palm up on his thigh. "Sometimes she *knew* things. I think I told you that."

"Yes, you did."

His eyes lifted to hers. "She believed in Heaven." The expression in his eyes intensified. "Do you?"

"Yes, I do. Don't you?" she asked softly.

"I—" He shrugged. "I...don't know. That is—" Wrenching his glance from hers, feeling like a fool, he faced the steering wheel and tapped a finger against it.

"I guess I used to—once. But that was a long time ago," he added almost inaudibly, and, starting the car's engine, he ended the uncomfortable conversation without saying anything further.

Cassandra studied him, wanting to ask more about his parents, knowing all there was to know, but knowing, too, that he needed to talk about them—about his feelings for them—to someone. For a few moments she'd thought he was about to open up to her and let all the bitterness of the past come pouring out. He'd brought the subject up on his own, and that realization had given her a glimmer of hope.

Was she making progress with him after all, despite her fears to the contrary? How was she to know for certain?

Oh, Barnabas, what am I to do? How can I help him? He's hurting so much inside.

Whatever choice he makes, all I know is that I wish I could stay with him, be with him, throughout eternity.

Chapter 10

Cassandra turned to take one last glance at the town as they left the quiet valley behind. The sun was slowly sinking behind the ravaged mountains, bringing a curtain of black to veil the shattered hopes and dreams of the people who had once lived within their majestic shadow.

There was nothing more she could do for them, she reflected sadly. Soon even the evidence of their passing would fade and there would be no one left to mourn them.

Shifting around in the seat, looking for a more comfortable position for her tired body, she bumped her forearm against the armrest. A burning sensation raced up the arm and she twisted it to take a look at what had caused the pain.

With puzzled eyes she contemplated the raw, red scrape about two inches long located just below her right wrist. Wondering how that had gotten there, she suddenly recalled trying to lift a particularly large headstone and having it slip from her grasp. The injury must have occurred then.

It didn't look serious, and it hadn't bothered her until she'd knocked it against the door. But that wasn't what concerned her. The accident had taken place hours ago. The wound should have healed by now. Why hadn't it?

"What's wrong?" Will glanced over to where she was holding her wrist turned to the waning light coming in from the window.

"N-nothing really," she replied, laying her arms on her lap, smoothing her hands down over the colorful material of her skirt.

"Let me see this nothing," he said shortly, reaching for her arm, remembering the thorn that had been 'nothing,' too.

Reluctantly Cassandra lifted her arm so the sore area was facing him.

"That looks like more than nothing to me," he said in a tone of mild disgust. "Don't you know you should be careful with scrapes and cuts that you get when working around animals or dirt? Haven't you ever heard of tetanus? Take some of the drinking water in the bottle and clean it. Then get that first-aid kit out of the glove compartment and put something on it."

Cassandra did as she was told. She couldn't very well tell him it was unnecessary, that she was immune to infection and that injuries didn't last long with her—because at the moment she wasn't certain it was true.

The sudden deep gasp of surprise she gave as the antiseptic touched the raw area drew another quick glance from Will.

"Where are you from, anyway?" he asked, as though they were simply continuing a conversation already in progress, hoping to take her mind off the sting of the medicine.

Then he realized all at once that it was a valid question, because he knew very little about her. Up until now, it hadn't really mattered, but for some reason now it did.

"F-from?" she repeated, twisting the lid back on the medicine bottle with cold, faltering fingers.

"Yeah, where were you born? Where did you and your parents live when you were growing up?"

"O-oh..." She fumbled with the small black knob on the glove compartment, thinking furiously.

Will watched her antics for a moment before reaching over and removing her ineffectual fingers. He gave the small knob a firm twist, and the door fell open.

"Thank you."

After placing the plastic first-aid box inside the shallow recess, she hesitated before closing the door. "Would you like me to put some of this on your face?" she asked, indicating the antiseptic she'd used on her wrist.

She had offered the same thing the night before and he'd refused, but she was buying time, hoping to turn his thoughts in another direction, away from her past.

"You mean some of that stuff that burns like hell?" he asked solemnly.

"Y-yes," she answered faintly, uncertain about the expression playing around his firm mouth.

"Not on your life," he answered firmly, shaking his head and grinning.

Cassandra stared at him. How young he looked in that moment, with his lips turned up in a smile, the light of amusement in his dark gold eyes—and how breathtakingly handsome.

A moment later he asked, "Well, are you going to answer my question? Or is it some big secret?"

"S-secret?"

"Where you were born, where you grew up?"

"Oh, no—I was born in H—" She bit her lip to cover her slip. "You wouldn't know the place. I wasn't born in this . . . country. What about you?" she asked quickly, hoping to divert his attention.

"Me?" He shot her a quick glance.

"Yes. Surely you didn't learn about tetanus—" she stumbled a little over the word "—and infection working in the city."

Will cast a piercing glance in her direction. "I thought you knew all about me. Didn't you say you learned about me when you were studying Black?"

"Oh, yes, but—" She faltered. It was hard to be devious when you were forbidden to tell a lie.

"It's all right," he said, misreading her momentary confusion. "I'm not angry about it anymore."

He shrugged, leaned over and turned the dial on the radio, giving her a moment to collect herself. The soft strains of a romantic ballad filled the car. Will lowered the volume until it provided a delicate background for their conversation rather than becoming an intrusion on it.

"What about your parents?" he returned to the subject.

"W-what about them?"

"Where are they? Did either of them possess this—ability—you have?"

"I don't know." She'd never considered her beginnings. She had always taken for granted the fact that she simply was.

"Sorry," he murmured abruptly. "I didn't realize you were sensitive about your childhood. Were you an orphan? I know what that's like," he continued after a brief pause. "Losing your parents before you're ready for it to happen. If you ever are—ready, I mean, to let them go."

Cassandra felt his compassion, and it made her uncomfortable. She wished there was a way to tell him the truth, *all* the truth, about herself. In silence she stared into the darkness, the strains of the music swelling to a close.

"I grew up in Texas." The words were softly spoken. She had to strain to hear them over the sounds of the voice on the radio. "My dad worked on a big co-op ranch. My mother and I helped out."

"Didn't you have any brothers or sisters?" she asked.

"No," he answered when she was beginning to think either he hadn't heard or wasn't going to answer.

"Were you lonely as a child?"

"Lonely? No," he answered cryptically. "I don't think you could call my childhood . . . lonely."

There hadn't been time for loneliness. There had been too much work to be done and not enough hours in the day to do it.

"What were your parents like?" she asked. Now that she had him talking about them, she didn't want to let him retreat into his shell and away from her again.

"My mother was a little bit of a thing—like you—but strong. I guess she had to be, or she never would have lasted on the ranch. I used to wonder how she did it, day after day, year after year, putting in twelve, sometimes sixteen, hours a day.

"At least I had a reprieve—I had school in the winter. And unlike a lot of the other kids living on the ranch, my parents never kept me out of school to work."

"They must have loved you very much."

"There were two things my mom cared about more than anything else in the world. My dad—and me. She was only thirty-eight when she died, still a young woman. It isn't fair." His hands gripped the steering wheel tensely. "She was too young to die."

The memories were crowding in too close, but this time he couldn't stop them.

"Did she have a . . . heart condition?"

"Yeah." He looked out the window at the lights of a town in the distance, coming steadily closer. "She had a heart condition all right. It was broken—by me."

He left the highway and headed toward a concentration of bright lights and cars.

"I think it's time we stopped for a rest and had something to eat." There was a note of finality in his voice, telling her in no uncertain terms that he wanted to end the conversation.

Cassandra wanted to protest, but she knew it wouldn't do any good. He'd already revealed too much about himself, let her get too close to what was inside him, the thing that drove him to take extreme measures—dangerous measures—like risking his life in a blackmail scheme.

Will parked in a space near the front entrance of the restaurant, and they both left the car at the same time. A bright flash of light overhead, followed by a low rumbling sound, instantly caught Cassandra's attention.

She looked up. The clouds that had been gathering in the sky overhead while they were finishing their work in Serenity had built into a powerful storm.

Rain began to lash at the windows beside her as she settled down in a booth inside the restaurant and looked around her. She didn't feel much like eating, even though her insides were telling her it was past time for a meal.

She let Will order for her, noting that he ordered very little for himself. He hadn't spoken to her, or even looked directly at her, since they'd left the car.

Had she angered him by asking so many questions? Or was there another reason for his studied indifference?

She wished for the hundredth time that she could speak to Barnabas about everything. He'd said he would be around to keep her on the right track, so where was he?

Remembering their last encounter, she kept scanning the faces of the other diners, looking for a familiar one, wondering what guise he would adopt for his next appearance. But his withered visage wasn't anywhere in sight.

The food came, and they ate in silence, the cadence of the other diners' conversations rising and falling around them. After a few bites Will pushed his plate away and stood, still without looking at her.

"I'm going outside. When you're finished, we'll leave." He picked up the check and headed toward the cash register.

Cassandra sat for a little while longer, pushing the food around on her plate. There was a commotion at the entrance, and she looked up hopefully, but it was only a group of people trying to get inside, out of the rain.

The waitress came over to the table and removed Will's barely touched plate. Cassandra gave her a small smile, feeling as though she should leave, too, because there were people waiting for a place to sit. She rose from her seat.

Outside, the rain was pelting everything in sight. She looked toward the car and saw that Will wasn't there. Scanning the area in the glow from the outside lights, she thought she saw movement at the end of the building and walked beneath the overhang along the sidewalk in that direction.

Will was leaning up against the end of the building, one leg bent, foot propped flat against the wall, supporting him—a cigarette in his hand.

"I didn't know you smoked." Her voice made him turn his head in her direction.

"There's a lot you don't know about me," he remarked enigmatically, an underlying note in his voice she couldn't comprehend.

"I smoke...I drink...I chase women," he continued, throwing the cigarette into the rain and straightening away from the wall.

"You think Jordan Black has a heart the color of his name because of that town we visited today. Well, take a look at me." He moved away from the shelter of the overhang and into the rain, directly into the path of the light from one of the security lamps overhead.

With his arms spread wide, he said, "Take a good look at me. Can you tell what color my heart is? Can you tell whether it's black or not?"

He advanced toward her almost threateningly, the rain flattening his hair to his scalp and running down his face. When he was within a foot of her, he stopped. "Can you see the murderer in me?" he asked in a menacing voice.

She shook her head, refuting his words.

"No? Well, take a closer look—because it's true. I'm a murderer," he insisted, and she couldn't tell if the water running down his cheeks was rain—or tears.

"I don't believe you." She refused to be intimidated by him. "You didn't kill anyone. You aren't a murderer."

"No?" he whispered unevenly. "Well, you're wrong—I killed my father."

"I don't believe you. You're only trying to frighten me. You want me to think the worst of you so you can go ahead with your blackmailing scheme. You think if you tell me this, I'll think you're as bad as he is and leave you to it."

"Damn it!" He advanced another foot, grabbed her by the shoulders and jerked her toward him—and into the rain. "Damn you!" He shook her. "I'd put all that behind me— forgotten it—until *you* came along with your ESP and your ghost towns! What the hell are you? My conscience? Or some demon from Hell, sent to torture me into remembering the past?"

Drawing her up on her toes until her face was only inches from his, he whispered, "I thought—when I first saw you— that there was something familiar about you."

There was a wild look in his golden eyes; they seemed to capture the light from the lamp above and absorb it before reflecting any of it.

"Are you one of the demons that curses my dreams every night, taking on human form at last to destroy me?" he asked angrily.

He shook her until her head flopped back and forth like a limp rag doll's, but she made no protest, only looked up at him, her blue eyes full of compassion, hiding the slight edge of fear trembling down her spine.

"Oh, God!" Letting her go, he whispered, "What am I doing?" He pushed past her rigid figure and ran toward the back of the building.

Cassandra stood still only long enough to catch her breath, and then she was following in his footsteps, calling his name. "Will! Will—please—wait!"

She caught up with him beneath an open-sided shed located behind the restaurant. He was backed against a stack of empty boxes and crates, head down, shoulders bowed.

"I'm not here to torture you," she whispered in a voice that could barely be heard above the sound of the rain. "Or to remind you of things you would rather forget. I sought you out because I knew you felt you had a score to settle with Jordan Black and I needed your help to bring him to justice."

If he was listening to her, he didn't show it, but at least he hadn't immediately run away from her again.

"I don't believe you killed your father," she continued, wondering how she could get through the wall he'd built around himself and reach the real man hiding on the other side. "There must be some other explanation for what happened to him."

"I *killed* him. It's my fault he's dead."

"Why? How?"

"I was supposed to fix the tie-rods on the tractor. I didn't do it. I went fishing instead. The next day Dad asked me if I'd done it—and I lied." His voice broke, and it was a few moments before he could continue.

"The next time I saw him, he was lying beneath it—beneath the tractor I was supposed to have fixed—covered in blood."

"You didn't kill him," she told him in a soothing voice. "It was an accident."

"It shouldn't have happened! I shouldn't have lied! I shouldn't have lied," he repeated in a softer tone, almost to himself.

"You were a child—"

"I was seventeen! That isn't a child!"

"You didn't do it deliberately—"

"I resented all the work—I hated the ranch. All I could think of was how I'd finally be getting away from there when I went to college."

"Your parents don't blame you—"

He didn't catch the slip. "You think that makes it any better for me? My mother knew! She knew it was my fault—that I was the one responsible for his death. The instant the accident happened she turned and looked at me with those huge, soft eyes of hers—and she knew!

"But she didn't say a word. She just hurried from the house and ran toward the field. I followed—but it was too late." He shook his head sadly.

"After that, all through the next few days, after the funeral, I waited for her to come to me and accuse me of his death. But she didn't. She never once, in all the months after that day, accused me by word—or deed—and it was killing me inside.

"I felt so guilty. I couldn't eat, I couldn't sleep, I couldn't stand to be in the same room with her—because I couldn't look her in the eye.

"All I wanted was to get away from there. Everyone on the ranch was so sympathetic. Mr. Barton, the owner, gave Mom a job in the big ranch house and let her keep the house we lived in, despite the fact it was the foreman's house and went with the job.

"All I wanted was to run and hide those first few days. Then I wanted to turn and scream my guilt at anyone who offered me sympathy. Finally I just wanted to get away. I didn't go home for vacations after I left for college if I could help it—and then one day Mr. Barton called me. Mother had died—peacefully, he said—in her sleep.

"But, you see, I knew that wasn't true—because I knew she never had another peaceful moment after the instant she realized what I'd done. I know she died of a broken heart because Dad was gone—and her *beloved* son was responsible for it. So, you see, I killed her, too, as surely as I killed my father."

Wiping his hands across his eyes, pushing the wet ends of hair from his face, he continued, "I went a little crazy after her funeral. I quit college, ran with a wild crowd, got into a lot of things I shouldn't have. And I visited...psychics, one after another.

"I ran through the insurance money left after Mom's death very quickly. For a while I believed that if I could reach her—and my father—I could explain, tell them both how sorry I was for what I'd done....

"But I found out there wasn't any way to reach the dead. They were gone, and that was it. And then I met Jordan Black. Maybe he saw something of himself in me." He shrugged. "I don't know. He offered to see me through school and give me a job afterward, let me learn how to make money from the master, so to speak. I agreed. By then I'd decided the only way I could repay my father for what I'd done was to fulfill his dreams for me. He'd wanted me to have all the things he'd never had, and I did. And it was wonderful—for a while."

Cassandra listened to his story, her heart breaking in two as he finally revealed the thing that had been slowly eating away at him for the past fifteen years. Now she wanted to comfort him, reassure him that with all the poison out of his system he could heal, but she didn't know how to do it without giving too much of her own secret away.

"You loved both your parents very much, didn't you?" she asked softly.

"Yes." She had to strain to hear his words. "Yes, I did."

"Did you deliberately set out to kill your father that day?"

"What kind of a question is that?" he asked angrily, raising his head, drawing himself up to his full height.

"It's the kind that's supposed to make you stop and take note of what really happened, make you blot out the pain and see the past for what it was—a tragic accident."

"No—" he protested.

"I'm not removing the blame for what happened from your shoulders. You should have done the work or confessed that you hadn't, but you aren't guilty of murder—only of being young and thoughtless.

"Haven't you punished yourself enough for your careless act? Do you think you father would want you to beat yourself up over this for the rest of your life? He loved you—you said so yourself. Don't you think he would have forgiven you long before now?

"Forgive *yourself*, Will," she urged. "If you want to do something for atonement, then stop more senseless deaths. Don't let anyone die due to someone else's carelessness—and greed. Help me stop Jordan Black. It's what your father and mother would have wanted."

"That won't make up for their deaths," he repudiated, fighting against giving up the guilt he'd lived with for so long.

"You don't have to make up for their deaths. They were your parents. They loved you. They would forgive you anything. They wouldn't have wanted you to suffer this way. And they would have agreed with me about Jordan Black."

He stared into her eyes, trying in the faint light to read what was behind their intent expression. "You sound so certain. How can you be that certain about everything—about how they'd feel?"

"You knew them. What would your father's opinion be of a man like Jordan Black?"

"Dad didn't like dishonesty of any kind."

"There, you see? It's your duty to see that he's brought to justice."

"And what about *my* crimes? Who's going to bring *me* to justice? How do I pay for what I've done?" he asked in an inflexible tone.

Cassandra stared into his pain-filled eyes and felt her heart twist inside her breast.

"Forgive yourself, Will." Touching a hand to his cheek, she whispered, "Judgment for our sins is God's sphere, and his alone."

"What about Black? Aren't his sins supposed to be judged by God, too? Aren't you judging him?"

"God has judged him—don't you think? And besides, it isn't his sins against God that I want to see him punished for but those against man. One of God's laws is that we follow man's law as well as His own."

Will wanted to believe her. He wanted to believe that all he had to do was give in to her wishes, do a good deed and everything would be made right. But he knew better.

For the rest of his life he would carry the stigma of having been in large part responsible for both his parents' deaths. That would never go away, no matter how much good he did in the world.

She was right about one thing, though. His mother and father would have wanted to see Black put behind bars.

But at what cost to her? Had she considered that aspect of it?

"Have you any idea how dangerous a man Black is?" Will asked, sounding more like his usual self. "Do you realize that he won't rest until he sees that I pay—and you, too, now that you're involved—for putting him behind bars?

"By now he must know we've rented a car. Before long he'll know about the cabin—if he doesn't already. And then neither one of our lives will be worth a plugged nickel."

Taking her gently by the shoulders, he held her gaze. "Even if I wanted to stop him, I can't—not now. And I can't be responsible for someone else's death. Not again."

"But we'll be safe—for a little while, at least—in your cabin, won't we?" Her concern was for him; her own safety was inconsequential.

"Only until Black finds us—and make no mistake about that. He *will* find us, however long it takes."

"Then what do we do?" she asked despite herself, feeling a shiver running down her spine at the tone of finality in his voice. He sounded as though his own death was a foregone conclusion.

"I'll turn the evidence over to the authorities—just like I promised you I would. Only this time I agree to testify to everything I know about him. Does that satisfy you?"

"I—yes."

"But there's one condition. I won't do it until I know you're safely out of the picture. It will take time to get the stuff I have sent to me in Arizona, anyway."

"Oh, but—" she tried to protest.

"That's the deal," he cut her off. "My way—or not at all."

He wasn't pretending to be noble. He was simply determined that no one would be hurt because of him. This way, if he did a good enough job of covering up, maybe Black would never learn her identity.

"Deal?" he asked, wishing he dared to give in to the feelings that her hand alongside his cheek was arousing inside him.

"Deal," she answered in a voice barely above a whisper.

He had thought she would be happy about his decision, but she sounded almost sad.

"The rain is letting up," Will said after a moment. "We'd better get going."

"Yes, I suppose you're right."

But neither one of them moved. With his eyes holding hers, Will's head slowly descended. Cassandra rose on her toes to meet him halfway.

It was only supposed to be a light kiss, a seal for the deal they'd struck, or so he told himself. But when his lips touched hers, all at once he was on fire. He wanted her with an intensity he'd never known before, not even the first time they'd made love.

Maybe it had something to do with the fact that she'd shown him a way out of the maze of self-recrimination he'd been living with, or maybe it was because he knew that the next few days would in all likelihood be all they would have together.

Whatever the reason, his arms wrapped around her like bands of steel. His lips opened over hers, and he drew the sweetness from her, taking it inside, feeling it begin to heal his shattered soul. And all he could think was that it was too late—he'd found her too late.

"Hey—you folks ain't supposed to be out here."

Will let her go reluctantly and, keeping an arm around her, turned to confront the owner of the voice.

"We were sheltering from the rain," he explained, keeping Cassandra's face turned from the man's view.

"Is that what you call it?" came the man's derisive reply. "Well, the two of you better *shelter* someplace else. We've had some things come up missing around here lately, and we got a guard that patrols this area. He's apt to shoot first and ask questions later—if you get my meaning."

"Yes, I get the picture," Will answered. "We'll be moving along."

The rain had stopped, and a few stars were showing through a thin covering of clouds. Cassandra walked at Will's side, skimming the puddles of water standing in the parking lot. At another time she might have enjoyed splashing through them, but she had a lot to think about just now.

Her job was technically at an end, and she'd been successful. Why wasn't she happier about it? She should be ecstatic; she'd finally done something right. Barnabas would be proud. She'd earned a promotion.

Only one thing was wrong with all that. She didn't want it. She didn't want to leave Will.

And something else was bothering her, too. What would it do to him—to Will—to wake up in three days' time and find her gone from his life without a trace?

Back in the car, Will drove with one hand, holding Cassandra close with the other. She drifted into sleep after a while, and even then, when the feeling left his arm, Will didn't move it. For as long as it was possible, he wanted her near him. The time would come soon enough when they would have to part.

He considered what it would be like to have this woman always at his side. With his newfound acceptance of the past, he even went so far as to contemplate what the future might be like with her as his wife. He would want a real home—children.

He had to admit that the idea of him as a happily married man, with children, sounded strange, even to himself. Those were the trappings of a life he'd never wanted until now.

He supposed the reason for that was all tied up in some way with a belief that he didn't deserve to be happy. Or perhaps he was afraid that somehow the curse he'd carried around inside for so long would come back to haunt him—taking his new family away just as his parents had been taken away from him.

Whatever reason in his past for his remaining alone, now he yearned for someone of his own. His heart and mind overflowed with a strange new feeling for the sleeping woman cuddled beneath his arm.

With a blinding flash of insight, he knew the feeling for what it was. So this was how his mother had felt when she'd contemplated the future without his father.

Dear God, what a terrifying prospect it was to know you would have to face the rest of your life without the one person beside you who could make it worth living. *I'm sorry, Mother. Forgive me.*

The sudden blare of a horn jerked his attention back to the road. He swerved in the nick of time to miss the twin beams of light speeding toward him.

Heart in his throat, hand shaking on the wheel, he realized that they might both have died just now.

And just like his father, killed instantly when the tractor overturned on him. Cassandra would never have known what hit her.

She had placed her safety in his hands, trusting that he would be up to the responsibility. And from now on he would be.

Once again he wished they had met under different circumstances—in another life? Did he really believe in that? Did he believe in good versus evil, in Heaven and Hell?

Cassandra murmured softly in her sleep, and he pulled her closer. It was a sure thing that, as of this night, he believed in guardian angels.

Because if Cassandra wasn't his guardian angel—after the way she'd charged into his life, turned it upside down, then crept into his heart and made life worth living again—then surely there was no Heaven, and God didn't exist.

Cassandra awakened slowly to the cessation of movement and heard a new sound—the sweet tones of a bird's song. For a brief moment she was filled first with a sweet peace and then with a blind panic.

Had she returned to Heaven so soon? Without even being aware of it? Without the opportunity to say goodbye to Will?

Opening her eyes wide, she looked around her, then slumped in relief. She was in the car, not in Heaven!

Through the window she saw that the sun was high overhead but had gone past its zenith. Had she slept the night and more than half the new day away?

The last she remembered, they'd left the mountains and had been traveling in a region of desert. But the countryside around her looked very different.

Her eyes went from the tall green mountains in the distance to a small log cabin set in a stand of tall pines beside a running stream.

The day was waning, and the thought of the hours she'd spent in mindless sleep, and missed spending with Will, filled her with deep sorrow. There was so little time left.

Two more days—that was all she had left here on Earth. She couldn't bear to calculate the hours as Barnabas had done.

And then another even less palatable thought entered her head. What if Barnabas came for her before then? After all, her job was done. Will's mind had been changed, he was no longer willing to condone Black's evil plans for destroying more lives to make money.

Not enough time! She wasn't ready to leave...

A slight sound turned her attention toward the trees—and Will. Her heart leaped at the sight of his tall, muscular body. He looked so strong, so fine—so precious.

Thoughts of his arms around her, his warm lips on hers, made her yearn for things beyond her reach. She wanted earthly things, like a home, a husband—children...

It was beyond her understanding, how she, an angel, a guardian to those who lived on this planet, kept watch over it and its inhabitants, should now want to become one of them.

But she did—oh, she did!

Shouldn't this body have come with a built-in resistance toward that? Something that would have made it impossible for her to become...enamored with life down here—and her charge.

And then another thought crowded out the first. Perhaps she *had* been given the ability to resist the lure of Earth and its inhabitants, but for some reason it had failed.

There was so much she didn't yet understand about being an angel—about mankind.

They had the world at their fingertips. From birth they had the ability to *feel*—to experience deep, soul-wrenching emotion. And those feelings continued to grow until death took over, changing their essence.

Cassandra left the car and turned her eyes toward the heavens where she spotted a flock of birds and followed their path of flight until she could no longer see them.

Taking a deep breath of clean mountain air, filled with the fresh scent of flowers and trees, she suddenly remembered the large, dark red, velvety petals on the roses growing outside Jordan Black's estate.

There was so much beauty surrounding the people of Earth, all of it put there expressly for them to enjoy—*and did they?*

No! Not all of them. It was something they called wealth that they sought. Money, she thought sadly, money with which to buy the things they only *thought* would make them happy.

And were they happy?

Look at Jordan Black—look at Will.

She *was* looking at him. He was moving toward the car, and she was filled to bursting with the need to touch him. This churning turmoil taking place within her was something she had never known in Heaven. A kind of headiness, like that she'd experienced from too much sun, mixed with anticipation—and just a little fear.

It was true, what she'd told Barnabas within her first few hours as a human. There *was* a loneliness about being mortal, a separateness she found frightening—but there was also this wonderful spiral of sensation she'd found she could share with Will. And it more than made up for the loneliness.

There was something so exciting about the tingling, explosive passion she had experienced when Will had made love to her. The damp palms, the breathless sensation in her lungs, the curling knot in the pit of her stomach—they all made her feel so *alive!*

There were many sides to the passionate nature of man, and she wanted to experience them all—*at Will's side.* He needed her—and she was just beginning to realize something even more astonishing: *she needed him, too.*

Her eyes had been following Will's progress while this profusion of thoughts had been running through her head. She watched as he stopped a couple of yards from the vehicle, his eyes on the ground, forehead wrinkled in thought. He looked tired, like a man who had been battling long and hard with his conscience.

She wanted to run to him, smooth the frown from his brow, take away the pain of his bruises, his melancholy thoughts. She wanted to make him forget every unhappy thing in his life and remember only her.

Will glanced up at that moment and caught his breath. There was a look of such yearning on her face, a glow of blue fire in her eyes, and her golden hair seemed to stand out around her head, creating a kind of radiance. He wanted desperately to make love to her.

Even though he'd just spent the better part of last night and today convincing himself that, considering what he would have to do to ensure her safety, it was best he keep his distance from her, he wanted her in his arms, joined with his body—now.

Without a word he opened his arms wide to her. And without considering if what she was doing were right, Cassandra flew to him, feeling his arms close hard around her.

For whatever time was left to them, she would make a Heaven for the two of them right here on Earth.

Will scooped her up in his arms, cradling her against his heart, and found her mouth with a purpose that disregarded everything but his need for her. His mouth locked with hers, his feet took them unerringly toward the cabin.

Without taking his lips from hers, he grappled with the doorknob until his impatient fingers finally managed to twist it. At last they stumbled inside.

Will stood Cassandra on her feet beside the bed, lifted her face up to his and slanted his mouth over hers. For now, the rest of the world could wait—he had his world in his arms.

Chapter 11

Cassandra leaned her elbows on the windowsill, a dreamy look in the blue eyes fastened on Will's back. The muscles rippling beneath the blue denim shirt quickened her pulse.

He was fishing, casting his line into the stream, reeling it in slowly, then casting again. The movements were swift and sure, full of grace and virility.

He was catching their supper because the cupboards were bare.

His friend, Tex, had done a good job keeping the cabin clean and aired, but he hadn't left any stock in the larder.

Will had told her that Tex had no doubt figured he would rather slip into town and fill his own list of supplies. Even though the cabin appeared isolated and miles from civilization, it really wasn't far from the town of Bisbee.

Her heart fluttered in her breast. He had stopped to strip the shirt from his back, and now he was wearing nothing but the low-riding jeans. With his long, muscular legs spread wide, feet bare and toes curling in the grass, he rocked back and forth on his heels, casting, reeling and recasting the line.

His attention was totally focused on what he was doing, reminding her deliciously of the last few hours and how he'd made love to her as though nothing in the whole world existed except the two of them. As if he wanted her to remember it forever.

You're right to enjoy it while you can, a small voice whispered in her head, *because it's later than you think.*

She knew the voice was right. Soon she would have to secure Will's promise to give the information he had on Black to the authorities. He hadn't told her where he was keeping it, only that it would take a little time to get it.

She knew that at any moment Barnabas could come for her, and that knowledge filled her with panic. Will had come to mean so much more to her than just an assignment.

Not even the promotion awaiting her in Heaven made her feel better. She had discovered something so precious in her feelings for this man that everything paled by comparison.

Shooting a swift glance toward the sky, she prayed, "Don't be angry with me, please. I can't help how I feel. I can't explain what—or how—it all happened. It just…did."

Had Barnabas suspected that something like this might happen? That might explain the unusual note of nervousness in his voice when he'd first mentioned the assignment to her. And the way he'd kept telling her, over her protests, to remember that whatever happened was for the best and all a part of God's greater plan.

She watched Will turn to pick up a new fly for his line and saw again the bruised face and swollen lip. Her heart ached at the sight. His lip looked more swollen than before, she noted with a guilty flush.

A while ago, when she'd kissed him in a flurry of passion, raining kisses all over his face, she should have known that he would be the one to pay for it later.

At one point in their love play he'd given a slight jerk, then tried to hide it when she'd apologized for hurting him. Will had listened to her offer to heal his injuries with her kisses and, grinning indulgently, told her that she had already *healed* him several times in the past few hours.

She'd been tempted for a moment to wipe the smile from his face by doing just that—taking away his pain with her touch—to prove that she could. But a cautioning voice sounding in her head had warned her against the folly of giving in to temptation.

It was a good thing she had listened to the voice, she reflected now, leaning back from the window. How would she have explained her ability?

She couldn't tell him that she was an angel, not again. He hadn't believed her the last time—and now she didn't want him to.

Her arm scraped along the surface of the windowsill as she moved back, and she gave a sudden gasp. Lifting the arm, she stared at the puffy red scratch marring the white skin. What was wrong with it? It throbbed with pain, and there was a darker red area around the original scratch.

Why hadn't it faded? It was such a small wound to still be giving her trouble.

She would soon be seeing Barnabas; she would ask him.

No—wait—she backtracked in her thinking. When Barnabas showed up again, it would mean it was time for her to leave.

"Well, sleepyhead, I see you've finally decided to join the ranks of the living."

Cassandra's head shot up in surprise. Will had moved, unbeknownst to her, from his place beside the stream to stand on the other side of the open window, looking in at her.

"Oh—yes—" She dropped her arm guiltily to her side.

Will saw the almost furtive movement and frowned. "What's wrong?"

"Nothing."

"Come on, let me see." Resting a forearm on the windowsill, he motioned with his fingers toward the arm hidden at her side.

"It's nothing," she maintained, feeling foolish. It wouldn't mean anything to him that the scratch hadn't yet healed.

"If it's nothing, then you won't mind if I see it, now will you?" He wiggled his fingers insistently. "Give."

Cassandra placed her arm reluctantly in his hand, unable to hide the tiny shiver of shock at the contact. His touch filled her with a sweet longing she couldn't quite hide.

Will's eyes lifted from her arm to her face, their gold taking on a more brilliant hue as the same shock of awareness that was racing through her fired his own blood.

Cassandra held her breath, her eyes locked with his, but he only swallowed tightly after a moment and dragged his glance back to her wrist.

"I told you that you couldn't ignore an injury like this," he muttered, trying to get a firmer hold on his emotions. He'd had the poor woman in bed all afternoon; it was too soon for either of them to be making love again.

"It's infected—"

"No!" Cassandra withdrew her arm quickly from his grasp. Seeing his surprise, she continued in a softer tone, "It can't be infected. It's only a small scratch."

"Well, it is," Will informed her, wondering at her vehemence. "It looks as though it's going to need more than the iodine you put on it last night. I think we'd better take a trip to town sooner than I'd planned. There's a pharmacy there where we can get something stronger to combat the infection, before it becomes serious and you lose the whole arm."

Cassandra clutched the arm protectively to her chest, eyes going wide with alarm.

He was smiling!

"Hey," he sobered instantly, noting her real fear, "I was only kidding."

He'd been trying to lighten the tension between them with a bit of humor. "You aren't really going to lose your arm from that little scratch. But it is infected, and you do need to get some stronger antibiotic on it."

His words appeared to have little effect on her fear. Berating himself for jesting about something that must be some kind of phobia for her, he raised himself up onto the window frame and climbed through the window.

Cassandra backed away.

"Come here." He held his arms out to her. When she stayed where she was, he coaxed, "Come on, I'm sorry if I frightened you. I was only teasing. I didn't expect you to take me seriously."

She gave in, moving toward him a step at a time.

Will reached out and pulled her the rest of the way into his arms. Holding her against his chest, he rested his chin on the top of her head and closed his eyes. In moments her very essence had the power to envelop him in a cloud of passion. Which he did his best, under the circumstances, to resist.

"I really am sorry," he murmured softly, kissing her hair. "I wouldn't let *anything* hurt you."

Squeezing her tightly against him, his arms like steel bands around her shoulders and waist, he maintained firmly, a glint of steel in his eyes, "Nothing—no one—will ever hurt you. I promise."

He'd been trying to come up with a solution to the problem of getting her away before Black and his crew descended on him. Now he wondered if the plan he'd devised was good enough, and decided to go back to the plan that had begun forming the night before in the back of his mind.

The only way to stop an attack from a mad dog was to kill it. Would Black have to die before either one of them would be safe?

He'd considered bargaining with Black—his life for hers. But he knew there was no bargaining with a man like that. It was impossible to trust him. If Black ever got his hands on Cassandra, Will knew, he would never let her go again—at least, not alive.

There was only one way to ensure her safety, and he knew what it was. He would have to see that the information was on its way to the authorities first—and then he would have to kill Jordan Black.

Tex would help him. Will knew he could trust the man to see to Cassandra's safety. Tex would see that she got to the hotel in Los Angeles to pick up the packet without being followed, and that she put it in the right hands. If Will asked, Tex would also get her safely out of the country for a while.

Will dropped a light kiss on the side of her neck. They'd better pay a visit to town—to Tex's place—and soon.

"How about a quick shower, a change of clothing, then a trip to town for dinner?" he asked, hiding what he was really feeling, pushing her away from him so he could look down into her face.

"I think I might be able to find you something to wear that won't be too awful until we can get you something better in town."

"But—what about your friend? I thought you wanted to wait until he came to you—not go to town—because of Mr. Black."

"We'll drop by his place on the way into town and invite him to join us for dinner. I've never known Tex to refuse an invitation to a meal. About the other, keeping away from town, I guess it doesn't matter that much, now that I've decided to turn the evidence over to the authorities." He turned away to hide anything she might be able to read in his eyes.

But Tex wasn't home when they stopped at his place a couple of hours later, so they headed into town anyway. Bisbee was about twenty miles from Will's cabin, and about ten from where Tex lived. It sat among the mountains, only a short distance from the Mexican border.

Many of the streets in town were so narrow and winding that only one car at a time could pass. It was the only city in the United States that didn't have home mail delivery within the city limits, Will informed her as they drove down the main thoroughfare.

At a small café situated in the center of town, Will pulled over to the curb and parked. He escorted Cassandra from the car to the glass doors, carefully keeping his distance.

He was discovering that his willpower when he was with her was almost nil. And it was going to take all his reserves of strength to go through with the plan he'd concocted to get her to safety so he could take care of Black.

If he gave himself half a chance to think about it, he knew he would change his mind, bundle her up and, with or without her knowing it, somehow get the money from Black as originally planned, then *run*—as fast and as far as his resources would take them.

He wanted her more than he'd ever wanted anything in his whole life—except to change the past for the sake of his parents.

As they entered the restaurant, Will glanced around the room, spotting several of the older men whom he recognized from previous visits. He nodded to each of them as they passed, then took a seat at the back of the room, facing the door.

The waitress, a tall, busty redhead, came over to take their order, smiling at him and calling him by name. In a short time they were served with steaming cups of coffee, mixed salads, steak, baked potatoes, and biscuits.

Cassandra ate slowly, occasionally turning to cast an eye on the door, on the lookout for a familiar figure, still wondering what part he would be playing this time. She felt a blob of butter from her biscuit drip down her chin, reached for her napkin and glanced up to find Will watching her.

"Is something wrong?" she asked, removing the butter carefully from her face.

"No." He shook his head, grinning, and leaned over, touched his own napkin to a spot on her cheek. "It's just that I've never in my life seen anyone enjoy their food as much as you seem to do."

"Shouldn't I?" she asked, glancing toward the table beside them, where two couples were talking and eating.

"Yes, of course you should. It's just . . . most women are too worried about their figures to really eat." He was thinking about Janice.

"Figure?" She glanced down at her lap. "Is something wrong with it?" she asked seriously.

Will hid a grin and shook his head. He never should have started this. If he'd learned anything about her at all in the past few days, he'd learned she took everything he said literally.

"You have a perfectly gorgeous figure."

He could recall all too vividly how perfect, and he dropped his napkin across his lap in response, then picked up his water glass and took a quick sip from its icy depths. His eyes moved from her to the tall figure coming in the door.

"Well, it's about time," he muttered beneath his breath. He'd left a note, without telling Cassandra about it, on

Tex's front door, urging him to meet them, because he had something crucial to discuss with him.

"Tex!" Will set his water glass down and stood, his hand going out as he moved across the room.

Cassandra lowered her napkin and turned to look at the man Will had hailed with a wide grin. He was huge! An imposing figure, dressed like a cowboy, who reminded her of someone.

Michael! He reminded her of the angel Michael, who sat on God's right hand; except when he was seeing to matters of importance for Him.

This man, Tex, possessed a commanding presence that drew all eyes, just as Michael did. Cassandra glanced around the room; as she had expected, everyone's attention was focused on the two men at the door.

She watched Will and the other man shake hands, then slap each other affectionately on the back, before making their way to the back of the room, and Cassandra.

She recalled nervously that she'd always felt uncomfortable in Michael's presence, as though she wasn't quite good enough to warrant his exalted attention. She felt the same way right now.

"This is Cassandra." Will indicated her with a smile and a nod. "And this is the man I've told you about, Tex Manetti," he added proudly. "We've known each other for a hundred years or more."

Cassandra frowned, her eyes on Will's beaming face. After a moment of uncertainty she glanced at the other man. A hundred years? She knew Will wasn't that old. But this man, she thought, regarding him closely, *might* be. She knew some men lived to be that old; she'd seen a few, some even older.

"Pleased to meet you, little lady." Tex nodded to her, grabbing her hand and pumping it up and down. "Yes, sir, it's a real pleasure."

Her eyes widened slightly in shock. He wasn't imposing at all! In fact, he was very sensitive about his size. And shy about entering a room this crowded.

She sensed a great capacity for gentleness in his touch. The only imposing thing about him was the way he appeared from a distance. When he'd first entered the room and stopped, it had seemed as though he was taking measure of everyone in the room, gauging their importance.

But in fact he'd been gauging their reactions to him. It was to bolster his own courage that he had hesitated on the threshold before entering.

Could the same, she wondered, be true for Michael?

"I was surprised to get your note, ol' buddy." Tex turned his attention to Will, gripping his shoulder with one hand while taking a seat between the two.

"I—we—just got in a few hours ago," Will explained.

His eyes rested intently on the other man's face, warning him to be careful of what he said. "I wanted to talk to you about a few things before we get settled in."

A light of understanding sprang to the older man's faded blue eyes, and he nodded, letting Will know that he'd received and understood his message.

"Sure thing. I'll be glad to talk with you anytime you like."

Cassandra, sensing something in the atmosphere, finished her meal in silence. She was tempted to do a little eavesdropping, mind to mind, but managed to restrain the impulse.

To make it easier to stick to that decision, she made an excuse about visiting the ladies' room and left the table. It would give them some time alone to discuss whatever it was they wanted to discuss.

And it would give her the opportunity she needed to search the place for Barnabas. The questions she had for him wouldn't wait much longer, and even at the risk of having to leave Will before she was ready, she felt the need to make contact.

Will watched her make her way across the room before turning his gaze to his old friend's sun-weathered features.

"I'm in trouble," Will stated baldly.

"I guessed that," Tex replied matter-of-factly.

They went back a long way. Will's father and Tex had been close friends when they'd worked the rodeo circuit together. Tex had been an employee on the ranch where Will had been raised, and he'd known Will since birth.

He was the only person who had ever really spoken to Will, beyond offering condolences, about his father's accident—or its cause.

After the accident, he'd tried to reason with the boy, to take some of the blame off his young shoulders by telling him that his father should have looked at the tractor himself and made certain that the equipment was safe before using it. The responsibility for what had happened wasn't Will's alone to bear.

But Will hadn't listened; he'd turned on Tex in anger when he'd suggested his father was in part to blame for his own death. It was the only time in their relationship that Will had refused to listen to the other man—or raised a hand to him in anger. He'd hit him—once—then, with tears in his eyes, had turned and run away.

Hours later, when Tex had gone searching for him because his mother was worried about him, neither had mentioned the blow. And they'd never spoken about it to this day.

"I need a favor." Will spoke quickly, his eyes on the entrance to the rest rooms. "Actually," he qualified, "I need four."

"Is that all?" Tex commented sardonically.

Will ignored his sarcasm and explained. "I need you to get Cassandra out of town without anyone knowing about it. I want you to take her to Los Angeles, to a hotel I'll give you the name and address of, and make certain she picks up a package I left for her there.

"After that, see that the package gets to the police and Cassandra gets safely out of the country."

"That's a tall order," Tex commented softly.

"I know—but it's important. You have to trust me on this one. Will you do it?" he asked tautly.

"You haven't told me what the fourth favor is yet."

"I need a gun."

The older man let his breath out in a whistle. "Damn it, Will." He shook the graying curls that reached his shoulders. "I can't—"

"I need it badly, Tex." He gripped the man's arm with urgent fingers. "You know me—I wouldn't ask without a damn good reason."

"Has it got anything to do with that crook you worked for a while back?"

Will shook his head, a slight grin on his face. "I should have known I wouldn't be able to keep anything from you. How does an old varmint like you know what's going on in the rest of the world when you never leave this place?"

"I keep an ear to the ground, boy, that's all. And I want to know what the hell you're planning to do with a gun."

"See that I live long enough...maybe...to keep Cassandra alive."

"Hell and damnation, boy, even I know that man's as dangerous as a cornered rattler."

"I know." Will ran a hand over his bruised face. "Believe me, I know."

"Yeah. I wasn't going to mention it," Tex motioned toward Will's face, "but now that you've brought the subject up, so to speak, what happened?"

"Black and his hired guns—they're what happened." Will hesitated before going on. "I can't say I didn't actually deserve this, though."

Will met the other man's eyes. "I asked for it," he stated blatantly, "by trying to blackmail him. I had planned to extort money from him to withhold information I have about something he's planning to do that could hurt a whole lot of people."

Tex stared him straight in the eye and asked in a hard voice, "You over that foolish notion yet?"

Will gave a wry grin and nodded. "Yeah, I'm over it. I don't know what I was thinking at the time. I had some crazy idea that I deserved to wallow in the filth Black lives in because of the past."

"Aw, boy, I thought you'd got hold of the right end of the stick about that by now."

"I have," Will hastened to reassure him. "Or at least I've come to terms with it—thanks to Cassandra."

"Anything I need to know about the two of you?" Tex asked, curious about the relationship between this man who was like a son to him and the woman he hadn't yet figured out.

"Only that she's the best thing that's ever happened in my whole life. And she's come too late."

"Listen." Tex leaned closer across the table and spoke in a conspiratorial tone. "You want *me* to take care of Black and his crew?" He gave Will a steady, meaningful stare.

Will hesitated. It would be an easy way out for him. Tex could dispose of Black without anyone ever knowing what had happened to him. Black would simply disappear like Jimmy Hoffa, never to be heard from again.

Will's father had told him once that Tex wasn't really from Texas at all, that he'd come from somewhere back east and was related to a high-ranking member of the "family."

But Will couldn't do that to his old friend; he couldn't ask him to become a murderer for his sake.

"No, thanks. Just keep them away from Cassandra while I figure out what to do, that's all."

"You're sure?"

"I'm sure," he answered without hesitation.

"Is your lady friend agreeable to the plans you've made for her? She might not want to go with me."

"She has to. There's no other solution to the problem. There's only one thing..." He hesitated, wondering how to put what he was about to divulge.

"She's kind of—" He shrugged "—different. She's not like a run-of-the-mill woman. When you get to know her a little better, you'll realize there's something—a fey quality—about her."

Tex peered at Will through narrowed eyes. "You telling me she's got *the gift?*"

"She reminds me a little bit of my mother," was Will's way of answering.

"Ah, she was a real beauty, your mother." Tex nodded, remembering not so much the detail of each feature but the overall gentleness of manner with which she treated everyone. "You're right. This little lady of yours does remind me of her," he murmured, seeing the fact now that it had been pointed out to him. Pushing the stained white Stetson back on his head, Tex leaned back in his chair. "I promise you, she'll be safe with me."

"Thanks. I owe you one—"

"Naw—"

"Yes, I do. I've taken stock of my life in the past few days and learned a few things about myself in the process. I regret a lot of the choices I've made and the things I've done over the years. One of the things I regret most took place in a barn, fifteen years ago."

"I don't know what you're talking about," Tex muttered, taking a quick sip of coffee, his eyes on the table.

"You know, all right." Will's voice was barely above a whisper. "I've wanted to apologize for that punch since the instant it happened."

"Forget it. I have." Tex glanced up.

Will shook his head, opened his mouth to try to explain his state of mind at the time, then closed it with a snap. Throwing the other man a quick look, he smiled as he rose to his feet.

"You're back," he said to Cassandra. "We were just finishing up here. Are you ready to leave?"

"Yes, if you are." She nodded, giving the older man a shy smile.

Will took her arm, gave Tex a purposeful look behind her back and strode toward the cash register situated near the front door. After he'd paid the check, he left Cassandra by the door and walked back to the table, ostensibly to leave a tip for the waitress.

"I need an answer," he said in an undertone to Tex. "About the gun."

"I'll do my best."

"Good. Keep an eye out for any strange-looking visitors to the area in the next few days. Especially if they happen to be wearing three-piece suits with extra padding *beneath* their shoulders.

"And the gun," he reminded him. "I need it as fast as you can get it. That means within the next day or so," he added with an eye on Cassandra, who was watching him from the door. "When I get the gun, or when any strangers show up, that's the signal that it's time to get Cassandra out of here real fast.''

He made as though to turn away, then turned back. "You know," he gripped the other man's shoulder with a firm hand, "I wouldn't trust her with just anyone. And whatever happens, stay out of it. If you know about Black, then you know he has friends in very high places."

"I got a few friends of my own," Tex commented. "But I'll keep it in mind," he added dryly. "You know," he said, "there's always the possibility Black won't find you. Not many people know about your cabin down here."

"You're right—but Black knows I used to spend a lot of time in Arizona. He'll keep looking until he finds out why— and it won't take him long, either."

Tex offered his hand by way of telling Will he would live up to his promises—all of them—and Will turned away. At least now he could do what he had to, knowing Cassandra would be safe. If he trusted his life, or that of anyone he cared for, in anyone's hands, it was in Tex Manetti's.

The day of his father's accident Tex had literally lifted the tractor off him. And he'd done it single-handedly. Cursing and crying, he'd called on God—anyone's God—and everyone within hearing distance to help him save his friend.

But despite his prayers, despite his great strength, and despite all his labors to the contrary, he hadn't been able to breathe life back into his old friend's broken body.

"I like your friend," Cassandra murmured as they drove along the dusty road out of town.

They'd stopped to buy a few supplies at one of the local stores and some medication for her arm. It was well after dark when they finally left the town behind them for good.

"Yeah, he's a good man to have with you in a tight spot."

"What are we going to do now? About Jordan Black?"

Will didn't answer right away. If he had any sense, he would put her on the nearest bus, plane, or train out of Arizona. But if he'd had any sense, he wouldn't have been in this fix in the first place.

"I have a few things here, around Bisbee, to take care of in the next few days," Will answered.

"You mean before we go to the authorities?" she asked anxiously. She wanted to get the business part of their relationship over and done with—and spend what little time she had left without that hanging over her head.

"I'm not backing out of our deal, if that's what you're afraid of," he answered a bit testily, worried about his own part in the next few days, wondering if he could have mistaken her real feelings for him.

Maybe the attraction he held for her was more tied up in what she wanted from him—the evidence against Black—than he wanted to believe. And maybe it would be better for them both, given that he had to kill Black, to do as he'd first intended and back off from her, let their relationship cool down a bit.

"I trust you," she whispered softly, finding his hand clenched on his knee and slipping hers beneath it.

She did that so easily, he thought, the same way she'd slipped beneath his defenses, managing to get under his skin before he knew it. It was like the way a burr worked its way into a horse's hide, and once that happened there was no getting it out. It could drive a horse crazy.

He hadn't used the word love—so far—in conjunction with what he felt for her, not even in his thoughts. But it was a good word for what he was feeling at that moment.

Without answering, he steeled himself against the onrushing tide of feelings breaking him apart inside, slipped his hand from hers to grip the steering wheel and pushed down harder on the accelerator. The rest of the ride was accomplished in silence.

He knew that he'd hurt her, and that every now and then she threw him a glance of bewilderment. But he couldn't seem to force himself to throw off the shackles of bitterness he was feeling at life's latest thrust.

Fate had brought her to him just when he'd made it impossible for them to have a future together. And he couldn't pretend at the moment that he was anything but unhappy.

When they had reached the gravel driveway in front of the cabin and he'd stopped the car, instead of immediately going inside, he sat staring through the windshield at the night sky.

It was a beautiful night; the heavens were aglow with millions of tiny points of light. The warm night air was filled with the sounds of nature. He could hear the deep croak of a bullfrog near the stream and the noise of a score of crickets spreading their harmony on the night air.

"What is it, Will?" Cassandra couldn't keep silent a moment longer. "Why are you so sad?"

It was long moments before he took one of her small hands in both of his and raised it to his lips.

"Why didn't you ask why I was being a jerk instead of why I was sad?"

Cassandra shrugged, using a gesture that she had discovered could cover a whole scope of answers without need of any further explanation.

"Any other woman would have asked why I was being such an idiot. But you ask why I'm sad," he murmured, rubbing his fingertip along the back of her hand. "I think that's one of the things I . . . like most about you, your sensitivity to other people's feelings."

He was in a strange mood, Cassandra discerned, one she didn't quite understand. He'd been in high spirits at the restaurant when he'd been talking to his friend. What had happened to put him in this dark mood?

"I've met a lot of women in my time." He lifted her hand to his cheek. "But I have never met one quite like you." Moving her hand to his lips, he kissed her fingers one at a time. Then, opening her hand, he pressed a kiss to its center. "I thank whatever God exists that He sent you to me."

"Oh, Will—"

She pulled her hand from his, cupped his cheek with it and leaned forward, wanting to put her arms around him, on the point of confessing all—but he held her off.

She might not know it yet, but he'd just told her goodbye.

"It's been an eventful few days." He held her by the forearms. "I think we both need a good long—uninterrupted—night's sleep."

Cassandra drew back in confusion. He acted as though he didn't want her to touch him, when only moments ago he'd been holding her hand and kissing it.

She watched in silence as he climbed from the car, removed the grocery sacks from the back seat and strode toward the cabin.

She wished she dared to tell him how little time they had left. But she couldn't. There was nothing for her to do but follow him, hoping he would become more approachable once they were together inside.

But he only placed the groceries on the table and began to put them away. When he'd finished doing that, still without even so much as a glance in her direction, he made for the bedroom—where they'd loved the afternoon away.

There he took blankets and a pillow from the chest at the foot of the bed, keeping his eyes off the rumpled sheets, turned and left the room.

Cassandra stood against the closed cabin door.

"Here." He picked up the medicine for her arm and offered it to her. "See that you put some of this on that scratch before you go to sleep. I'll sleep here." He indicated the long couch. "You can have the bedroom."

Without a word, without taking the medicine from him, wondering what she had done to cause him to withdraw this way, she rushed from the room, closing the door between them with a snap.

For the next eight hours Will tried unsuccessfully to shut the picture of blue eyes, bright with unshed tears, out of his mind.

Chapter 12

Cassandra rolled over on her side in bed and stared at the bright sunlight coming through the window. The same window where she'd stood the evening before and watched Will fishing.

Her glance moved around the room, from the double wardrobe against one wall to the painting of Indians in the midst of a herd of buffalo to the padded wooden rocker sitting next to the closed door to the living room. A large round multicolored rug covered the center of the wooden floor.

The room was rustic, as was the whole cabin, but comfortable, filled with a sense of peace, uncluttered by the trappings of modern civilization. There wasn't a television, radio or telephone in the place.

The only concession Will had made to modern comfort was a bathroom and running water. Heat was provided by a large double-sided fireplace, one side in the living room and the other at the end of this room.

She loved the place. If she were human—a real human being—and not an angel she couldn't think of any place she would rather live than here, with Will.

Before melancholy at the thought of how little time she had left to spend with Will could get her in its powerful grip, a loud rapping noise coming from the front of the cabin had her rising onto her elbows and cocking her head in a listening attitude. It seemed Will had a visitor.

In the next room Will, who had been up since dawn, opened the door at the first knock. But instead of inviting his visitor inside, he followed him out, then closed the door softly behind them.

They were several yards from the cabin, walking along the water's edge, before either man spoke.

"I wasn't expecting you so soon," Will began.

"I figured this might come in handy." Tex handed Will a pearl-handled gun in a leather holster, the kind cowboys used in television Westerns.

"It belonged to your daddy a long time ago. He gave it to me when we was nothin' more than kids, still wet behind the ears. He was mighty good with it, put on a real good show in rodeos down south of here, near the border. It was always good for attractin' the ladies—course, we was both single in those days.

"Then one day some crazy kid, even younger than we was at the time, decided he wanted to try a quick draw with your pa."

"What happened?" Will asked, withdrawing the gun from the holster, his eyes on its shiny barrel.

"Your daddy told him to get the hell away from him and had him pitched out on his rear. The kid swore vengeance, but he was all mouth. We never saw him again. But your daddy refused to wear the thing after that, said it was only asking for trouble from some young punk like that one had been.

"He gave it to me. I told him to save it for the son he'd have one day. But he hadn't met your ma yet, and he said he didn't figure he'd ever have a son."

Will gripped the handle of the gun tighter, a lump the size of a goose egg in his throat. He'd had a son all right—and that son had been the death of him.

"I can't take this." He shoved the gun and holster back at Tex.

Tex saw what was in his mind written in the lines of his face. "Don't you go gettin' stupid again, boy. You've done worked your way through all that once, don't wade through it again. Your pa was proud of you. You was always a son any man could be proud—"

"You don't know—" Will interrupted, only to be interrupted in turn.

"I do," Tex insisted. "And I know you'd never do something to make your father think any less of you than he did the day he died."

Will looked at him sharply. "Are you saying I should let Black live?"

"All's I'm sayin' is you better think hard and long on it— make real certain you're doin' the thing for the right reasons. That's all."

Will took a deep breath. "To want to go on living, to want to keep someone you . . . care . . . very much about alive. Is that the right reason?"

"It'll do, as long as there's no other choice," Tex answered.

"If you knew Jordan Black as well as I do, you'd *know* there's no other choice. I'm not making it lightly, Tex. I'm not—" Will looked down at the gun, his eyes darkening with memories better left forgotten. "I'm not a killer by nature," he continued, before looking up at his old friend again. "But even the most peaceful creature fights for its life when it's backed into a corner."

"Yes." Tex nodded, laying a hand across the younger man's shoulders. "You're right, boy."

And that was that.

"I guess you haven't come across anyone looking for us yet?" Will asked tensely.

"Nope, no new faces this morning when I was there. I put the word out around town, though, and I'll be among the first to know if anyone shows up."

"Not if," Will corrected in a hard voice. "When."

They walked in silence for a dozen yards before Tex nodded toward the gun and cautioned, "You better put that where your lady friend won't see it. Most women don't cotton to firearms."

"You're right. I'll put it away before she gets up."

"Have you told her yet that you're sending her with me?"

"No. It's not an easy thing for me to do—" he said, able to admit it to this man "—to send her away—even with you."

"Maybe that's because you don't *want* her to go. You know, the offer is still open. Let me take care of Black."

"*No.* This is my fight."

"Well, it's up to you—" Tex broke off, his eyes on the figure walking out the door and down the stairs. "I think we're about to have company." He gestured toward the cabin.

"Damn! Here, take this. Head on back to the cabin through the trees over there and put this in the closet by the front door. I'll wait for her here and tell her you had to go."

Tex took the holster and gun and carefully kept them at his side, facing away from Cassandra as she came to meet Will.

Her greeting to Tex was soft and shy. But the smile she gave him warmed his old heart, reminding him clearly of what Will had said about her resemblance to his mother.

"Where is he going?" she asked Will, watching the bear of a man hurry out of sight around the corner of the cabin.

"Oh, he had an errand in town, and he just stopped by a minute to see if we needed anything.

"I've told him about Black. He knows we don't want any unexpected visitors out this way, and he'll be keeping an eye out for us."

"Good." She walked along at his side, at peace for a few moments, until the tension began to seep into the air between them once again.

"Are you hungry?" Will asked for something to say, hoping to clear the air. Once they were back at the cabin with something mundane like cooking a meal to do, things would be all right.

"No," she answered simply, unhappily, not at all adept at hiding her feelings, sensing there was something he wasn't telling her.

"I . . ." Will paused, breaking a dead twig off a tree and tearing it into small pieces. "Don't get the idea that just because Black hasn't found us so far it will last," he cautioned. "I've asked Tex to look after you when the time comes. He's going to see that you get out of the valley—"

"But what about you?"

"I'll be fine. I'll lead Black and his men away from you. He'll be so smug at the thought that he's cornered me, he won't be thinking about you for a while."

"I don't like the idea—"

"It doesn't matter," he cut across her objections. "It's settled."

"And the information? What about that?"

"Tex will take you to it. I've told him where I hid it. He'll see you get it and stay with you until you turn it over to the police."

"Me? But you're supposed to be doing that."

"Right," he answered quickly. "I'll join you as soon as I can, and we'll both take it to the police. After I've made certain Black hasn't followed you. I promised I'd keep you safe, remember?"

"And you?" she asked softly, taking a step in his direction. "Will you be safe, too?"

"I'll—be all right. Don't worry about me."

He looked away, unable to sustain the resolve to keep his distance from her when she was looking at him the way she was now.

"But I do, Will. I worry about you all the time when you aren't in sight."

"Don't," he pleaded, hanging on to the tail end of his resolve to keep a distance between them.

Cassandra retreated before the agony in his voice. Lowering herself onto the grass beside the stream, she crossed her legs and dipped a hand into the water, feeling its bracing coolness against her sweaty palm.

Something inside Will snapped. He didn't want to be noble and save her from whatever heartache she might experience once they were parted.

He wanted her, wanted to make love to her now, this moment. And for the next few hours if that was possible—for the next few days—whatever time they had left until Black's arrival on the scene parted them for the last time.

Cassandra felt him behind her, felt the hand he lowered to touch the top of her head before it actually made contact. Closing her eyes, she rested her cheek against his knee.

Will stroked her soft cheek before slipping down beside her, his hand turning her face up to his.

"For a little while, let's forget tomorrow and all the tomorrows to come. Let's live for this moment."

"Can we do that?" she asked gently, her eyes on his face.

"I can," he murmured as he leaned closer. "Can you?"

Her answer was smothered beneath his lips. And then her arms were sliding around his neck and she was transported to that place above the clouds, so close to Heaven in her heart that it was almost the same as being there.

A gentle breeze blew through her hair; the crisp, cool air wafted nature's perfume to her nostrils. So close to Heaven. Did any man ever figure it out? she wondered as she gave herself over to Will's capable hands. Did any man ever come to realize just how close he really was to Heaven—on Earth?

With gentle hands and ardent lips Will brought her to the brink of fulfillment before drawing back, his heart in his eyes, to whisper, "Have you ever made love in the grass beside a river?"

"N-no."

"Would you like to?"

"Would you?"

"I asked you first."

"What about your friend? What if he comes back?" She was learning at last about being human.

"He's gone," Will assured her. "He won't be back today."

The pink tip of her tongue appeared to moisten her lower lip, then disappeared again almost immediately. She glanced with shy eagerness into his dark, glowing eyes.

"Yes, I'd like to," she answered, tempted beyond refusal.

Without further words, Will pulled her up into his arms, lifted her and whirled her around, feeling young and carefree, full of his feelings for her. He put all thoughts of Jordan Black out of his mind and concentrated only on this woman who'd changed his whole way of thinking about life—and love.

Cassandra floated, drifted, her head back, arms spread wide, her hair bouncing around her shoulders. Feeling giddy at last, she wrapped her arms around his neck and hid her face against his chest with a laugh of pure joy.

Will's steps slowed, stopped, the grin of delight on his face slowly changing to a look of pure passion. He lowered her, sliding her gently down his length until first her toes, then her heels, touched the ground.

Disengaging his arms from her waist, he stepped back, took a quick breath and, eyes fastened onto her face, began to unbutton his shirt.

Cassandra looked away, feeling a strange new emotion. This was different than what they'd done in the past. That had been spontaneous, a sudden combustion of the feelings they generated in each other.

"Look at me," Will demanded.

Cassandra looked up, and then she couldn't have looked away if her soul had depended on it. He was so beautiful. The muscles of his chest and shoulders were well-developed yet trim, bursting with health.

The skin covering his chest was tanned the color of birch leaves. A light sprinkling of soft, curly hair spanned that broad expanse, then narrowed as it disappeared toward the waistband of his jeans.

With a firm flip of finger and thumb, the snap of his jeans popped open. Cassandra held her breath as he skinned the jeans down over his narrow hips and long, muscular thighs. Kicking them off onto the ground, he stood, arms at his sides, all his secrets laid bare for her eyes to see.

A shaft of sunlight found a meager space between leaf and branch and cast a shaft of light across his face. The sherry-gold eyes smoldered with banked fires.

"It's your turn," he whispered hoarsely.

Cassandra lifted tentative fingers to the buttons on the shirt he'd loaned her to wear, her eyes riveted on his face. Slowly, she began to unbutton one button at a time, heart pounding, pulse jolting.

There was nothing teasing or erotic in her behavior, only a touchingly sweet naïveté. She saw nothing wrong in her nakedness. There was intense beauty in God's creation of the naked human form. But these new and exciting feelings she'd developed for this man lent more meaning to the state of being unclothed.

As she slid the shirt away from her shoulders and her unrestrained breasts became visible, Will made an involuntary sound deep in his throat. She was pure poetry in human form.

Cassandra halted, thinking that her lack of traditional human undergarments bothered him. "I...don't like... undergarments...." she explained haltingly. "They're uncomfortable."

"You don't need them," Will managed, his hands curling at his sides to keep from reaching toward the pale, mauve-tinted breasts thrust so unexpectedly into view.

The shirt slid off her shoulders and fell to the grass. She had difficulty with the belt. Will stepped up to assist her.

He pushed her hands gently aside, his own fingers trembling, yet he made short work of unfastening it. And then he couldn't stop himself from sliding his hands around her slender waist and pulling her to him, fitting her to his hips.

His lips drifted down over the side of her neck, the fragrance of her skin like sweet nectar, her taste like honey on his tongue. Pressing a long kiss against her jaw, his hands slipping below the waist of the jeans, he rubbed her flesh gently.

With a downward movement, he slid the loose jeans over the curve of her hips. They fell, forgotten, at her feet.

Cassandra basked in the warmth of his palms caressing the bare skin of her hips and thighs. Pressing herself against him, eyes closed, she heard the uneven beating of his heart as his hands explored the curves and hollows of her back.

She finally permitted her own hands to conduct an exploration of their own. They rested against his bare back before skimming the rough textures of muscle and bone. And once she'd touched him, she wasn't satisfied with that.

His kisses, the sensitive areas he'd found to test and tease, were filling her with a yearning she couldn't resist. Resting fully against him, she kicked the confining jeans from around her ankles and drew back, standing on tiptoe, to find his mouth with hers.

The kiss deepened as, without taking his mouth from hers, Will lowered her gently to the grass. It tickled her bare skin, and she loved it, a new sensation to add to the store she'd built up in the past few days.

But nothing she'd experienced yet compared to Will and the glorious sensations his touch produced within her. Never had she known anything so divine as his touch. It burned, feeling more fierce than the heat of the sun's rays against her skin, branding her forever as his.

Nothing in Heaven had prepared her for the deep desire growing within her to give and give until she was completely drained. Leaving her empty, waiting for him to fill her with his love.

"You're like...a fever...burning me up...inside," Will panted against her breast, teasing her with the tip of his tongue. "I can't...think of anything...night or day...except you."

His lips drank from hers again and again. "I don't want...anything..." His hands smoothed the skin of her face, her shoulders, her breasts. "Except you.... For the rest of my life..." He pressed her head back, finding new areas for his lips to baptize "...you'll be a part of me...in my heart...in my mind...a part of my soul...forever."

Cassandra's heart pounded so hard in her breast that it hurt. She couldn't stop the all-pervading sense of deep sadness his words brought her.

Soon there would be no more touching, no more kissing, no more joining as one. Soon Will would be alone, facing Black and his anger, pursuing a life without her. And she...

No! Cassandra nearly jerked her head away in denial. She mustn't think about that. This time was for Will—for them.

Her hands captured his roving face and held it so she could press her lips to his. Today she belonged to him, only to him, and he to her.

This was all she would ever have of him, so she had to make the most of it.

Pressing against his shoulders with her hands, she rolled over until she was lying atop him, her blond hair a cloud of silk drifting around them. The sunlight bouncing off the strands of gold was so bright it brought tears to Will's eyes.

He blinked, telling himself that was all it was, the brightness hurting his eyes. While his eyes were closed, Cassandra kissed him—open-mouthed—and the world stood still.

The world as he knew it ceased to exist, and he floated up among the clouds in a world completely of Cassandra's making. He could feel every cell in his body, every hair follicle, every nerve ending, every living part of him, become attuned to her touch.

The fish in the river swam and jumped, the birds in the sky sang and flew, the bees in the afternoon sun buzzed around the flowers gathering nectar to make honey—and Cassandra made love to Will.

Life around them continued with its normal cycle, but for the two of them, nothing would ever be the same. They forged a bond between them stronger than life or death, a bond that would never be broken.

The afternoon became evening, and when the air grew cool they moved inside. They pretended to act normally, made a meal from the supplies they'd purchased in town, even pretended to eat. But they never strayed more than a few feet from each other's side, their eyes preoccupied with keeping each other in sight.

When night fell, they fell into each other's arms as though they had been apart for weeks. The cabin was alive throughout the night with their whispers of love and long sighs of pleasure.

"Cassandra?"

She opened her eyes slowly, focusing them on Will's face.

"Good morning—or should I say good afternoon?" He grinned.

"I was dreaming," she whispered in a sleepy voice, a hint of wonder in it. She'd never dreamed of being mortal before, it was—unexpected. "I dreamed we lived here—always."

The smile on Will's face disappeared. "Tex was here a little while ago. Some of Black's men were spotted in town yesterday evening. It's time for you to leave."

"What day is this?" she asked, alert all at once.

"Day? Saturday, why?"

"Saturday," she repeated sadly, biting her lip.

"Yes, Saturday. Come on." He straightened and turned away from the bed. "Get up and get dressed. Tex will be back in a little while, and I want you to be ready to leave when he gets here. I want you as far away as possible before Black arrives."

"I'm not going," she announced in a firm voice, without moving from the bed.

Will's back stiffened. He turned slowly to face her, lips compressed in irritation. "What did you say?"

"I said I'm not going." Tucking the blankets beneath her arms, she folded her hands atop them and leaned back against the headboard.

"You don't have a choice in the matter. *I'm* not giving you one. Now, get up and get dressed—before I dress you myself."

Though she trembled at the thought of his anger being directed toward her, she refused to budge. She knew something he didn't. She had no choice, all right—but not about this matter. She *did* have a say in where she went until Barnabas came for her.

"I'm staying."

A muscle quivered in his set jaw. The fingers on the hands at his sides clenched spasmodically. "I know you don't want to go—" he exploded, then clamped his lips firmly shut on whatever else he'd been going to say.

Taking a deep breath, releasing it slowly, he moved toward the bed, took a seat beside her and lifted one of her hands to rest in both of his. He played with her fingers as though his fascination with them had already made him forget their recent altercation.

After a few moments he looked up into her face. "I don't want you to go. Don't you know that? But if you want to save the world from Black, then you have to. You're the only one besides me who can get possession of the information.

I've left it in the safe at the hotel where we stayed in Los Angeles, with instructions to give it to no one but you.''

"But—"

"No.'' He shook his head, laying a finger against her lips. "Don't argue with me, please. There isn't time. You must go with Tex, get the package—''

"But I told you, you have to be the one to turn it over to the police.''

"I know,'' he told her, hating what he was about to do. "I'm only staying behind to keep Black busy while you slip away.''

He knew he was lying to her, but what could he do? He couldn't tell her, *I won't be joining you, because I'm going to kill Jordan Black to keep him from killing you.*

"I'll fly out and join you later in Los Angeles. We'll go to the police together—I promise.''

No, we won't, Cassandra corrected him silently. *Because I won't be in Los Angeles.*

What was she to do? What would Barnabas's reaction be when he learned the package was still in California? Surely that wouldn't make any difference to Will's standing with God. He'd decided against blackmail and agreed to see that Black was stopped. Surely that would be enough to please the powers above.

As for herself, and his promise to fly to her side, today was Saturday. And that meant that at midnight she would be making a flight of her own. . . .

Chapter 13

The sound of a vehicle speeding down the driveway drew Will to the front window. Pushing the curtains back, he peered outside. The familiar sight of Tex's beat-up Jeep lessened some of the tension that had been building inside him since Tex had arrived on his doorstep that morning with the news of the strangers in town.

Now that Tex was here to get Cassandra, Will would be able to rest easier in his mind about her.

He stepped outside and strode down the steps to meet the older man halfway. They shook hands.

"Everything go okay?" Will asked. "Did you have enough money?"

"No problem. I keep a bit stashed aside in case of an emergency. It was more than enough to get the tickets and make a few arrangements."

"I'll pay you back—"

"Forget it," Tex interjected gruffly. "Just don't get yourself killed, that's all I care about."

"Don't worry, I'll do my best not to."

"Is she ready?"

"She's getting that way. I'd better warn you, she doesn't want to go. You'd better keep a close eye on her. She has a penchant for slipping through defenses that would stop people like us," he warned the other man, recalling how she had managed to get past Black's guards—man and beast—to rescue him on the man's own estate.

"I'll keep an eye on her. Look, are you sure you want me to leave, too? I can see to the woman and come back—"

"No." Will shook his head. "You stay out of this as much as possible. If anything should happen . . ." He paused. "I don't want you on my conscience, too."

"Aw, hell—"

Will rested a hand on the big man's shoulder and squeezed. "Thanks, but no thanks," he added with a grin.

Tex met his glance and, defeated by the light of determination he saw there, nodded in surrender. "Okay, have it your own way. Just remember, don't turn your back on him, boy. And don't shoot unless you have to—but if you do, shoot to kill."

Will nodded as the older man gripped his hand tightly and patted him on the back. "Your father would be a proud man if he were alive today, knowing you were his son."

They stood, hands gripped, staring at the ground, both wanting to say something more, but neither knowing how.

Will wanted to thank Tex for all the years of his friendship, for being there for him even when he hadn't appreciated it.

And Tex wanted to tell Will how he'd always thought of him as more than his best friend's son, as the son he'd never had.

"I'm ready," Cassandra said from behind them, drawing both men's attention.

She was dressed in an unbleached cotton blouse and wide cotton skirt, an Indian print in various shades of red, blue and yellow.

In the past couple of days she had done her best to remove as many signs of travel from the outfit as possible, but it still managed to look as though she'd worn it to bed.

But Will's attention was on her face, and the beauty of her large, sad blue eyes. He knew they would haunt his dreams until the day he died.

Leaving the older man, he went to where she stood on the topmost of the three steps leading to the cabin.

"I'm going to miss you," he whispered, on eye level with her for the first time.

Cupping his hands at the sides of her face, he leaned forward and brushed his lips lightly against hers.

Cassandra couldn't keep the tears gathering in her eyes from spilling over onto her cheeks.

"I'll miss you, too." She swallowed a sob, diving past him while she still could and hurrying toward the car. His last words, "Don't forget me," rang in her ears.

Climbing into the Jeep beside Tex, she felt her lips begin to tremble and raised a hand to hide her face.

He didn't need to worry about her forgetting him; she had so much to remember, and a long, long time to do it. Every sweet kiss, every gentle touch, every loving gesture, every tender word he'd ever spoken to her, would remain locked in her heart for time immortal.

Will stood watching for as long as he could see a cloud of dust marking their departure, feeling as though this, and not the bullet Black was certain to have with his name on it, was the final end to his existence.

How could he go on, when his only reason for living was speeding down the road at this very moment, on her way out of his life?

Hands in his pockets, he turned toward the cabin. The gun Tex had given him, and the bullets he'd bought for it this morning, were waiting for him on the top shelf of the closet.

Would he really be able to use it? Could he cold-bloodedly take another man's life—even to save his own?

Instead of heading up the steps to the cabin door, his feet took him toward the stream, to the spot where he and Cassandra had made such sweet love the day before.

He stood for a long time staring down at the grass, searching his heart—remembering.

All at once he began to speak in a soft, hesitant voice.

"I'm not sure if I believe in You, Lord." He lifted his head and stared at the blue sky overhead.

"It's hard for me to believe in someone I can't see or touch. But my mother believed, and maybe my father did, too, though he didn't have much to say about religion. And I know Cassandra believes, so..."

His voice faltered, and he remained silent for a while, glancing uncomfortably around him, as though expecting to see strangers hidden among the trees or in the long grass, listening to him.

"I feel pretty foolish, talking to someone who isn't there, someone who can't answer me back."

He stared down at the toe of his boots for a while before continuing.

"I'm going to ask You something—a favor, I guess. Maybe You don't feel like You owe me one. And I can understand that, things being the way they are and all. But I'm going to ask anyway. All I'm asking—and I'm not asking for myself—is that if there is a Heaven, if You do exist, You'll see that Cassandra is kept safe. I don't know much about Your work and all that, but if ever there was someone who went about it—Your work, I mean—then it's her.

"She fought me, and she's fighting Black, and I guess there's not many she wouldn't fight for a cause she believes in—and she believes in You.

"Black is corrupt, about as corrupt as you can get. He wouldn't find anything too low to stoop to, even murdering a woman. He wouldn't think twice about...hurting her."

Fists clenched at his side, teeth gritted at the thought, he paused, unable for a moment to go on.

"See that it doesn't happen. Keep her out of his damned—sorry. Keep her out of his clutches.

"I know I stayed behind, prepared to do whatever was necessary to keep him from finding her, but knowing him, he's probably already got her address and telephone number and has someone waiting for her to return home.

"I'm not a killer. I don't know if I can bring myself to shoot a man—even the likes of Black. I wish, now," he muttered in a rush, placing his balled hands in his pockets, "that I hadn't decided to play this macho game. The big man and all that," he added in self-contempt, "staying behind to protect his woman. I'm not even sure she is my

woman. And I don't feel very macho at the moment, just
kind of... scared.''

He was talking more to himself now than to an entity
somewhere in the vast reaches of time and space.

"I wish I'd gone with them," he muttered. "All I want is
to live out my life—whatever time I have left—with Cassandra."

Lifting his eyes to Heaven again, he asked in a taut voice,
"Is that too much to ask?

"Maybe I don't deserve to be happy, after the things I've
done." He shrugged his shoulders. "I don't know.

"But I know Cassandra cares about me—maybe even
loves me. So, if You won't do anything for me, will You do
it for her?

"I'd give anything, Lord, anything at all, just to be with
her." His voice deepened. "To see her, touch her, one more
time." The words trailed into silence. Will was staring at the
sky so hard, his eyes began to burn.

"Give me a sign, Lord, if You're there. Tell me what to
do. Should I go after her, or stay and wait for Black?"

Nothing moved, not so much as a breeze stirred the leaves
on the tree overhead. He held his own breath, waiting.

The palms of his hands began to itch with sweat; the
muscles in his legs and back, held so rigid for so long, began to quiver.

After a few seconds he saw a black-and-yellow butterfly
out of the corner of his left eye. A fish jumped in the stream
at his feet, splashing a few drops of water on his forearms
and legs.

He doubted either one of them was a sign from God.

Feeling disappointed, angry with himself because he'd
been so foolish as to stand there and make a fool of himself, he turned on his heel and stalked away.

And suddenly the mournful sound of a bird's lonely cry,
coo-ooh, coo, coo-coo, drew his eyes to the branches of a
pine tree.

He could see the brownish gray feathers of a bird, a
mourning dove, through the pine needles and branches way
up high toward the top of the tree.

The bird bent its head, tilting it to one side as though it were examining Will, and he could see the blue ring around its beady little eye. For a moment he had the crazy thought that it was trying to tell him something.

And then, as though having captured the man's attention was what it had wanted, the bird lifted its head and gave the same melancholy cry that had captured Will's attention in the first place.

At the end of the sound the bird lifted gracefully from its perch and flew up in a swooping arc, flapping its wings a few times and then diving down in a movement that ended in a gentle glide.

With its tail spread wide in a flamboyant display of white-tipped feathers, it made straight for the spot where Will stood. At the last minute it changed course and veered to the left, ascending higher and higher, until Will could no longer see it—heading in the direction Tex had taken when he'd left a short while ago with Cassandra.

Will took it as a sign—maybe it was and maybe it wasn't—but it was the impetus he needed to do what he really wanted. His will to survive, along with his need to be reunited with Cassandra, was stronger than any need to see Jordan Black punished.

Cassandra was worth living for, and he wanted very much to live. But he wouldn't do that if he waited here, like some poor excuse for a Western hero, and made it easy for Black to kill him.

Somehow he and Cassandra would manage to defeat Black—and do it legally—without guns, without violence. Violence was Black's way—not his.

For a while he'd forgotten that, but something about the strength of the bird, one of God's most delicate creatures, managing to survive in this great big world all alone, had reminded him of the fact.

The first thing he had to do was get away from the cabin. Black and his henchmen were sure to show up before long. Secrets had a way of becoming common knowledge, and his presence here wasn't really a secret, anyway.

Will made a quick dash toward the cabin, pausing just long enough to lock the door. He didn't want to make it too easy for Black when he arrived to search the cabin for the documents.

Will climbed behind the wheel of the small rental car, turned it around and headed toward Tucson. Maybe if he broke a few speed limits along the way, he might have time to catch Tex and Cassandra before their flight took off.

Cassandra stared around at the horde of people thronging the airport. It had taken Tex an hour and a half to reach Tucson and another twenty minutes to get to the airport.

All along the way she had watched the road, expecting Barnabas to pop up and delay them. But he hadn't, and now she was sitting in the corner of one of the airline's waiting rooms, waiting for a flight Tex had booked the two of them on to Los Angeles.

A voice over the loudspeaker announced an incoming flight, and she watched as a stream of people passed by the corner seat where she was awaiting Tex's return. He'd left her with a mumbled explanation about a necessary stop he *had* to make before getting on the plane.

The flow of passengers had thinned to a mere trickle when she noticed something familiar about the shorter of two men at the tail end of the group. He was dressed in a black suit, white shirt and black tie. He wore a pair of wings on the cap perched jauntily left of center atop a head of deep red hair.

As his cocky strut brought him closer, he spotted Cassandra and gave her a wink.

It was Barnabas! She would recognize those blue eyes anywhere. Casting a quick look behind her to make certain Tex wasn't in sight, she jumped to her feet and hurried to her mentor's side.

"Where have you been?" she asked quickly. "I've been watching for you."

"Not here, child," he muttered out of the corner of his mouth.

Smiling pleasantly, he took her arm. As though he were escorting her to her destination out of courtesy, he guided her along the corridor, up a ramp and through an exit door to the outside of the terminal.

A large jet was taxiing down the runway to the left of them, and Cassandra watched it with wide eyes, the noise so loud that conversation was impossible. When it had lifted off, she turned to her companion and asked, "Did you really fly one of those?"

"Yes." He sighed, watching it become smaller in the distance, eyes filled with regret as it disappeared. "It was the best of all my experiences down here this time. Have you any idea how fast one of those babies can go?"

"Babies?" Cassandra asked, eyeing him curiously.

"Oh, never mind, that's pilot's lingo. Come along, child, the job is done," he murmured ruefully. "It's time for us to go."

"But it isn't done, Barnabas. I don't have the information, and neither does Will. It's in California. How can Will turn it over to the authorities when it's there and he's here? Does that make a difference to his future?" she asked anxiously. "Does that count in his favor?"

"Yes, of course it does, child. He atoned for his sins just by agreeing to give up this blackmail scheme and in *wanting* to turn the evidence over to the authorities."

"Then it doesn't matter that we don't have it?" she asked with a puzzled frown. "What about Jordan Black? What about his plans for the town and the people who will suffer if we don't stop him?"

"But we will. I have the information right here." Barnabas opened a black satchel he'd carried off the plane and removed a manila envelope.

"How did you get that?" Cassandra asked in surprise.

"I took it from the hotel safe the day you saved Will from Black at his estate."

So that was where she'd seen it, before. It was the package Barnabas had started to give her, then changed his mind about.

"I don't understand. If you have it—if you've had it all this time—then why did I have to try to get it from Will?"

"It isn't the information itself that's so important to Will. It was his coming to terms with the past and his finding the *desire* in himself to do what was right."

"I see," she answered slowly. "Then my job really *is* finished," she whispered woefully.

"Yes, child, I'm afraid it is."

He patted her hand, sensing the reasons for her sad face. He led her to a taxi parked near the front of the terminal and opened the door.

"Where are we going?" she asked.

She came out of her fog of despair long enough to notice the beat-up Jeep Tex had abandoned in such a hurry because he'd been afraid they might miss their flight. It was sitting behind the taxi Barnabas was ushering her into.

"Surely we aren't returning in that?"

"No, no. We're going to the police station. This information must be placed in the right hands as quickly as possible. Someone is waiting there to do just that."

"But I thought you said it wasn't necessary?"

"For Will, child, only for Will. It *is* necessary that it be made clear what Jordan Black is up to—and as speedily as possible."

Cassandra had barely closed the taxi door when she looked up and spotted Tex's bearlike figure coming out of the terminal. He spotted her at the same time and, with a shout, hurried toward them.

"Oh dear—Tex."

Barnabas glanced up, spotted the man and turned the key in the ignition. He bore down on the accelerator in much the same way Tex was bearing down on them, and, tires squealing, the taxi shot away from the curb.

Cassandra watched with regretful eyes as the figure of the other man diminished in the distance. Tex was a good man, a good friend to Will. And that comforted her, because she knew Will would need the man's friendship in the near future.

"What about Will?" She finally broke the silence as the police station came into view.

"Don't worry about him—his soul is safe."

"Yes, but—"

Barnabas had parked near the front of the building and was scanning the other cars closely, his attention on what he was doing and not on her conversation.

"Barnabas, what about Jordan Black? How is Will going to get away from him? The man is a killer."

Barnabas saw the person he was looking for and lifted a hand. In a moment the man was leaning in the window and Barnabas was passing him the envelope.

Cassandra recognized the man as another angel, one of those who had been pointed out to her above as a veteran of many trips to Earth.

"All is well, child," Barnabas reassured her when the other angel had entered the police station. "Now our job is well and truly done. We can both leave at midnight, knowing we've accomplished what we were sent to do. I want to congratulate you now, before we return, on how well you've handled this assignment. Naturally He will want to congratulate you, as well, and much more elaborately, when we get back. You're going to make a fine archangel, my child, very fine indeed."

"But what about Will?" she insisted again.

It was nice to know she'd made this man proud of her, after all the heartache she must have given him in the past, but Will's welfare meant more to her than accolades on her own behalf.

"Is he safe from Jordan Black?"

"Jordan Black can't touch him, child. He's in God's hands now."

Everything around her became suddenly still; even the air in the car refused to move when she tried to draw it into her lungs.

"What do you mean?" she asked in a breathless voice. "What do you mean, *'He's in God's hands now'?*"

"Just that, child. No one can hurt him, no one can hurt the shell that was him, ever again."

"No!"

Eyes widening in shock, she shook her head in protest, fully understanding the meaning behind his words. "No—I—it can't be! You said I would be saving his life as well as his soul!"

"I didn't lie to you." Barnabas, unable to sustain the accusation in her eyes, looked away. "I didn't actually tell you that you would be saving his *mortal* life. It's his *immortal* soul that's important. You just assumed—"

"And you let me," she interrupted.

"He will be with you in Heaven—"

"I've betrayed him—"

"No, child!" He quickly glanced back to reassure her of that fact. "You have not betrayed him. You've helped him find a place in Heaven. You should be proud of that."

"I *have* betrayed him," she repeated in a soft, tearful voice. "He trusted me."

"He doesn't *know,* child." How his old heart ached to see her in so much pain. "He'll never know what happened."

"Is that supposed to make me feel better? Well, it doesn't, because *I'll know!*" Focusing tear-bright eyes on his face, she continued. "I'll know, Barnabas—I'll know."

The sound of tires squealing as they rounded the corner filled the night air. A car stopped alongside the taxi, and Tex Manetti jumped out. Leaving the engine running, he jerked Cassandra's door open, gave Barnabas a fulminating look, took her by the arm and literally dragged her from the vehicle.

"You okay, little lady?" he asked in a tight voice.

"Y-yes, I'm fine."

"Good, 'cause we got a plane to catch, just as soon as I turn this one—" he motioned with a thumb back over his shoulder toward Barnabas "—over to the cops for kidnapping."

"You don't understand," she started to protest, thrown into confusion by what she'd learned from Barnabas and now this man's misunderstanding of the situation. "H-he didn't—"

All at once she stopped. Maybe it wasn't too late. Maybe, if they were fast enough, they could save Will.

Or—if they weren't . . . Her eyes took on a bright glow at the thought. She had the power. She could return life to a body, as long as the soul was still intact. . . .

"Leave him, Tex." Cassandra laid her hand on the big man's arm. "He didn't hurt me—he's harmless."

But Tex wasn't so certain of that. He resisted the tug on his arm, eyeing the other man angrily.

"Come on." She tugged harder. "We have to get to Will. He's in grave danger—and I can save him. Please, Tex, come on."

"What are you saying?" Barnabas was out of the car on the other side. "You can't save him. It's too late!"

That did it as far as Tex was concerned. Shaking a finger at the little man over the top of the taxi, he gritted, "You better not be right about that, you little varmint, 'cause if you are, I'm goin' to hunt you down and break you in half with my bare hands." He made a breaking motion with both hands before turning to Cassandra. "Let's go, little lady."

"Cassandra!" Barnabas's voice boomed, seeming to expand as it filled the air around their heads. "Once a page has been torn from the *Book of Life* it cannot be returned—it's the Law. You know that! A soul *must* cross over."

"But *I* can stop it. If I get there in time, I can stop the crossing—you know that I can."

"It's forbidden!"

"I'm sorry," she whispered, tearing her eyes from his white face, climbing into the Jeep and determinedly facing the front.

Barnabas shook his head sadly. She was too softhearted at times, even for an angel; he'd known that from the first. That was why she was so good with the little ones, the new souls awaiting birth.

And that was why certain aspects of this journey had been kept from her—like the real reason for the urgency behind Will's repentance.

Well, it was in God's hands now; he'd done his duty, done his best. Climbing back inside the taxi, he sat for a moment and stared at the dash.

She wasn't as powerful as she thought.

His conscience smote him. He couldn't help it; he couldn't simply leave her to it alone.

With a whispered prayer, Barnabas started the car and tore off down the street in pursuit.

"You all right?" Tex asked when they'd left the police department and the strange little man behind.

"Yes, I'm fine. But we have to get to Will—fast!"

She didn't need to encourage him any more. The Jeep shot down the highway onto the freeway, then arrowed toward the cabin in the valley—and Will.

"You want to tell me what that was all about?" he asked in a gentle voice.

"I wish I could," she answered after an instant's hesitation. "I really do, but I can't. I want you to know, whatever happens tonight—whatever you see—I love Will, and I would never willingly do anything to harm him."

"That's good enough for me. That boy has had his share of grief. It's about time he found some happiness."

A few minutes later Cassandra asked, "What time is it?"

Tex turned on a light and pulled a round gold watch from his pocket. "It's going on to four. We should be at the cabin about five—or a little after."

Eight hours, Cassandra was thinking. She had eight hours until she would have to face God and explain her actions.

Forgive me, Lord, for what I am about to do, she prayed, *I know You could stop me, but please—please—don't.*

I'll answer willingly for my transgressions, just—please—please don't let me be too late to save Will.

Chapter 14

Within five miles of the cabin, Will rounded a hidden curve in the road and met two pickup trucks speeding toward him. He gunned the engine of the little car and fairly flew past them.

He watched in the rearview mirror as they both made a quick U-turn, one nearly flipping over, and were on his tail. The chase only lasted a few miles.

As though working to a prearranged strategy, one truck passed him, then pulled in front of him. The other one sped up to ride his rear bumper.

While the one in front slowed, the truck in back kept on his tail, giving him an occasional nudge to remind him it was there. There was no way out of the situation that he could see. This wasn't a scene in a movie, and he wasn't an actor guaranteed to go home at the end of the day, ready to take on another role the next day.

The little car slowed even more as the red taillights lit up on the truck ahead. In a few moments, like a caravan, all three vehicles were stopped at the side of the road.

There wasn't much Will could do outside of climbing from the car and making a run for it. And that seemed pretty foolish, under the circumstances. He didn't figure he could outrun a bullet.

The long barrel of a gun poked through the window beside him and a tall man wearing a dark suit and black-rimmed glasses bent to look inside.

"Where's the woman?" he asked, looking in the back seat and seeing it was empty.

"Woman?" Will asked innocently, knowing he wasn't fooling the other man.

The round black hole in the middle of the long barrel centered on a spot on Will's forehead. "You better refresh your memory real fast before I do it for you—with this." He poked Will's forehead with the cold steel.

Will felt his insides cringe, but all he did was shrug. He hadn't spotted Black yet, and he didn't figure this guy had the authority to out-and-out shoot him—unless he tried to escape—without Black's having first crack at him.

The gun was sharply withdrawn, then returned with force, the butt smashing against Will's jawbone. Will's head snapped back under the force of the blow, bouncing against the seat's padded headrest.

There was an explosion of pain inside his head, his vision went black for a moment, and he tasted the coppery tang of his own blood.

The door on the passenger side opened abruptly, and another man, one Will hadn't seen until then, climbed inside. He, too, had a gun, and it was shoved forcefully against Will's right side.

"Drive."

"Where to?" Will asked out of the side of his mouth that still worked.

"Your place. Mr. Black will join us there."

Will considered the possibility of jerking the wheel to the right and smashing them into the side of a mountain, but didn't figure he would fare much better in the accident than the man at his side.

And there was always the possibility that the man would squeeze the trigger before he died. A blast from that angle didn't leave much hope of missing something vital—like his heart.

Will kept his cool, refrained from making any heroic gestures that were certain to get him killed and did as he was told. Perhaps, if he was *real good,* he thought with an ironic twist, he would live to fight another day.

"Well, I see you haven't changed."

Jordan Black crossed the room when Will entered and gave him a wide grin that didn't quite reach the cold black eyes.

"Neither have you," Will responded, wiping a smear of blood from his face.

"I thought you were heartbroken about your fiancée cutting out on you," Black said mockingly. "I guess that didn't last long, though, did it? Who's the new woman in your life, Will?" Black's grin faded. "And exactly what does she have to do with your little blackmail attempt?

"Is *she* the reason you need the money?" The words were short and clipped, and any element of artificial goodwill disappeared from Black's face. "You're a fool, Will! You always were, only I missed seeing that in the beginning, because of the eagerness of your youth."

"You mean because of the blind stupidity with which I viewed you—don't you?"

The older man paced the room like a caged animal, stopping to give Will an angry glare. "You could have had it all. You'd be a very rich man today, if you had any sense. I offered to share my empire with you."

"I'd have had a little trouble sleeping at night with so many people in bed with me. You know what I mean, the ghosts of people you've killed over the years."

Black shook his head in disgust. "Yes, that's right, you have a *conscience!*" He said the word as though it were distasteful.

Bending to look Will in the eye, he asked, "Well, what's happened to it now, that conscience of yours? Did it only take a come-hither glance from a pair of mascaraed eyes, or the promises spoken by a pair of red lips to make you forget all about your *conscience?*"

"I don't want your money," Will told him aloofly, choosing not to comment on the man's references to Cassandra, knowing he was fishing to find out what he could about her.

"No?" Black raised a dark eyebrow and flicked a surprised glance toward one of the men standing guard over Will. "You hear that, Joe? Here—" he gestured toward Will with one hand "—standing before us, we have a man with so much money, he doesn't need any more.

"And when—" Black turned his attention back to Will "—did this ... change of heart ... come about?"

Will shrugged. "I changed my mind. That's all you need to know."

"Perhaps I've been mistaken in thinking it was the woman who talked you into blackmailing me. Is she the reason you've 'changed your mind'?"

Will stared back at him without answering.

"I think I'd like to meet her—this woman who cares nothing about money. Where is she? Who is she?"

"You mean you don't know?" Will asked in surprise.

"And if I don't?"

"That doesn't sound much like the Jordan Black I know. I thought you'd have her social security number by now," Will answered derisively.

Pushed to anger, Black gave more away than he normally would. "You think I didn't try?" he asked. "I figured she had to be staying at the same hotel as you. If not in the same suite, then in the adjoining one. So I sent people to check it out. But no one recognized her from the description my men gave. And they learned that the suite on one side of yours was empty, and a family of four was occupying the other.

"It seems that the only women fitting her description staying in the hotel when you were there have all been satisfactorily accounted for. I concede that you've hidden her identity very well." He gave Will a slight bow.

Will kept his expression blank, but his mind was whirling with a few questions of his own. How was it that the hotel didn't have a record of Cassandra's stay? And what about the package he'd left in their safe to be given to her after he'd gone? Where was it now?

"So, now that we've established the fact that you're a very bright boy," Black was speaking again, "tell me where she is," he demanded in flinty tones.

Will shook his head.

"You don't know—or you aren't saying?" Black asked.

"I can change his mind for him, or loosen his tongue." The man who had clipped Will on the jaw with his gun barrel spoke from the doorway.

Will slanted him a narrow-eyed look. He recognized him as the man who had worked him over with such thoroughness at Black's estate.

If he ever got the opportunity, Will thought, he would show the guy what it felt like, having your lip split with a pair of brass knuckles and your jaw nearly broken.

"Max, did you find the girl?" Black asked without commenting on his offer.

"No. But I did some checking and found out that he—" he nodded toward Will "—and some old coot who lives nearby, had their heads together over dinner in town last night. The girl was with them."

"Where's the old man?" Black asked.

"Gone."

"Damn!" Black slammed a fist against the wall above Will's head.

Will give him a quick glance. Black was losing it. Will recognized the symptoms, the red face and nervous tic near the corner of his mouth were a dead giveaway.

"Where—" Black suddenly turned on Will "—is the evidence? Who has it? The old man? Or the woman?

"You might as well tell me." He knotted a fist and raised it threateningly in Will's direction. "I'm not leaving here without it."

"It isn't here."

"I know that! Do you take me for a fool? Don't you think I had the place searched while you were trying to run away?"

Black turned to Max. "What about the old man? Has anyone searched his place?"

"Someone is doing that now."

"I'm losing my patience with you," Black told Will.

"That's tough on your blood pressure," Will commented insolently. "And at your weight and age, that could be dangerous."

The man next to him made a fist and punched him in the stomach. Will doubled over in pain, gasping for breath.

The glance he turned on the other man, when he finally succeeded, was murderous. "Try that…again…when you don't have a gun in your…hand," he whispered hoarsely.

"That's only the beginning," Black promised. "Unless you give me what I want."

"I'm not giving you a damn thing. Go to hell!" Will spat, getting fed up now himself.

The man who had punched him lifted a hand, drawing Will's angry stare, but Black stopped him with a shake of the head.

"I'm not the one who will go to hell," Black promised, his black eyes twin points of brittle light in his florid face. "That's where you'll be going unless you cooperate—and soon."

Will tore his eyes from the man beside him and gave Black a crooked glance. "Cooperate?"

"Yes, let's make a deal."

"Deal? Who do you think you're kidding? You don't deal—you send your goons here." He motioned to the man beside him. "To beat people up—kill them—and then you take what you want."

"Not all the time," Black answered tolerantly. "I have been known to strike a deal now and then—when it suits me.

"I want the papers you have, and you want your friends to live to see another sunrise. You give me the papers—they live. You don't—" He shrugged. "It's as simple as that."

"And what about me?" Will asked.

Black shrugged his answer.

"That's not much of a deal for me."

"Someone's got to pay for all the…inconvenience I've had, all the…mental anguish…you've put me through."

"What if I don't deal—what then?"

"Well, then, I guess you die, and so do your friends. As for myself, I'll take my chances, if and when that evidence shows up in the wrong hands."

"You're a liar, Black," Will snarled. "You wouldn't let me, or anyone else, live, even if I gave you what you want. I trust you to keep your word about as far as I can see you, and then only if you're naked and alone."

All eyes in the room were on Jordan Black's face as the echo of Will's words filtered through the air.

"So be it. Max, Joe, take him outside, shoot him and bury his body somewhere in the desert behind the cabin where no one will find it.

He glanced around at the rustic interior of the room. "This place offends my sensibilities. I want to get this over with and get the hell out of here."

Will stepped out of the cabin and walked between the two men toward the stream. The sun was a golden wash of color in the late-evening sky when the two men stopped him near the spot where he and Cassandra had made love only the day before.

Will looked around him at the familiar mountains in the background, listening to the sound of water running in the stream, smelled the pungent odor of the creosote bush growing behind the cabin, and thought about how wonderful it all was, the sights and sounds and odors of life.

Was this a good day to die? Was any day? Ever?

"That will do," Black called, stopping them about fifty yards from the building, drawing Will's attention.

Both men, guns pointed in Will's direction, moved back to stand between him and Jordan Black, waiting for the man's signal.

"One last chance," Black offered, pausing before he continued, eyes narrowed as if in thought. "I'll tell you what. I'll let you live—my word of honor, I swear—but the other two, the old man and the woman, have to die. Because you have to be punished for what you've done—and they know too much. On my honor." He crossed himself. "I'll let you live. What do you say?"

Will stared into his black eyes, knowing the man's heart was even blacker. Yet this time he believed him. Black would let Will live and kill the other two. He would do it because he knew that for Will to save his own life at his friends' expense would be a death sentence in itself. How could he live, knowing what he'd done?

"Take your deal and shove it," Will answered clearly. "I'd rather be dead."

"If that's your choice." Black raised his hand and the two men took aim.

"No!"

"Cassandra—"

"Will—"

Black's men whirled in surprise. Cassandra was standing near the far corner of the cabin—and one of the guns went off.

No one moved.

Jordan Black looked down in surprise at the front of his shirt, where a large red stain had begun to blossom. "No-o-o," he murmured in protest. "It—isn't—supposed to happen—this way—"

Like a kite without wind, his immense body fluttered slowly to the ground and lay there without moving.

"Will!" Cassandra flew across the distance separating them and into his arms.

"Thank God you're all right," she whispered over and over, capturing his face between her hands and covering it with kisses. "I was afraid I'd be too late."

Will picked her up and held her against him, burying his face against her neck. She was here in his arms, safe and sound, and Jordan Black was dead. There really was a God in Heaven, after all. Hugging her to him, he vowed silently never to let her out of his sight again.

"Sorry, folks." A laconic voice interrupted their joyous reunion. "But I don't think I'd order a wedding cake just yet."

Will stiffened, twisted his head from Cassandra's gentle grasp and looked into the barrel of a gun.

"It's a little too late for that, isn't it?" he asked the man called Max without fear. "Your boss is dead. You might just as well pack it in."

"He's dead, but I'm still alive."

"Max!" Joe called, his eyes wide and staring, his face pale. "I shot him. I don't know what happened. The gun just went off in my hand."

"It's all right. Don't worry about it. Now's our chance to take over the boss's operation," Max told him. "Quit your sniveling and get over here. All we have to do is take care of these two and get the hell out of here.

"Wait." Max smiled coldly. "Instead of shooting them, why don't we have a little bonfire? Way out here, so far from town, by the time somebody shows up to put the fire out, there won't be anything left.

"Go and drag Black's body inside the cabin."

"B-but—"

"Do it! Now! Come on." Max waved the gun in the other man's direction. "Get a move on. We haven't got all day. There's still the old man to take care of before we leave.

"After you get Black inside, get on the car phone and find out if Les is through searching the old man's place. Tell him to stay there until we get there. And if the old man shows up—shoot him."

"Put down your weapons and raise your hands!" a loud voice growled all at once from the direction of the cabin.

Max whirled, crouching down, searching for the speaker.

"I said put your weapons down or I'll shoot!"

Joe was staring around him, knees bent, the hand holding his gun stretched tensely out before him. "I'm putting mine down. Don't shoot."

"Don't do it," Max snapped, his gun still wavering from Will to Cassandra.

"I'm not going to get shot because you've got some crazy idea about taking over the boss's business," Joe told him stubbornly, laying his gun down on the sandy ground.

"You fool! We don't know who's out there. It's probably just one man."

"I don't care—I'm out of it." Joe raised his hands, and stood up. "Don't shoot. I'm unarmed."

Max whipped the gun around and fired once in Joe's direction. The small wiry man fell to the ground, clutching his left shoulder.

"All right, this is the sheriff speaking, put the weapon down or I'm going to shoot."

"Sheriff? I don't believe you. Is that you, Les? Come on out and face me."

A tall hatchet-faced man, flanked by two companions, moved into sight. The three wore the khaki uniforms of the county sheriff's office. As they moved closer, the two men at either end distanced themselves from the sheriff, flanking Max on both sides.

"Do you believe me now?" the sheriff asked. "Believe this, if you don't drop that weapon on the count of three, my men are going to draw a bead and drop you in your tracks."

Max knew he was outmaneuvered. Lowering the weapon in the same manner Joe had done, he raised his hands and stood waiting for the sheriff's men to handcuff him.

Will stood with his arm around Cassandra's shoulders and watched them take him away. Joe was helped to his feet by another deputy who had been hiding behind a large outcropping of rock a few yards away.

It was all over, it was finally over.

And Jordan Black was dead.

Chapter 15

"Well, folks, I think I'll be heading on back to my own place."

Tex stretched out his long legs and took another sip of the lemonade they were all drinking without moving from the step.

"I want to thank you again for getting the sheriff," Will said from his place on the step beside him. "I don't know what we would have done if you hadn't shown up when you did."

"You can thank your little lady there for saving your hide. She's the one who insisted I leave her off here first before going into town to get the sheriff."

Will rested his cheek against the top of her bright head and hugged her to him. He hadn't let her leave his side once since she'd thrown herself into his arms.

"I know what I owe her. I owe her my life. She stopped Max and Joe from shooting me in the nick of time."

"Well, it's a sad day when anyone dies," Tex commented, getting to his feet. "But if ever a man deserved what he got, Jordan Black had it coming to him.

"Goodnight, you two. I'm going to take these tired old bones home and give them a good soak before I put them to bed. I'll see you in the morning, I guess, when we go talk to the sheriff about tonight's ruckus."

"Wait a minute." Will stood and, with a murmured word to Cassandra that he would be right back, hurried into the cabin.

"I'm not goin' to ask you about your friend—if he is your friend." Tex spoke in low tones, one eye on the cabin door, referring to Barnabas. "Because, whatever he was after, somehow I don't think he had anything to do with Jordan Black." He shoved the Stetson back on his grizzled head and scratched at one ear. "I don't know what part you've played in all this, either, and I don't want to know," he rushed to assure her.

"I like you. You got grit, and I like that in a person, man or woman. Will there, he's got grit, too, just like his daddy. He...cares a whole lot for you, but I 'spect you already know that. Just do me one favor." Tex peered down intently at her face. "Don't hurt him—okay? He's been kicked around by life enough as it is."

Cassandra took a shaky breath before speaking. "I can't explain about Bar—my friend," she answered softly, twisting her hands in the folds of her skirt. "But you're right. He didn't have anything to do with Jordan Black.

"Tex..." She didn't quite know how to put what she had to say next. "I need a favor from you..." She paused, looking up at him, her lips trembling.

"I'm listening."

"I—if Will should mention the...evidence he had against Jordan Black, could you assure him—no questions asked—that its been put into the right hands?"

"This something to do with your friend?" Tex asked without answering.

"I can't tell you anything except that he—my friend—wasn't working for Jordan Black."

"Yeah, well, I wondered if maybe he was from the government, till I saw him in that sheriff's uniform."

"You saw him in a sheriff's uniform?" she asked quickly.

"Yeah, he was already Johnny-on-the-spot when me and the sheriff and the other deputies arrived."

"Here." Will stepped out the door onto the porch and offered what he held in his hand to Tex. "I can't keep this. It rightly belongs to you—and I want you to have it."

Tex took the pearl-handled gun and leather holster from Will and stared down at them for a moment without speaking. When he looked up, there was a sheen of moisture in his eyes.

"I have to admit, I hated to part with it. But it's yours if you want it, I meant it when I said that."

"Thanks," Will answered, putting his hand on the older man's shoulder and giving it an affectionate squeeze. "But I know Dad must have wanted you to have it or he wouldn't have given it to you—and so do I."

"Right." Clearing his throat, Tex brushed a hand across his face and nodded. "Right—thanks. And now—" he straightened the hat on his head "—as much as I enjoy good company like yours, I'm an old man, and it's way past my bedtime."

"What time is it?" Cassandra asked with a catch in her voice.

Tex withdrew his pocket watch and turned toward the light from the porch. "It looks like—" He squinted. "Yeah, half past eight."

"That late?" she whispered.

Will gave her a puzzled glance before walking his old friend to his Jeep.

"Goodnight, little lady," Tex called, giving her a wave.

"Goodbye," she answered softly, waving back.

Will watched the red taillights disappear before turning back toward the porch—and Cassandra.

She'd been strangely quiet and jumpy since the sheriff had left. Sheriff Alvarez had assured them that the morning would be soon enough to take their statements.

"Are you tired?" he asked, coming to a stop below where she stood on the top step.

"Yes. Are you?"

"Some." He shrugged.

Hands knotted at her waist, she kept darting small glances at him, then looking quickly away. Her face looked paler than usual, and she'd bitten her lip until a small dot of blood could be seen.

"What's wrong?"

"N-nothing."

"You know, there's nothing to be afraid of now." He took her hands in his, pulling them apart, feeling their coldness, though the night was very warm. "It's all over and we're together." He stepped up on the first step, holding her gaze with his. "Nothing can hurt you as long as I'm alive."

"Oh, Will!" she cried. The tears that had been just below the surface for the past few hours came bubbling to the fore. "Hold me. Hold me tight!"

Gathering her into his arms, his face pressed to her breast, Will held her, savoring the warmth of her body in his arms.

"I'm holding you, my darling, and I'll never let you go. You're mine, and I'm yours, two halves of the same whole. We belong together—for eternity."

She felt ice spreading through her veins at the sound of the word. *Eternity.*

"Love me," she whispered as he allowed her to slide slowly down the length of his body until her feet touched the wooden step. She was aching unbearably for his touch.

He took her face gently in his large hand and turned it up to him. "I do, you know. I love you with every breath in my body." His lips hovered over hers as he spoke.

"Would you love me—no matter what?" she asked tentatively, holding her lips away from his.

"No matter what," he repeated, kissing the hollow at the base of her throat.

"And . . . if I should ever . . . leave . . ."

"I'd die," he vowed, covering her mouth with his, his hands smoothing down her shoulders and back.

"No!" She wrenched her lips from his. "Don't say that—don't ever say that!"

Tearing herself out of his arms, she pushed past him and ran down the steps to disappear in the darkness.

"Cassandra?" he called in stunned surprise. "Cassandra!" he repeated louder. "Cassandra!" he shouted in sudden fear. "Come back!"

He followed her, dashing across the ground in her wake, catching sight of the pale color of her blouse in the moonlight. His footsteps slowed when he caught sight of her stationary figure up ahead. She was standing near the stream, staring up at the full moon, her profile toward him.

Coming up behind her, he leaned close, without touching her, and whispered near her ear, "I love you. Why did you run from me? Does the intensity of my feelings frighten you?"

"Yes," she whispered after a moment.

"It shouldn't. I don't want to frighten you. But how can I tell you I love you any less when it isn't true?"

She took a step back and turned to look up at his face, pale in the moonlight. "There are things about me you don't know—"

"They don't matter," Will assured her swiftly.

"But what if they do?" she insisted.

"What—are you married?"

"N-no."

"Are you an ax murderer?" he asked half-jokingly.

"No," she answered seriously.

Taking her suddenly by the shoulders, a hint of unease creeping into him despite his determination that nothing should mar this night, the first night of his confession of love, Will asked, "Are you—terminally ill?"

"No—of course not."

"Then there's nothing, not a thing under God's Heaven, that you could tell me about yourself that would make me unhappy."

He gripped her shoulders a little desperately, drawing her up onto her toes. "Unless—" He watched her expression closely. "Unless it's that you don't feel the same way about me."

She hesitated. Perhaps if she denied the turbulent feelings running rampant through her body...

His eyes darkened with the beginning of pain. She could feel a slight trembling in the hands holding her so close.

"I love you more than all the angels in Heaven," she answered with the simple truth.

That was enough for him. Sweeping her up into his arms, he kissed her so sweetly that the world stood still.

"I want to make love to you. I want to worship your body with mine," he breathed feverishly against her neck.

Stepping back from his embrace, taking his hand in hers, she led him toward the cabin. They walked without speaking, passion seething just below the surface.

Leaving the door open so that the sounds of the night filtered into the cabin, still without speaking, in perfect accord, they moved to the bed.

A shaft of moonlight slanted into the room from the window facing the stream, falling across their bodies. As if it were a signal, Will took the hem of her blouse in his hands and lifted it carefully over her head.

His heartbeat accelerated at the sheer beauty of her. Unable to wait any longer, needing to touch her, he pressed his hands flat against her shoulders and slowly drew them down over her breasts, feeling her nipples harden against his palms.

Taming the wild blood flowing in his veins, Will leaned forward and lifted one small breast to his lips, kissing it with restrained ardor.

"You are so lovely—a magnificent work of art." His lips lingered against her nipple, tantalizing the small bud until it became even more rigid against his tongue.

A soft liquid feeling moved through Cassandra, and she pressed her legs together against it. Her knees became weak, and she had to hold on to something or drop down onto the bed.

Her hands reached out, touching Will, finding the solid wall of his chest. She wanted to make him feel what she was feeling, but she was uncertain about how to go about it.

One of her hands encountered a button and unfastened it, and then another and another, until his shirt fell open, baring his chest to her touch. With trembling fingers she explored his muscles, sifting through the curls of hair, sliding her hands lower until she encountered his navel.

That spot fascinated her. She slipped through his fingers and bent to run her lips over it, her tongue delving into the shallow space. She felt him draw in his stomach with a slight gasp, and she smiled.

Will caught his breath and pressed her face against his belly, his legs becoming shaky. When he couldn't stand the pleasure any longer, he pulled her back up to him and covered her mouth hungrily with his.

While his mouth explored hers, his hands were working at the fastenings of her skirt. It fell gently to the floor, exposing all her charms to his ravenous eyes.

Easing her down onto the bed, Will quickly shed his jeans and joined her, lying beside her, examining her beauty with smoldering eyes. His hand outlined the circle of one breast before searing a path down her taut stomach to her thighs.

Cassandra couldn't control the quivering of her body as she felt first hot and then cold. The muscles of her legs trembled spasmodically as his hands smoothed the inside of one leg.

"Are you cold?" he whispered against her lips, knowing she couldn't possibly be, because he was burning up inside.

"N-no—yes—I don't know," she answered in confusion, feeling first one way and then the other. "When you touch me—ah!" she gasped. "—like that, I feel like I'm burning up inside."

"And so am I, my darling, so am I."

Finding her hand, he placed her fingers against him, and closing his eyes, he felt his desire swell against her.

Cassandra moaned softly as his hands slowly traced over her stomach, hip and thigh. Aroused almost past the point of reason, she drew herself closer to him, slipping one leg over his, pressing her soft stomach to his lean hip.

Will rose on one elbow and leaned over to press a series of kisses against her slender throat, then moved his lips to her shoulder and finally to the tops of her breasts. His other arm slid beneath her, lifting her to his chest.

A wave of passion flowed between them, binding them with a golden cord. Will eased over onto his back without haste, taking her with him, until she lay with her soft curves fitted along his angular length.

"Now," he panted, having reached the end of his self-control. "It must be now."

Cassandra could feel the heat of his body down the entire length of hers. She adjusted her position and felt the rigid tip of his passion invade her. She gasped in surprise, then sighed, filled with a sudden sense of completeness.

She was utterly his at that moment; she belonged to him as she never would again. Because this was the last time—the very last time—she would ever feel his passion driving into her this way.

Will clasped her to him, sensing something in her manner, yet unable to define what it was. And then, catapulted over the edge of his own passion, he was unable to stop to ask what was troubling her.

Rolling her over onto her back, he held her to him, rocked her against him, filled her with his mounting passion until they were both soaring—flying toward an awesome, soul-shattering, ecstasy.

The world splintered into a million tiny pieces, then came together again, securing Will and Cassandra into the puzzle, two interlocking pieces joined together forever.

For a while the only sound in the room after their cries of ecstasy had ceased was the short, rapid panting of their breathing. Will moved to lie beside her, tucking her against him, pulling the sheet over their sweat-dampened bodies.

He'd never felt so at peace with himself, or with the world around him, as he felt at that moment.

Cassandra knew by the angle of the moonlight slanting in through the window that it must be nearly midnight. Will was snoring softly at her side, his arms, even in sleep, wrapped protectively around her.

It was time to go, yet how could she leave him?

Never had she faced such a hard test of her strength and courage. One part of her—the human part—was telling her to stay where she was, that if she ignored the time somehow she wouldn't have to leave.

But the other part—the part still in tune with Heaven—knew differently. She had asked God to assist her—to let Will live—and she had promised to make amends for disobeying Him. It was time to pay up.

Carefully she removed first one and then the other of Will's arms, and slipped from the bed. Pulling the sheet up to cover him, she paused to place a tender kiss on his brow. The time for passion was done—now there was only tenderness and remorse.

Cassandra slipped into her clothing and moved toward the door. Should she leave him a note?

No, what could she say?

Outside, she glanced around, wondering where to go. Barnabas must be waiting for her somewhere close by. In the distance, out toward the desert, toward the mountaintops, she saw a bright shaft of light.

Barnabas...

Will gave an abrupt snort in his sleep, then sat straight up in bed. A sudden deep fear was pumping adrenaline through his system so strongly that his heart was pounding, and he felt dizzy and short of breath.

"Cassandra?" He stared at the empty bed beside him. "Cassandra, where are you?"

Thinking she might have gone to the bathroom, he climbed from the bed and moved toward the door. But the door opened easily beneath his touch. The room was empty.

"Cassandra?" he whispered, unable even to shout, filled with the terrible knowledge that she wasn't anywhere in the cabin. "Where are you?"

He grabbed a flashlight from the drawer in the night-stand beside the bed and hurried toward the door. Realizing that he hadn't any clothes on, he stopped and turned impatiently back to dress.

With every passing second, he had the feeling that, somehow, Cassandra was moving farther out of his reach. He had to find her quickly, had to get to her before it was too late.

The certainty that she was moving beyond his grasp didn't make sense to him, but he didn't stop to analyze it; he simply reacted to it. He couldn't take the chance of losing her when she was all that made life worth living.

Outside the cabin, he flashed the light around, looking for signs of her passing. He found nothing.

Behind the cabin, he stood near the stream, staring into the darkness toward the mountains. Something was telling him that she hadn't headed down the road toward town but had instead taken off across the desert in that direction.

Following his instinct, he moved at a fast pace toward the peaks barely visible in the moonlight.

Cassandra climbed the last few feet, then turned and stood at the top of the ridge; the valley where Will's cabin stood lay stretched out before her. She could barely make out the cabin's indistinct lines in the distance through the mist in her eyes.

Tearing her unhappy eyes away from the sight, she lifted her head toward the heavens. "I'm here, Barnabas, waiting for you."

"Yes, child, I see you've come—at last."

Expecting him to come from the sky, Cassandra whirled around in surprise at the sound of his voice coming from the rocks somewhere behind her.

"B-Barnabas!"

"I'm sorry if I frightened you. I've been waiting for some time now—you're late."

"I know—I'm sorry." She dashed a hand across one cheek, swallowing back a sob.

"What's this?" the old man asked, stepping closer to take a look at her face. "Tears? Oh, child," he murmured, clicking his tongue.

He was reminded of the very first tears she had shed; they had been at Will Alexander's instigation, too.

"Are you ready to leave?" he asked.

"I...don't want to go," she mumbled quickly, before her courage failed her. "I want to s-stay." She hiccuped, then asked, "Is He very angry with me?"

"Angry?"

"Yes, about what I did."

"You mean about Will's staying and Jordan Black's...crossing over?"

"Yes, are *you* angry with me? I didn't get you into trouble with Him, did I? I wouldn't want to do that."

"No. You know that no matter how badly you wanted it, it couldn't have happened without His approval. And the need was met. A soul passed from one realm to the next. Everything is once more in balance."

"I want to thank you," Cassandra whispered, "for helping me."

"Helping you?" he asked with a raised brow.

"Yes, I don't know if my power would have been strong enough to stop Will from dying, but thanks to you, I didn't have to find out. You're the one who saved Will's life tonight."

"I saved *both* your lives tonight, you silly child."

"W-what?"

"Take a look at your wrist, is the scratch yet healed?"

"How did you know about that?"

"I just know. Now take a look at it."

Cassandra twisted her arm up and peered at it. "I can't see in the dark—" She broke off and gave a tiny gasp.

"Exactly." Barnabas nodded.

"But I don't understand. I should be able to see without light. I could when I came to Earth—"

"And now you can't. Here." He lifted her arm and passed his hand over it, leaving a trail of light. "Can you see your wrist now?"

"The scratch is still there." She peered closer. "But the medicine Will got for it seems to have worked. It isn't as red—"

Barnabas *tut-tutted* and let go of her arm. "Medicine..." He shook his white head.

"What's happening to me, Barnabas? Why can't I see in the dark? Why hasn't my arm healed?"

"The answer is simple, if you think about it," he replied gently. "All angels have those abilities—"

"You mean—I'm not an angel anymore?" She was afraid to believe what she was beginning to suspect. "What does that mean?"

The instant of excitement dimmed as she asked in horrified tones, "Am I banished from Heaven because of all the rules I broke?" Banishment meant—no, she couldn't even contemplate a fate as horrendous as following in Jordan Black's wake.

"No, of course not." Barnabas put her fears to rest in a peevish voice.

"Then it must be that I'm—" She was afraid to say the word for fear it wouldn't be true. "Human?"

"Yes, child, that's exactly what you are, Human. You've been becoming more human every day. Haven't you noticed your powers waning?"

"Barnabas—did you do this for me? Did you see how I was coming to feel for Will and intercede on my behalf with Him—talk Him into letting me stay?"

"Oh, child, I can't *talk* Him into anything. Any decisions made above are made strictly by Him without interference from anyone. It's His plan—it must have been His plan all along," Barnabas muttered almost to himself.

"I knew nothing about it until very recently," he added on a note of mild indignation.

"Oh," she whispered in disappointment. She'd always thought Barnabas liked her, but he only sounded irritated with her at this moment.

"Not that I wouldn't have—if I'd thought it would do any good," he admitted gruffly.

"Cassandra-a-a—"

The sound of her name, sounding like the cry of an animal in great pain, echoed across the valley floor below.

"Will!" She turned to peer into the darkness, looking for him.

"He's on his way to you, child. He'll be here soon enough. I must go."

"Oh, Barnabas—I'll miss you." Hugging him, she planted a kiss on his withered cheek and tried to smile.

"I'll miss you, too, child. I can't think why you'd prefer Earth to Heaven." The old man paused. "Of course, there is the matter of the conveyances they have down here. I do so like flying—and speeding along on the ground..." His voice trailed off.

"Well, don't be upset, child," he said, returning to their previous conversation. "It won't be for long. A lifetime here on Earth is only the blink of an eye in Heaven. I'll watch for you."

"Does that mean I won't ever see you again, until—"

"We never know what He has in store for us, now do we?" he asked mysteriously.

His dry fingers touched her soft cheek. "It won't be the same up there without you."

"Cassandra-a-a—"

She glanced over her shoulder toward the sound of Will's voice. How she wanted to go to him, but there was one more thing she needed to ask Barnabas.

"Are all my powers gone?" she asked curiously, turning around. "Barnabas?"

He was gone. For an instant she felt terribly alone. Then the sound of her name, echoing across the valley, came to her, and she thought only of Will.

She was his! She belonged to *him* now.

"Will! Will!" she began to cry, the joy of knowing she wouldn't have to leave him filling her voice, bubbling up inside her.

She descended the mountain ledge with eager, incautious steps and covered the ground separating them as quickly as possible, given her newly human vulnerability.

They almost collided, but Will caught her, whirled her around, holding her so tightly she could hardly breathe, needing to make certain she was really there in his arms, where she belonged.

When he was finally satisfied that she was real and not a figment of his tortured imagination, he held her away from him to ask, "Why did you leave me? Why did you come here?"

"There was something I had to work out by myself," she answered carefully.

"And did you?"

"Yes, I did, and everything is going to be all right."

Will let his breath out on a long sigh, not realizing he'd been holding it until then.

"I love you. I know we haven't known each other long— I can't believe it's only been a few days."

"Six, to be exact," Cassandra interjected.

"Six days, long enough for God to create Heaven and Earth, and long enough for me to know I can't live without you. Will you marry me?"

"Marry, as in a home—and babies?" she asked with repressed excitement.

"As in a home and babies," he agreed.

"Yes—oh, yes. I love you, Will Alexander. I'll marry you, and you'll never regret it—I promise."

Throwing her arms around his neck, she kissed him fervently. After a few moments of exchanging kisses, they turned toward the cabin and moved across the valley floor, the sound of their excitement drifting behind them on the night air.

"We're going to be so happy," Will promised. "I have a feeling life has a whole lot of good things, and maybe a few surprises in store for us."

"I'm certain of it," Cassandra agreed, hugging his arm against her side, recalling the question Barnabas hadn't answered concerning her powers.

Life for the next fifty years or so was going to be very interesting indeed—and quite possibly full of far more surprises than Will Alexander had ever imagined.

*   *   *   *   *

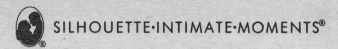

COMING NEXT MONTH

#409   TWILIGHT SHADOWS—Emilie Richards

When a friend's wedding party ended with bullets being exchanged instead of just ordinary vows, Griff Bryant discovered someone was out to get him, and he needed help—*fast*. However, capable *and* gorgeous private investigator Kelley O'Flynn Samuels gave "bodyguarding" a whole new meaning....

#410   NOWHERE TO RUN—Mary Anne Wilson

Psychiatrist R. J. Tyler had chosen to focus exclusively on the teaching side of his field. Yet, drawn by the vulnerability and fear in Lyndsey Cole's eyes, he made an exception. He had to help her remember who her attacker was, before it was too late. But was his heartfelt determination professional . . . or personal?

#411   LONG WHITE CLOUD—
Marilyn Cunningham

When Kiri MacKay inherited an island from the father who'd abandoned her as a child, she wanted nothing more than to sell the entire estate and be done with it. Then she met wildlife biologist Noel Trevorson, and her determination wavered. His arguments against the sale were persuasive, his kisses seductive. But was he after her—or her island?

#412   BAD MOON RISING—Kathleen Eagle

Schoolteacher Frankie Tracker thought she'd gotten over her adolescent crush on Trey Latimer. But the moment he returned to town, she knew trouble lay ahead. For Trey the man was twice as exciting as Trey the boy. And this time, *she* was a fully grown woman.

AVAILABLE NOW:

#405 PROBABLE CAUSE
Marilyn Pappano

#406 THE MAN NEXT DOOR
Alexandra Sellers

#407 TAKING SIDES
Lucy Hamilton

**#408 ANGEL ON MY
SHOULDER**
Ann Williams

Angels Everywhere!

Everything's turning up angels at Silhouette. In November, Ann Williams's ANGEL ON MY SHOULDER (IM #408, $3.29) features a heroine who's absolutely heavenly—and we mean that literally! Her name is Cassandra, and once she comes down to earth, her whole picture of life—and love— undergoes a pretty radical change.

Then, in December, it's time for ANGEL FOR HIRE (D #680, $2.79) from Justine Davis. This time it's hero Michael Justice who brings a touch of out-of-this-world magic to the story. Talk about a match made in heaven . . . !

Look for both these spectacular stories wherever you buy books. But look soon—because they're going to be flying off the shelves as if they had wings!

Take 4 bestselling love stories FREE

Plus get a FREE surprise gift!

SILHOUETTE®
OFFICIAL SWEEPSTAKES
RULES

NO PURCHASE NECESSARY

1. To enter, complete an Official Entry Form or 3"× 5" index card by hand-printing, in plain block letters, your complete name, address, phone number and age, and mailing it to: Silhouette Fashion A Whole New You Sweepstakes, P.O. Box 9056, Buffalo, NY 14269-9056.

   No responsibility is assumed for lost, late or misdirected mail. Entries must be sent separately with first class postage affixed, and be received no later than December 31, 1991 for eligibility.

2. Winners will be selected by D.L. Blair, Inc., an independent judging organization whose decisions are final, in random drawings to be held on January 30, 1992 in Blair, NE at 10:00 a.m. from among all eligible entries received.

3. The prizes to be awarded and their approximate retail values are as follows: Grand Prize — A brand-new Ford Explorer 4×4 plus a trip for two (2) to Hawaii, including round-trip air transportation, six (6) nights hotel accommodation, a $1,400 meal/spending money stipend and $2,000 cash toward a new fashion wardrobe (approximate value: $28,000) or $15,000 cash; two (2) Second Prizes — A trip to Hawaii, including round-trip air transportation, six (6) nights hotel accommodation, a $1,400 meal/spending money stipend and $2,000 cash toward a new fashion wardrobe (approximate value: $11,000) or $5,000 cash; three (3) Third Prizes — $2,000 cash toward a new fashion wardrobe. All prizes are valued in U.S. currency. Travel award air transportation is from the commercial airport nearest winner's home. Travel is subject to space and accommodation availability, and must be completed by June 30, 1993. Sweepstakes offer is open to residents of the U.S. and Canada who are 21 years of age or older as of December 31, 1991, except residents of Puerto Rico, employees and immediate family members of Torstar Corp., its affiliates, subsidiaries, and all agencies, entities and persons connected with the use, marketing, or conduct of this sweepstakes. All federal, state, provincial, municipal and local laws apply. Offer void wherever prohibited by law. Taxes and/or duties, applicable registration and licensing fees, are the sole responsibility of the winners. Any litigation within the province of Quebec respecting the conduct and awarding of a prize may be submitted to the Régie des loteries et courses du Québec. All prizes will be awarded; winners will be notified by mail. No substitution of prizes is permitted.

4. Potential winners must sign and return any required Affidavit of Eligibility/Release of Liability within 30 days of notification. In the event of noncompliance within this time period, the prize may be awarded to an alternate winner. Any prize or prize notification returned as undeliverable may result in the awarding of that prize to an alternate winner. By acceptance of their prize, winners consent to use of their names, photographs or their likenesses for purposes of advertising, trade and promotion on behalf of Torstar Corp. without further compensation. Canadian winners must correctly answer a time-limited arithmetical question in order to be awarded a prize.

5. For a list of winners (available after 3/31/92), send a separate stamped, self-addressed envelope to: Silhouette Fashion A Whole New You Sweepstakes, P.O. Box 4665, Blair, NE 68009.

PREMIUM OFFER TERMS

To receive your gift, complete the Offer Certificate according to directions. Be certain to enclose the required number of "Fashion A Whole New You" proofs of product purchase (which are found on the last page of every specially marked "Fashion A Whole New You" Silhouette or Harlequin romance novel). Requests must be received no later than December 31, 1991. Limit: four (4) gifts per name, family, group, organization or address. Items depicted are for illustrative purposes only and may not be exactly as shown. Please allow 6 to 8 weeks for receipt of order. Offer good while quantities of gifts last. In the event an ordered gift is no longer available, you will receive a free, previously unpublished Silhouette or Harlequin book for every proof of purchase you have submitted with your request, plus a refund of the postage and handling charge you have included. Offer good in the U.S. and Canada only.

SLFW-SWPR

SILHOUETTE® OFFICIAL SWEEPSTAKES ENTRY FORM

4-FWSIS-4

Complete and return this Entry Form immediately – the more entries you submit, the better your chances of winning!

- Entries must be received by **December 31, 1991.**
- A Random draw will take place on **January 30, 1992.**
- No purchase necessary.

Yes, I want to win a FASHION A WHOLE NEW YOU Sensuous and Adventurous prize from Silhouette:

Name _____ Telephone _____ Age _____

Address _____

City _____ State _____ Zip _____

Return Entries to: Silhouette **FASHION A WHOLE NEW YOU,**
P.O. Box 9056, Buffalo, NY 14269-9056   © 1991 Harlequin Enterprises Limited

PREMIUM OFFER

To receive your free gift, send us the required number of proofs-of-purchase from any specially marked FASHION A WHOLE NEW YOU Silhouette or Harlequin Book with the Offer Certificate properly completed, plus a check or money order (do not send cash) to cover postage and handling payable to Silhouette FASHION A WHOLE NEW YOU Offer. We will send you the specified gift.

OFFER CERTIFICATE

Item	A. SENSUAL DESIGNER VANITY BOX COLLECTION (set of 4) (Suggested Retail Price $60.00)	B. ADVENTUROUS TRAVEL COSMETIC CASE SET (set of 3) (Suggested Retail Price $25.00)
# of proofs-of-purchase	18	12
Postage and Handling	$3.50	$2.95
Check one	☐	☐

Name _____

Address _____

City _____ State _____ Zip _____

Mail this certificate, designated number of proofs-of-purchase and check or money order for postage and handling to: **Silhouette FASHION A WHOLE NEW YOU Gift Offer,** P.O. Box 9057, Buffalo, NY 14269-9057. Requests must be received by December 31, 1991.

ONE PROOF-OF-PURCHASE

4-FWSIP-4

To collect your fabulous free gift you must include the necessary number of proofs-of-purchase with a properly completed Offer Certificate.

© 1991 Harlequin Enterprises Limited

See previous page for details.